1991

... The conception and execution of *Katha Prize Stories* ... represents a unique and special moment in Indian publishing history.
– *The Economic Times*

... an excellent collection ... the range of craftsmanship and technique is amazing ... – *The Hindu*

Fastidiously hand-picked with an accent on the inherent heterogeneity and cultural complexity of contemporary India ... – *Sunday Chronicle*

... refreshing ... transcends but does not erase linguistic character.
– *Times of India*

1992

Prize Catch ... The best of India translated. – *India Today*

... a publishing feat ... The stories ... have the earthy vitality of a live language and the advantages of a refined narrative technique.
– *The Daily*

1993

... the pioneering effort to bring out translated versions ... moistens the barren patch of short fiction in English ... near flawless end-products.
– *Indian Express*

... an anthology which serves as a good shop-window of the literary happenings in India. – *Business Standard*

A fundamental collection. – *The Book Review*

... has established itself in a surprisingly short period of three years as an anxiously awaited yearly event watched alike by discerning readers in India and abroad as well as by writers, translators and literary journals.
– *The Economic Times*

KATHA

PRIZE STORIES VOLUME 4

The best short fiction published during 1992-94 in thirteen Indian languages, chosen by a panel of distinguished writers and scholars.

Edited by
Geeta Dharmarajan

KATHA

Rupa . Co

Published by
KATHA
Building Centre, Sarai Kale Khan,
Nizamuddin East, New Delhi 110013
Phone: 4628227; 4628254

First published in December, 1994

Distributed by
RUPA & CO.
15, Bankim Chatterjee Street,
Calcutta 700070
94, South Malaka, Allahabad 211001
P.G. Solanki Path, Lamington Road,
Bombay 400007
7/16 Ansari Road, Daryaganj, New
Delhi 110002

KATHA is a registered non-profit society devoted to enhancing the pleasures of reading. KATHA VILASAM is its story research and resource centre.

KATHA VILASAM
Asst. Director Keerti Ramachandra
Editors Meenakshi Sharma
Gita Jayaraj
Bindu Nambiar

Cover design Taposhi Ghoshal
Colours Arvinder Chawla
Logo Design Crowquill

Typeset in 9 on 13pt Bookman
by Ramesh at Katha
Printed at Print Perfect, New Delhi

ISBN 81-85586-14-4 (hardback); ISBN 81-85586-15-2 (paperback)

CONTENTS

The Katha Awards
have been made possible
by a grant from
The East India Hotels Ltd.

THE NOMINATING EDITORS

Assamese
PANKAJ THAKUR

Bangla
SARAT KUMAR MUKHOPADHYAY

English
RUKMINI BHAYA NAIR

Gujarati
SHIRISH PANCHAL

Hindi
VIJAY MOHAN SINGH

Kannada
RAMACHANDRA SHARMA

Konkani
CHANDRAKANT KENI

Malayalam
K. SATCHIDANANDAN

Marathi
G. N. DEVY

Oriya
SACHIDANANDA MOHANTY

Tamil
GNANI

Telugu
ALLAM RAJAIAH

Urdu
ANISUR RAHMAN

THE KATHA AWARD WINNERS FOR 1994

THE WRITERS

Bibhas Sen	Bolwar Mahamad Kunhi
Gauri Deshpande	Kanji Patel
Madhuranthakam Narendra	N. S. Madhavan
Manoj Kumar Goswami	Meena Kakodkar
Mithra Venkatraj	Prakash Narayan Sant
Pratibha Ray	Priyamvad
Sethu	Surendra Prakash
Swapnamoy Chakraborti	Thanjai Prakaash

Vandana Bist

THE TRANSLATORS

Nivedita Menon

Dhananjay Kapse	Gauri Deshpande
Gopa Majumdar	Jayeeta Sharma
Narendra Nair	C. N. Ramachandran
C Revathi	Sacheen Pai Raikar
Sachidananda Mohanty	Sarala Jag Mohan
H.Y. Sharada Prasad	Lakshmi Kannan

Vijaya Ghose

THE JOURNALS

Aajkaal	Chitrangi
Gadyaparva	India Today
Jhankara	Kala Kaumudi
Mauj	Prajavani
Saptahik Sakal	Subhamangala
Udayavani	Zehn-e-Jadeed

INVITING TRANSLATIONS

KATHA publishes *Katha Prize Stories* in December each year. We invite nominations for stories, in the original language and in translation.

POINTS TO KEEP IN MIND:

- Stories should have been published between January 1 and December 31 of the preceeding year in a magazine, journal or small magazine.
- They should be "excellent."
- They can deal with any topic.
- They may have been written by either an established or an upcoming writer, though we encourage you to nominate stories by women writers, without prejudice to quality.
- The story should not have been translated before.
- We prefer stories that are less than 5000 words.

DETAILS YOU SHOULD INCLUDE: Name, date and address of the journal/magazine which first published it. The editor's name. The address of the writer (if possible). Your name and address. **Please send us a good xerox copy of the story.**

IF YOU ARE A TRANSLATOR: In case you would like to try your hand at translation, also, please keep in mind the requirements of Katha: Please do not leave anything out of a story. Put footnotes wherever a word is not translatable directly into English without losing its meaning. Keep all kinship terms in the original language, again giving footnotes where needed.

IF YOU WRITE IN ENGLISH: Stories should be original (no translations!) and should not have been published in India.

DEADLINES : Every year –

For nominations	January 31
For translations	February 28
For stories written originally in English	March 31

ADDRESS: Please send nominations to: Katha,
Post Box 326,
GPO, New Delhi 110 001

TREADING EUCLID'S LINE

Thoughts are ephemeral. Language slips through the crevices of the mind to create a ripple that is almost atavistic, taking its source not in the word itself but in something experienced long ago, to create a story, a thing of magic. It is a magic that India has woven with consummate ease for the last 3,000 years and more. That's precisely why the short story can never be a "minor" art form in our country.

This year too, as in the previous years, the stories in *Katha Prize Stories 4* reinforce the fact that good fiction is being written in the regional languages. These *KPS 4* stories were initially picked by discerning editors of regional publications – small, literary journals to mass circulation magazines – and were chosen for the Katha Awards through a rigorous and eclectic process. The range of stories is as wide. From Bolwar's simple tale to Surendra Prakash's complex narrative; from the gentle old-worldly story of Prakash Narayan Sant to the disturbing brindled beauty that is Pratibha Ray's. The two stories written originally in English were chosen from more than 200 that were received in response to advertisements.

To recreate the magic of one story with words from another language is not an easy task. This becomes even more difficult when we translate into English, since most stories are unable to cross the synapse between the language they were written in and this target language. Many writers still believe that the best is that which is untranslatable into English, and most readers who read regional fiction only through English, are apt to judge Indian stories by the translation, concluding that our stories are not worth reading, and can never be "world class." Often, it's not our writers who fail their readers, but translators their writers.

To translate ourselves, any form of English we have today seems grossly inadequate. The only way we can change this is by creating our own English – an English that can and will accomodate all that we Indians want to say, in a way that we want to say it. Good stories must get out of the confines of their own language through translation into other languages. And this necessarily has to include English. I would like to argue a case for an English that can stand right royally along with the other modern Indian languages – those that are called bhashas by Prof. G.N. Devy in his book, *After Amnesia* (Orient Longman, 1992). Such an English bhasha would be its own and yet capture all the immediateness that other Indian languages are capable of; it would refrain from being "bad" yet be able to let us be ourselves, without having to hide our deepest sentiments and emotions behind the restrained facade of "proper" English.

Katha's books are made primarily for the Indian who would like a deeper engagement with regional fiction through translation, and the creative genius our country nurtures. We strive to match excellent stories with good translations, even if this means "fracturing" English so as to retain the original flavour of the story, as much as possible. So Katha's idiosyncracies continue into this volume also. When we started we were alone in our belief. It takes time for such ideas to gain a certain respectability! Of course, we still flounder over, for example, the second person pronoun in Indian languages – "tum," "tu," "aap"; "nee" and "neengal" – wishing we could dare to create new words.

But till we manage to evolve such an English, do we *not* translate – as we have been advised for some stories? Or, leave out all that is "untranslatable" – as some translators believe? We agree that each translator has a special understanding of the story and each translation should be seen also as the translator's story. Yet, when a translation comes to us, I do tend to agonise over every word; have resource people whom I sit with to see that the translation does justice to the story, the writer, and, at the same time, is pleasing to the reader. But, as always, what divides scrupulousness from nit-picking is a mere Euclid's line.

We urgently need more translators who can devise their own

standards, who will provide the best, regardless of the payment – which *is* poor now, but which is bound to go up when we have more and better translations and more readers for the same. We need techniques that are creative, and responsive to the story. We need universities to prescribe translations, but more, to teach translation, as part of their curriculum. Today, with the rapid migration of people within the country and students willy-nilly learning languages other than their mother-tongues right from school, multi-language skills should not be difficult to rustle up.

We also need language courses that are more practical and train students in the art and craft of editing. An author whom I admire, once told me that no writer worth his salt would accept suggestions from an editor. We need to redefine the role of the fiction editor, though it may not be immediately possible to think of her or him as "a combination doctor, teacher, coach, and conscience who could benefit any writer," as Thomas McCormack, Chairman & Editorial Director, St. Martin's Press, New York would have us do. Katha instituted the JOURNAL AWARD last year, precisely for this reason: To applaud the editors of journals that publish quality fiction, for their sensitivity, their sensibility.

This book would not have been possible without the continued and warm support of many. We sincerely thank our Nominating Editors. Special thanks to the Friends of Katha, especially Abdul Naseeb Khan, A.S.K.V.S. Sharma, Dipankar Basu, Mahasweta Baxipatra, Olivinho Gomes, Raji Lakshmiratan, Renuka Ramachandran, Revathi and Vishwapriya Iyengar, Sandhya Bhandare, Sasi Bhushanam and Sukanya Dutta.

I would especially like to thank the East India Hotels Ltd. and Shri P.R.S. Oberoi and Shri K.K. Sharma, for their support. Without their grant, this book would not have been possible.

I would like to believe there is something here for every taste, for every reader. I hope you enjoy the variety!

November, 1994 Geeta Dharmarajan

THE SELECTION PROCESS

The KATHA AWARDS were instituted in 1990.

Katha requests an eminent writer, scholar or critic in each of the regional languages to choose what she/he feels are the three best stories published in that language, in the previous year.

Our Nominating Editors sift through numerous journals and magazines that promote short fiction. Many of them consult friends and other friends of Katha in the literary world to help them make their choices. The nominations made by our editors are translated and from these are chosen the final stories.

Each author receives the KATHA AWARD FOR CREATIVE FICTION which includes a citation, Rs. 2,000 and publication (in translation) in that year's *Katha Prize Stories* volume.

The editor of the journal that first published the award-winning story receives the KATHA JOURNAL AWARD.

The translators are hand-picked from the list of nearly 2000 names we have at Katha. Each of them gets the KATHA AWARD FOR TRANSLATION which includes a citation and Rs. 2,000.

The A. K. RAMANUJAN AWARD goes to a translator who can, with felicity, translate between more than two Indian languages, as Ramanujan himself was able to. A.K. Ramanujan was a friend of Katha and this award was instituted last year.

Every other year or so – as and when we can afford it! – Katha holds a literary workshop and the Award-winning translators, writers and editors are invited to it.

PRIYAMVAD

THE BED

TRANSLATED BY NIVEDITA MENON
NOMINATED BY VIJAY MOHAN SINGH

THE TRANSLATOR IS THE RECIPIENT OF
THE A. K. RAMANUJAN AWARD

First published in Hindi as "Palang" in *India Today,*
Sahitya Varshiki, 1993, New Delhi.

When the first bloom appeared that year on the bare scattered branches of the palaash, Ma was perfectly healthy. By the time the tree was aflame with blossom she had fallen ill, and the night the sudden fierce storm tore every flower down, turning the ground below into a trampled crimson swamp, she died.

It was a small three-cornered room – the walls scabbed and stained with seepage – in which we lived. My mother had one corner, I had one, and in the third, there was a large bed on which Ma and I slept. Each of us had absolute rights over our own corners, and neither would dream of interfering in the other's. In her corner Ma had established her empire. A small platform, on it her gods ... two ancient, old-fashioned tin boxes ... two bundles ... a few vessels ... some old clothes ... a couple of japmalas ... a torch ... a hand-fan ... old coins and things like that. My corner didn't have much. Books, an old wooden cupboard in which lay some bottles of cheap liquor, a few clothes and over it all, the indescribable air of defeat that hung over my middle-aged existence – something between indifference and disappointment. Near a small window was the third corner and in it, the bed, which dominated the entire room with its sheer personality. Ma had brought it along when she got married and she was enormously proud of it. A large old-fashioned bed in which she had once slept with my father. The memories of her past clung to that bed, coming alive at night, hovering over her. Night after night I had lain silently, watching Ma in conversation with those memories. Suddenly smiling. Then in tears. Sometimes, turning shyly away. I often felt she was closer to the bed than to me, and shared with it what she could not reveal to me.

On holidays and during the early hours of the morning, I would lie watching Ma. She would get up very early and complete all her work. She took great pains to ensure that her movements did not disturb my sleep, but often I would be awake and watching her. So regular and predictable were her activities that even with my eyes closed I knew exactly what she would be doing. Now she'd be cleaning the house ... now washing clothes ... now telling her beads ... Or sometimes first thing in the morning she would clean up her corner, then mine, and then bathe. She took a long time bathing. She was almost insane in her desire for cleanliness. Every little thing was cleaned two or three times – the floor, the walls, the bucket, the clothes, her body. Every once in a while she would come out of the bathroom and into our room, to pick up something she had forgotten or to clean something she had overlooked. I would watch her silently ... her bent back, her wrinkles, her shrivelled mouth, her look of perpetual uncertainty. She would be wearing just one piece of cloth, oblivious of her near-nudity. Then I would close my eyes and turn my face away.

Seeing Ma in this condition always aroused a strange sort of aversion in me. I wanted to stop her from being so careless, to make my distaste evident ... but I could never bring myself to say anything. After all, this had been Ma's routine for years. I felt that if I said anything she would be so ashamed and awkward about it that her entire sense of balance would be shaken. The calm and self-assured way in which she led her life would be destroyed forever. So I would say nothing. But I couldn't hide my disgust. After getting up I would ignore her and my face would bear traces of my agitation. She would watch me silently in sadness and fear. Sometimes she would pluck up enough courage to ask, "What's wrong?"

I would say nothing. Head bent, I would continue to smoke. I wouldn't want to speak. One word from me and she would feel encouraged and then she would talk and talk. And that would destroy the silently accepted protocols that governed our interaction. But my tension-filled silence brought to the surface all her suppressed worry, sharpened the pain on her face.

"Aren't you well?" she would dare to speak once again. I would raise my head angrily to say something bitter, but seeing the fear on her face, or perhaps moved by the fragility of her age, I would remain silent. She would be trembling ... what if I answered, Yes. She couldn't bear to think of me in pain.

Perhaps she drew some meaning from my silence. I never understood how Ma figured out exactly what went on inside me. What was this magic she had? Anyway, for some time she would be very careful. She would not come near me when I was in that condition or would make very sure that I was asleep. Perhaps she stood for a long time behind the door watching me.

One day I was a little more drunk than usual, because I had quarrelled with the woman I wanted to marry, and who wanted to marry me. We had been in love for a long time ... so long that she too, like me, had begun to age. Her hair was streaked grey and her breasts had begun to sag. Tired out, she had become passive, uncreative in her love. If the room had had a fourth corner I would have married her. This was precisely what she and I quarrelled about. She said that we could remove the bed and live in that corner. But I knew that Ma would not be able to bear this. Whenever I thought of Ma without that bed, I would sense a collapsing of foundations. When she lay with me on that bed at night, she was able to escape from her day-long silence, from my indifference, her failing sight, her wrinkles. She would touch my hand or run her fingers over my head. I would pretend to be unaware. She would start murmuring to herself, and even then her worries were about me ... my tired face, my advancing years, my loneliness. If I sometimes smiled in response, she would get excited and start telling me stories about her glorious past, how she used to lie on this very bed, and how after my birth I used to lie on the same spot. In a way that bed was the expression of her existence, it established the fact that her presence on this earth had meaning. It was only on that bed that she could be close to me, the last remaining joy of her declining years.

Actually, Ma knew that woman. I would often bring her to our room. Ma enjoyed meeting her. She would take her to her own corner and chat for a long time. Perhaps she spoke of the things she told the bed at night, or of what she suppressed within herself because she could never tell me of them. It may have been that Ma felt guilty knowing why our relationship could proceed no further, and tried to make up for it by being particularly nice to her. I would sit in my corner, smoking silently, listening to them and occasionally smiling. On seeing me smile, Ma would become even more animated and talk a lot. If I participated in the conversation, she was relieved and happy. She felt then that I was healthy and contented, and that I valued her presence in my life. In fact, filled with self-importance, she would even start ordering me around. I put up with it, though unwillingly. But slowly this would become unbearable, and sensing the change in my mood, she would get up and go away to the neighbours'. She knew why I brought that woman home. She knew why we wanted to be alone. She would return only when, after a long while, I had left the house with her.

So that night I had quarrelled with that woman. It was a cold night. So cold that I had taken a few gulps of the liquor in the shop itself and carrying the remainder with me, had gone to her house. I was filled with desire for her body.

She was lying in her room. Perhaps she had been crying and had only then become quiet. Her eyes were rheumy and on her cheek a tear lingered. I told her to come home with me. She turned me down harshly, saying that unless I removed the bed and made space for her in the room, she would never come home with me again. The heat of the liquor and my desire for her body went to my head. I pushed her to the ground, biting her lips and scratching her body, and then walked away in disgust.

I came home and threw myself on the bed. Ma smelt the liquor on my breath and screwed up her face. "You have started drinking far too much," she muttered. "The stink hangs over you till the morning." I opened my eyes and looked at her. Her wrinkles and whitened eyes were right next to my face. She looked lovely to me. All her love, her compassion, her innermost pain were laid bare on her face. She stroked my head slowly and looked at my aging body intently.

"She's not worth it," I mumbled. "Go to sleep."

Ma got up groaning and settled down on her side of the bed.

I had drunk too much and couldn't fall asleep. Twice I threw up and then lay there rubbing my chest.

That night I looked at Ma closely. She had grown old. Her hair was completely white, her face a maze of wrinkles, her cheeks sunken. As she slept, her flabby mouth had fallen slightly open and a soft strange sound came from it. I looked at her for a long time. The only woman in the world who loved me. To me, she seemed holy.

I did not sleep at all that night.

As usual Ma got up very early. It was totally dark. She started doing her routine jobs. I lay with my eyes open watching her. In her usual way she cleaned the room, then went for her bath. Suddenly she emerged, probably to get something she had forgotten. I saw Ma at that moment and was so shocked that I screamed. She was entirely naked. She had not thought that I might be awake. I leapt from the bed and started pushing her out of the room. "Get out, get out of here exactly as you are!" I was shouting like a mad man.

Ma saw the disgust on my face and in that instant it was as if she died. She stood before me completely naked. Like a skeleton, her skin falling off her bones. She looked at me for a while with her empty white eyes and then suddenly fell at my feet. She was holding on to my feet with all her strength, begging, "Please, just this once, just once, forgive me."

She lifted her head. She was crying. She looked devastated, utterly defeated. That day I saw the kind of pleading on her face that appears only when the very essence of the soul has dried up. Everything was transparent, everything was revealed, her shame, her fear, her remorse, her sense of worthlessness. I pushed her aside with hatred and left the house. I went straight to that woman and told her that very soon we would be married.

It was on that day that the first flower bloomed on the bare and scattered branches of the palaash.

After that it was as if Ma had turned to ashes. Silent, curled up in her corner, no longer did she look at me with those yearning eyes. She did not even meet my glance. A sort of cloudiness had descended upon her face. Whenever I was in the room she was terror-stricken. Her head bent, she would do something or the other, fearful of calamity, trying to deny her very existence. Her confidence in herself had disappeared. She would serve my food without a word. She slept on the bed with me, but had stopped touching me as she used to. She no longer talked to me about her past. She would squeeze herself into one corner of the bed. Perhaps she had even stopped talking to the bed. I no longer heard her murmuring to herself at night or laughing quietly as she used to. It was as if everything inside her was dead. Even the bed.

In those days, a crimson jungle had begun to spread across the palaash, and Ma fell ill.

That night it rained heavily. I had been drinking since evening. Ma was lying quietly in bed, covered with a sheet, crimped into her corner. I went and lay down by her side. She was breathing with difficulty. I got up and looked at her. It was after a long time that I was really looking at her. Her wrinkles had deepened. I touched her gently. For the first time after that day. She trembled, and turned her head to me. She looked at me for a while and then started to murmur, "You have become so weak. You look like an old man."

I was silent for a moment, and then said softly, "I'm getting married."

She said nothing.

"To her ... she's growing old, too."

Ma was still looking at me. She did not speak but there was a question in her eyes. And uncertainty.

"She'll live here. We'll move the bed," I said, quaking.

Ma said nothing. Slowly, she closed her eyes. And that night she died.

After Ma went, that corner became empty. We removed all her stuff – the old tin boxes, fan, torch, gods, japmalas – wrapped them all up and dumped the bundle in the loft. She arranged her own things in Ma's corner. There was nothing left of Ma anywhere. Ma was nowhere.

That night she lay with me on the bed. On the same side as Ma used to sleep. She was very happy. Teasingly, she nibbled my nose, and slowly undressed herself. I turned and saw her naked body sprawled on the bed. And at that instant a scream rose in my throat. There she was. Ma.

SWAPNAMOY CHAKRABORTI

THE SAGA OF BIMALASUNDARI

TRANSLATED BY GOPA MAJUMDAR

NOMINATED BY SARAT KUMAR MUKHOPADHYAY

First published in Bangla as "Bimalasundarir Upakhyan" in *Aajkaal*,
Puja Special Issue, October 1993, Calcutta.

Along the railway track walks Bimalasundari. Black stones lie by the side of the black steel. Little wild flowers grow in timeless profusion between the stones. Bimalasundari urges her eyes to look carefully. Are there any traces of blood anywhere?

Adinath, the barber, had said there was a dead body near Signal No. 2. He'd seen it himself, he had stressed. Mahim Ghosh's second son had stuffed her Shabitri into a sack and left her on the track. The ten fifty-six had whooshed past only moments later.

Bimalasundari passes the second signal and walks on to the fourth. It's the last signal on this line. There's nothing. No signs of blood or anything ghastly, not even torn pieces of sack. She stands between the tracks and cries, "Shabi ... Shabi ... Shabitri-i-i-!"

Dozens of office-going babus, rexine bags in hand, are running along the track towards the platform to catch the eight thirty-six. A few women who work as part-time domestic servants, are returning home to their shacks on the other side of the track. They walk on the pebbles between the tracks, their feet weighing lightly on the countless, nameless flowers that grow there.

Bimala does not notice them. She's staring at the lane that runs parallel to the railway tracks, on the other side. The Ma Manasa Mishtana Bhandar stands there. Mahim Ghosh owns the sweet shop. That's where Shabitri had gone and Mahim Ghosh's son had ...

One of the men slaps her shoulder with his folded newspaper. "What do you think you are doing, Mashi? Want to get killed?"

It is then that Bimala hears the train, huffing and puffing its way out of the station. She steps aside, just in time. "Have you," she asks the noisy train, "seen my Shabitri? Did you meet her last night?" But the train just keeps going and disappears

I thank Aruna Bhowmick for her help in translation of this story – G.D.

behind the green of wild bushes and the grey of shacks that line the tracks.

Bimala makes her way to the sweet shop.

The motherless "boy" who works in the Ma Manasa Mishtana Bhandar is standing outside, staring at a red kite in the sky. "Shabitri?" he says in reply to Bimala's question, wiping his nose on the palm of his hand. "That black cat? Yes, I know what happened to it. It was a scoundrel, Mashi, stealing milk and paneer from our shop almost every day. Mahim Babu's son caught it last night, stuffed it into a sack and took it ..."

"Where?"

"Beyond that last signal – yes, I saw – and further than that. The–re!" The boy points at some specks hovering in the distance.

Birds. Large birds. Vultures.

Bimala retraces her steps. She must walk on, but her feet refuse to obey. The water is no nearer; only the thirst grows, she thinks as she steels herself to walk beyond the signal. Its single red eye stares at her. Vultures wheel above her in the sky. Some others call.

Bimala's pace quickens. Here, beside the tracks, lies a torn sack with blood stains on it. There lies Shabitri ... Shabitri, my dear! A black, furry body torn to pieces by the vultures. She would have seen it the first time if she had walked just a few more steps. The white patch near the tail tells her all. She closes her eyes and quickly turns away.

It takes her a long time to return to the station ... black stones beneath her feet, black water within the potholes, but she'll never see her black beauty ever again.

Bimala sits down wearily on an empty bench, anger and grief thudding in her heart. May Mahim Ghosh die of cholera, she curses silently. May he die tonight. Now. And why is this "up" train still standing at Platform No. 2? Waiting for a line-clear signal?

May all trains come to a halt. May all shops pull down their shutters. May the whole town go to sleep. Let there be silence.

But life continues. The hawkers continue to shout – Oranges! Salted peanuts! The Chief Minister has shuffled his cabinet again! The train continues to hiss. People scurry about, pushing and jostling.

In the middle of it all, a voice suddenly says, "Why, imagine meeting you here. Do you recognise me?"

Bimala turns, to see first a finger wiping chuna on the back of the bench. Her eyes travel up to a hand with a paan in it, then, to a smile. A ray of sunshine that comes through a crack in the asbestos falls and lingers on that face.

"So, how are you?"

Just three words, but they are enough to make Bimala's heart beat faster. This man is her husband. Years ago, oh a hundred years ago, she used to live with him. A million words rise to her lips, but she cannot utter even one. Her mind begins to flow down the river of memories. She fails to stop it.

"Are you well?"

Bimala says nothing.

"Where do you live?"

"Here." At last she speaks.

"Here? Where?"

"Not far from here. On the way to the pickle factory, in a room in Bhuban Roy's house."

The train whistles. He slips his feet into his PVC shoes. Bimala watches his feet move rapidly towards a carriage. "I'm going to leave my daughter at her in-laws' ..." He's now gripping the handles of the carriage, pulling himself into the train. "I'll see you again ..." The train begins to move. "You didn't tell me how you are ..."

"I am well ... very well!" Bimala shouts at the departing train. Then she wipes her eyes. Tears wash away all grief. But the sands of the sea and the darkness of the heart, what can wash them away? She sighs heavily, letting her sorrow get lost in the aroma of brewing tea, the shouts of the hawkers, the howling winds in the railway station.

It had taken her a long time, but she had indeed put the past behind her. Why did she have to meet her husband today? For years and years, his face used to come back and haunt her. She would see it in the smoke that rose from chimneys, in the clouds that gathered in the sky, in the castles she built in the air, day-dreaming in her lonely bed.

It was also this face that had called her a "barren slut."

Of course Bimala was barren. Six years of marriage had borne no fruit. Visits to doctors and holy men, temples and dargahs had all failed. That face, distorted with rage, had once told her, "You can never give me a child. Yes, the doctor said so. I am going to marry again." There was nothing she could do to stop her husband from taking another wife.

How many years ago was that? She cannot remember. All she knows is that the paved road that runs from the Kali temple was little more than a dirt track then. The huge gulmohar tree that now towers over the station boundary wall was but two hands high. There were no double tracks then. There was a bamboo cluster where the cinema hall is now. And a pond where now stands the three-storied "Vasant Vihar." And, in a hut, near the pond lived her sister, Kamalasundari.

Bimala was present at the other wedding too, and had joined in all the rituals. In fact, it was she who held the oil pradeep and welcomed the new bride into the house. After all, her husband was not abandoning her totally. The idea was that both his wives should live together. But, once the ceremonies were over and the last wedding guest had left, her husband went into his room with his bride and suddenly Bimala could take no more. The sound of the latch still echoing in her heart, she walked out of his house and made her way through the dark night, carrying nothing but what she wore, to board the last train to her sister's house, fifty kilometres away.

"A rival in marriage is like a thorny bush," her sister said.

"It's much worse than a step-child or rice begged from the neighbours. It's good that you came away."

Didi had been widowed three years ago. She ran a small grocery store her dead husband had left her. Her son – her only child – was in the army. She made room for Bimala in her little hut, offering her the sympathy and support she so desperately needed. "You can help me look after the store," she said, "and the few ducks I keep. We'll manage."

Bimala's husband did, in fact, trace her one afternoon. He met Kamala Didi near the shop and asked if Bimala had come there.

Bimala, inside the house, had sweated with hurt pride.

"Yes, she's here."

"Thank god. Where is she? I'd like to see her once."

Somewhere deep down inside her, her pride jangled. Hastily, she slipped out of the room and hid in the shadows of the Kali mandir, those shadows which hide entire lives of women. On the red-coloured stairs, the dhu-dhu bird let out a lonely cry.

Shortly thereafter, she had seen him go away, the sun shining on his back, his head bent. He had gone, leaving behind footprints on the rain-drenched earth.

Nights turned into days, the seasons changed, the crops rotated and the gulmohar showered its flowers on the platform. A few years later, her sister died.

Bimala's nephew arrived, a young man she hardly knew. Secretly, she hoped that he would ask her to go and live with him. She dreamt of being looked after by his wife, of playing with his children. Oh, but the drums of time seldom play to one's dreams. Her nephew told her, "I want to sell this land and the shop. I'm going to settle in Dehradun. I'll try to send you a little money every month, if I can."

Bimala had to start another life, this time floating from one job to another, each time looking for a new place to live in. She was a cook at the house of Ṛasamaya Haldar of Goruhata. Then at Bipin Chakraborty's house, to tend to his old father. She lived behind the ration shop for a while. A few months ago, she had rented a tiny room in Bhuban Roy's house, near the pickle factory.

Who would have thought that the face she had almost forgotten would greet her here again, so unexpectedly?

All her old love surges forth, wiping out the years of loneliness. Do you still get that gastric pain, she asks him silently. Wish you wouldn't eat so many paans, with tobacco in them. It's not good for you. You've lost weight, and your hair looks greyer.

With a sigh, Bimala rises and walks across to a stall selling biscuits. She buys two cream biscuits for Bablu. Shabitri's gone. At least she still has her dog. He would be waiting for her.

Bimala turns to go home. Normally, she would have gone to the local primary school to sell snacks to the children. Today, she simply can't make the effort. Besides, there's this niggling drizzle.

Nitai, the idiot, stops his singing to greet her. "Mashi, namaskar!" Haru, the rickshaw-puller, calls out, "Mashi, how are your children?" Bimala does not speak. "And your grand-children?" Haru asks, ringing the bell of his cycle-rickshaw. Bimala continues to walk away. It was this same Haru who once took her all over town in his rickshaw, during Puja. On her lap were Antul and Bantul, two of Shabitri's little ones. Shabitri sat by her side on the red seat, and Bablu at her feet, his tongue hanging out. "Look at the lights!" Haru said to her animals, "See, see the giant-wheel. Just look at the colours and the people and ... oh, if you were little children, I'd have bought you ice-cream and taken you for rides on the giant-wheel!"

Bimala opens her door. A small puddle has formed just outside her verandah. Yellow flowers of the kalabati tree that grows in the adjoining house are reflected in the water. A lone frog leaps out of the shadows. There's still enough beauty left on this earth, if one knows where to look for it. Bimala's heart feels a little lighter.

Bablu barks as she walks in, straining on the rope he is tied with. His tail begins to wag. Antul-Bantul rush out and start meaowing. "Stop it!" says Bimala, breaking the biscuits into small bits for Bablu. "You have just lost your mother, do you know that?"

Her neighbour's wife – a graduate, no less – is watching over the fence. "Yes, I bought these biscuits with *my* money to feed *my* dog," Bimala mutters under her breath. Why should her neighbours mind?

On any other day, Bimala would have got busy by now. The pounding of coriander and cummin seeds would permeate the air and the chick-peas would be boiling in the pot. She sits outside the Bhagavati Balika Vidyalaya every day at tiffin time, selling cooked grams and potatoes, spicy and exciting. She could have found work in the pickle factory, but she'd have been on duty from eight in the morning to six in the evening. Then who would run her house?

Today, however, she goes in and lies down. The rain beats steadily on the tin roof. There's no hurry to make lunch. She'll get up later and cook something; her animals, those creatures of god, have to be fed.

"Bimala! Bimala!"

Someone's at the door. Bimala peers out. Oh, it's her landlord's son. "Do stop barking Bablu, you mustn't bark at any of the landlord's family," she says to her dog and opens the door.

"Baba wants to see you. Come at once," says the boy. He runs away, without waiting for her to speak.

Bimala shuts the door and follows him slowly, frowning. Why does the landlord want to see her again? She does not owe him any rent. She has started to keep her dog tied, and Shabi's dead. So what could be the matter?

Bhuban Roy had come from Bangladesh. Bimala can still remember him living in this small house with a tin roof. Then he got into the business of selling wheat. Goddess Lakshmi smiled on him. Soon came a trinket shop. He bought land; built a large house. A second storey followed; then came glass panes and curtains for the windows. Out of these windows now floats the aroma of pure ghee, and the sound of music. He let one of the three rooms in his old house to Bimala. The other two are packed with discarded furniture and such rubbish.

There was a time when Bhuban Babu's children used to call her Mashi. Bimala Mashi. Not any more. Today, even the youngest of them calls her by name. Perhaps he is just settling scores because she reprimanded him the other day. Oh, what a mess that was! She lost her temper, but with good reason. Could it be that her landlord was simply going to ask her to leave? But then he already had. She had asked to be allowed to stay for three months. He had agreed, hadn't he, after she apologised? "Don't make it four," was all he had said.

It was Bablu's fault, really. No. How can she think that? If Nature was going to have her way, who could stop her?

What happened was this: Bablu, in the prime of his youth, was courting a young bitch. The two were ... well, they were together out on the street, doing what Nature intended them to do. They should have been left alone. But this boy who had just come to call her, and two of his friends, had to go and interfere in a manner which, certainly in Bimala's eyes, was hideously cruel.

Bimala rushed out when she heard her dog howl in pain, to find the three boys laughing in glee. Bhuban Roy's son had rubbed a handful of salt on Bablu's body, on that precise spot where he was most vulnerable.

"You stupid bastard!" screamed Bimala, quite unmindful of who she was addressing.

"Ma!" the boy yelled, "Look Ma, she called me a bastard. She did, Ma, she did!"

The boy's mother – and many others – rushed out of the house at this. Amid their abuses, which included the word "whore," Bimala returned to her room with her dog. There was a little cream left in her kitchen, which she applied on the affected area. Cream was supposed to soothe irritation and burning. And suddenly, the sound of laughter made her look up. The graduate lady next door, clad in a maxi skirt, her adoring husband beside her, was watching her closely. Bimala saw her nudge her husband, who said something she couldn't catch.

Bhuban Roy summoned her the same evening.

"What is all this I hear?" Bimala heard him ask.

She made no reply.

"About your dog? What's your dog been up to?"

"Nothing that's unnatural."

"Not unnatural, hn? I see. What your dog does is perfectly natural, is it? I have a daugher, you know."

"The month is such, babu."

"Then keep him tied."

"From now on I will, babu."

"And what about yourself?"

"Me?"

"Reports have reached my ears about your perversion."

"Per ...?"

"Yes, yes. Don't try to act all innocent. You've been seen with your dog, doing unspeakable things."

Bimala could only stare. Bhuban Roy went on, "I won't stand this, I tell you. First it was your cat that would drink our milk, steal our fish and create a mess on our floor. Now it's your dog making a nuisance. Besides, you dared to call my son a bastard!"

"Only because ..."

"That's it. This is a respectable locality. You'll have to find some place else. I give you three days to clear out."

Bimala had to offer profuse apologies and promise to keep Bablu chained most of the time, before Bhuban Roy agreed to extend the three days' notice to three months.

Bimala has, in fact, been looking for another room. Many new buildings have come up in the town. But they are all modern buildings made with cement and concrete. Their rent is too high for her. Where can she find another house, old, with a tin roof maybe, but affordable?

She even went back to Goruhata. Rasamaya Haldar was older, but he recognised her instantly. He said, "Well dear, how are you?" She had been a cook in his house for three years. One day Rasamaya, true to his name, had become romantic. "Will you stay if I … I'll fix up another nice house for you." Bimala asked, "Do you think I'm crazy?" Rasamaya smiled. He asked her to not react so hastily, to think over the matter. "I am barren," Bimala told him. "That is why," he said with a grin, "there's no risk, you see." Bimala frowned, but Rasamaya was not looking at her face. "You are all the more desirable because your body has borne no children – heh-heh-heh! Food tastes better when the dishes are new, heh-heh-heh!" Bimala gathered her things and left that very day. She remembered him calling out from behind her, "If you are ever in need, come …"

She must go to the landlord's house. Why does he call, this Bhuban Roy?

The tall, iron gate of Bhuban Roy's new house opens as Bimala pushes it, with a screech that echoes inside her. As she steps into the ornate verandah, she hears a pressure cooker hiss.

"Have you found another room?" Bhuban Babu asks, coming straight to the point.

"No, babu. I've been looking, but …"

"Get out in seven days."

"But you said three months only the other day!"

"Don't talk nonsense. A week is all I am prepared to give you. Your cat drank our milk again. We won't put up with it."

"My cat? My cat … last night …"

"What about last night?"

"She died last night, babu."

"Rubbish! A lot of people saw your cat last night. We all know it, don't we? You may go now."

Bimala returns, her head bowed, twisting the anchal of her sari round and round her finger. As she opens the door, something soft and warm rubs itself against her legs, purring gently. A large, black, pregnant cat. Shabitri!

Bimala bends down quickly and gathers her in her arms, hardly daring to believe what she is seeing. How could Shabitri have escaped the certainty of death?

Bimala walks to the station. Her steps are light, like a girl's, her sari crisp white, its border a bright red. A fresh streak of sindoor in her hair-parting and alta on her feet, she walks like a queen. Bablu and Antul-Bantul, come frisking behind her. Shabitri comes last, her large body slowing her down. The last of the sun's rays falls on them.

At the station, Bimala buys a few pieces of bread. She dips some of the pieces in her clay tumbler of tea and offers it to Shabitri who likes drinking tea. Antul-Bantul get dry bread. She throws the crust of the bread towards Bablu and says, "Here, have some cake." Bablu sniffs at it and looks questioningly at her. Bimala laughs and then actually buys Bablu a small cake, picking out the raisin in it to give to Shabitri – she's pregnant after all.

A train pulls in.

Can *he* be on it?

If he is and if he gets down to see her, she'll not speak to him, even if he smiles at her in that special way. Let him think her heart has turned to stone.

Bimala waits a few moments. No, he isn't on this train. But he'll come one day. She's positive about that. She turns to go home. Shabitri's return has made her day.

It's morning again. The crows are up. Boonchi's Ma and Panchi's Ma are on their way to work, discussing their problems. Bimala stretches an arm sideways; it brushes against the bed-sheet, and nothing else. Bimala sits up. Where's Shabitri? She always sleeps in the same bed and rises only when Bimala does.

Bimala comes out and stands in her little verandah. The karabi shrub by the gate has started to bloom; a carpet of white flowers lie at the foot of the shiuli tree. The BA-pass daughter-in-law next door is up, making her way to the bathroom, her mouth full of toothpaste foam. Bimala turns away and looks out at the street. A number of people are out already, heading for the Mother Dairy milk-booth. Nitai the vagabond is out, too, sitting in his shorts and banian, singing a love song.

Out of the corner of her eye, she sees the graduate lady coming out of the bathroom. She returns to her verandah, and pulls out a cane chair. She prepares to lower herself into it, then gives a little shriek. Her husband bounds out of their bedroom, still tying his pyjama cords. "What's the matter?" he asks. "Look!" says his wife, pointing at the cushion. Then she turns and looks straight at Bimala. "Come here!" she calls. "See what your precious cat's done to our cushion!"

Bimala walks over with slow, measured steps. The lady and her husband haven't stopped talking. They are fed up, they say. They would quite happily kill that cat.

"How can you be so sure it was my Shabitri?" Bimala asks spiritedly. "Did you actually see her do it?"

"Don't argue," says the husband.

"Peel off the cushion cover and wash it," commands his wife, "No other cat ever comes this way. Of course it was yours."

Bimala does as she's told. There's a small lump of waste matter on the red cushion cover. She takes it off carefully, not really minding having to do this. It looks familiar. It can only mean Shabitri's alive, and not far from home.

The day wears on. Boonchi's Ma and Panchi's Ma return from work, discussing their problems. Nitai, through with his wanderings for the day, has sung himself back home. Where then is Shabitri?

The school being closed for the day, Bimala takes her basket of snacks to the station. What could have happened to Shabitri? Has someone beaten her up? She often came back with bleeding wounds. But now ... Bimala worries more. Shabitri's pregnant.

Bimala takes Bablu out for a walk in the evening. A new

two-storeyed house has come up nearby. Bimala doesn't know the people who live in it, but she knows their dog. It's a bitch, large and furry and clearly well-looked-after. She's out in the garden today, all by herself. Bablu stops. The other dog has seen him. She presses her face against the iron gate. Oh, so she finds my Bablu attractive, does she? Bablu begins licking the tip of her nose, the only part he can reach through the bars of the gate.

"No, Bablu, no!" Bimala drags him away. "Don't get involved with vilayati dogs. It can only mean trouble. I'll get another one for you ... yes, yes, I'll have to tempt her with food or something, to get her into the house. I'll lock the door from outside, then you can do what you must do, without any disturbance. All right? Come now, there's a good boy."

She asks a few children if they had seen her cat. No one has. Bimala walks for miles. She goes to the milkman's colony. There's no sign of Shabitri. She returns slowly, each step heavy with weariness, to find a group of young men near her house. One of them rushes forward when he sees her. Bimala recognises him. She has often seen him outside the local club.

"Ai, you old woman, when will you leave this town? Tell me!" he says angrily.

"Why, what's happened?"

"Go and find out from Kakoli's mother. Ask her what your cat's done in their house!"

A girl called Kakoli lives with her parents, only four houses away from Bimala's. What has Shabitri done in their house? Eaten the prasad? Or, Durga-Ma Durga, has she had her litter in their puja room? Kakoli's father is a devout Brahmin. Bimala has often heard the sound of bells and conch shells from their house. The puja room is a sacred place, after all. They *would* be angry.

Kakoli's mother screams at the top of her voice when she sees Bimala. "Your cat has ruined, absolutely destroyed, our well! Go and have a look. She's floating in the water, dead."

Bimala almost swoons. Then she runs to the well, not caring that one of her chappals has slipped from her foot, or that her sari has dropped from her shoulder.

A black body is indeed floating in the dark water.

Bimala closes her eyes.

"Who's going to pay for the loss? The well ... and all that water..."

"Pour a few kilos of bleaching powder in it."

"Not bleaching powder. Gamaxin."

"Don't be silly. That's poison. Bleaching powder will do."

"Let's argue later, shall we? The main job is to get it out."

"I've been trying with this bucket, but keep missing."

"Isn't there a hook? The hook to lift buckets with?"

Someone brings a well-hook and some rope. "Let me try. If I get it out, do I get a reward, or what?"

The hook is lowered. There are joyous cries. "It's coming ... It's coming!"

A black cat is brought up, dripping wet, as though its whole body is weeping. Bimala glances for a fleeting second at its bloated stomach, then looks away. The hook has dug itself into the body. How many kittens would she have had, had she lived? What a cruel waste!

There are excited voices everywhere.

"What do we do with this?"

"Throw it away by the pond."

"Are you mad? It'll start smelling, won't it? Far better to take it to the railway track."

Someone eager for a reward goes and gets a rope. Someone else ties it around the dead cat's neck. They then drag it away – Bolo Hari, Hari bol! – jubilant with their day's work. Crows fly overhead, cawing incessantly. All that is left is the trail of wetness on the ground. But that will soon dry.

Bimala gathers all the darkness in the anchal of her sari. She comes back home to lose herself in the emptiness of her room. How did Shabitri fall into the well? She could not have flung herself in, surely? She didn't have a single care in the world, did she? Was it an accident, or had someone pushed her in?

It grows darker and darker. Married women blow the conch of Laxmi in evening prayer. The puja bells chime from the homes of Brahmins. A cycle-rickshaw honks somewhere, a train toots. Nitai sings on. The sandhyamalati blooms. Someone's frying parathas; Bimala can smell the dalda rise and mingle with the scent of the flowers. Everything appears to be right with the world. The moon rises as usual, the stars shine, and trains whistle at the station. A few fireflies buzz in the darkness.

The light from a street-lamp falls at an angle near the karabi shrub. It merges with the faint glow of moonlight, creating strange patterns in the darkness. Bimala, still overcome with despair, is staring at the shadows under the tree when she notices a movement, and hears a sound a second later.

Meeaow!

Shabitri stands before her, her tail held erect.

Unable to believe her eyes, Bimala picks her up quickly, burying her face in the warmth of Shabitri's body.

"Well, here I am!" says a voice.

Startled a second time, Bimala looks up and finds her husband standing in the semi-darkness of her verandah.

"I told you I'd come, didn't I?"

"Yes, so you did. Come in."

"I had to look everywhere before I found your house. Took me over an hour."

"Do sit down."

"All I remembered was the name, Bhuban Roy. But it turned out that there's another person by the same name who lives towards Pathanpur. Then someone directed me here. It was only later that I remembered the pickle factory. Well, aren't you happy to see me?"

"Very."

"What are these? My God, why do you have so many cats? And a dog, too!"

"My pleasures and my passions."

Bimala raises the wick of the kerosene lamp. Then she looks

at herself in the mirror and applies a large red dot of sindoor. She bends to touch his feet.

"Would you like a cup of tea?"

"No. Just a glass of water. I bought some meat and rotis from the shop at the station," he says. "Here. Take it."

"Keep it on that table."

Bimala hands him a glass of water, her fingers touching his. When was the last time she touched him? Her fingers tighten into a fist. Bimala looks at the flame that rises from the lamp, her hand stroking Shabitri.

And it is that moment that Shabitri chooses to go into labour.

"How are you, Bimala?"

"I am well. Shabi is going to have her babies."

"Who's Shabi?"

Bimala does not reply. In the light of the lamp, her eyes shine with an odd tenderness.

"Oh, I see. Your cat. Short for Shabitri, is it? A cat called Shabitri? Ha-ha! Look, I want to stay the night. My family will think I stayed on at my daughter's house – I was going to, but I came here instead. Ha-ha. She's expecting, you know."

Bimala rises and washes her hands. The shadows dance on the wall. "Shabi's giving birth," she says softly.

A firefly comes in through an open window. The fragrance of the madhabilata flowers outside wafts in with the breeze.

"What I'd really like to do," her husband continues, "is to take you back with me. That is, if you agree. I mean ..."

"Sh-h!" Bimala whispers, "Don't speak now. Not a word. Even the TV in every house has fallen silent. Can't you make out?"

Then she turns to Shabitri. "Oh daughter, daughter of mine, don't cry," she consoles, "I know it's difficult, but you're a woman, aren't you? All this pain, all this discomfort is only going to lead to joy, fulfilment. You're going to be a mother again. You know that, don't you? Don't cry. It'll be over soon."

Bimala gathers her cat into her arms. The warmth of Shabitri's body fills her heart.

BOLWAR MAHAMAD KUNHI

THE FISHMONGER

TRANSLATED BY H. Y. SHARADA PRASAD
NOMINATED BY RAMACHANDRA SHARMA

First published in Kannada as "Meenu Maruvavanu" in *Prajavani*, Deepavali Special Issue, October 1993, Bangalore.

One could have sworn by any god that the young man in his twenties, who stood on the threshold seeking permission to enter, the man with wide eyes and a pleasant smile, did not have an iota of faith in astrology. If Adram Byari had not dropped in the previous evening at dusk and explained everything, Subraya Jois would have been more startled than puzzled by the visit of this man who had never before come to his house.

Jois gestured to the young man and bade him enter. He did so and sat opposite Jois on a straw mat with his feet tucked under him, like a man at namaaz. The radiance of youth was enhanced by the attar, Jannatul Firdaus, he had sprinkled on himself.

Jois took some cowrie shells in his hand and cast them on the floor. He pulled a few of them together, brushing the rest to one side. He bent his fingers and then opened them, one by one, obviously making some calculations. Then he shut his eyes in the manner of a man looking for the answer to a riddle. A moment or two later, he opened his eyes and, with the triumphant smile of a man who knew it all, asked the young visitor in a playful voice, "Isn't your name Razzak?"

"Yes."

"Weren't you watching a film at this hour last Friday?"

"Yes."

"And you didn't go to the theatre today because you wanted to be here?"

"Yes."

"And also, before coming here, you didn't go to the Liberty Hotel, as you do every Friday, but went instead to an Udipi eating place for a vegetarian meal?"

"Yes."

"And you are planning to buy a second-hand car and you are here because you want to consult me?"

"Yes."

"Now tell me, how did I come to know all this?"

"Because Adram Byari of the cloth-shop told you."

They both burst into laughter. There was no trace of reserve now. Razzak shyly placed before Jois a ten-rupee note he had hidden in his fist.

"Adram Byari hadn't told me about this money. Or did he give you special coaching?"

Razzak caught the disapproval in Jois's tone and did not attempt an answer.

Subraya Jois's reputation as an astrologer was well-known from Sakleshpur above the ghats to Kasargod on the coast. It was a matter of record that marriages made on the basis of the horoscopes he had studied and matched had endured without exception. When war had broken out for the second time between Pakistan and India, he had forecast, in the very first week, that India would score a swift victory, and the prediction had been widely reported in the newspapers. This wiry man with a bent nose, large ears and shining eyes, this man who was on the threshold of sixty and commanded instant respect from anyone who saw him ... such a person's disapproval was something Razzak did not know how to deal with. He wondered whether he had done the right thing at all in coming to Jois at Adram Byari's bidding.

It did not take Jois much effort to read what was going on in the young man's mind. His face revealed it all. Jois craned his neck towards the door at the back of the room and said aloud, "Oh, lady of the house, look, your Fish Clock is here in person."

Jois's wife knew someone had come in, and had been waiting behind the door for the summons. Even so, she was taken aback to see Razzak.

The young man who sat like a disciple on the mat was no stranger. She saw him every afternoon, barring the three or four months of the rainy season. A couple of minutes after four, his bicycle carrying baskets of fish passed in front of the house, Razzak announcing his progress by pressing the rubber horn attached to his bicycle.

From Jois's house one could see the knot of women and children waiting for the bicycle at the end of the street.

That was the terminus of Razzak's daily journey. By the time he arrived there, he would have sold the contents of the two baskets tied to the carrier of the bicycle and he would be left with the fish in the two palm-leaf bags that hung from the handlebar. It was not his habit to haggle and it did not take him much time to dispose of his stock. After that he went to the public pond at the end of Post Office Road for a bath.

It was not only Razzak's customers who knew the various stops on his daily route. The smell of his fish assailed the nostrils of everyone on his beat, whether they were fish-eaters or not. His punctuality had earned him the nickname "Radio Time Razzak." And Jois called him the Fish Clock.

Jois had publicly paid him a tribute a couple of years ago. This is how it had happened: Jois was giving a discourse on values in life and the meaning of devotion at the Ganesh festival in the main temple of the town. He had expatiated on the idea that devotion consisted, not in shutting one's eyes and singing hymns, but in doing one's work with utmost dedication and without any expectation of a reward. "Let me give you an example," Jois had gone on to say. "Take Razzak, the lad who sells fish. There is no difference between bhakti and the thoroughness with which he goes about his work." These words of Jois had become the talk of the town.

To recognize Razzak, you needed eyes only on one day of the week; on other days the nose would do. On Fridays, Razzak took a break from his work. From ten-thirty to twelve-thirty he was at the government pond on Post Office Road, giving himself a good scrub from head to toe. Why, even the white rubber sandals he wore were cleaned with the bath-soap he used. Then at the stroke of one, he was at the mosque. His clothes could serve as an illustration of the phrase "shining bright like lightning": A milk-white dhoti, a sparkling white full-sleeved shirt, and a white handkerchief with a green or blue border tucked around the nape of his neck to protect the collar of his shirt; and his presence on Fridays was announced by the perfume he used so liberally.

After namaaz he took a rickshaw and rode to Liberty Military Hotel (it was called "military," because it served meat). From there, again by rickshaw, he made his way to the Apsara movie-house, where a new film was released every Friday. The left corner seat on the front row of the balcony was reserved for him by the management. After the matinee show Razzak sat on the jagali of Adram Byari's cloth-shop until sunset, hardly talking to anyone. At eight, he rose and went back to the same eating place where he had his afternoon meal. And by nine, he was back home.

After the death of Razzak's mother, there had not been a single day when Jois's wife had not thought of sending for him to enquire after his welfare. She and Razzak's mother had been born in the same town and had come to Muthuppadi as brides around the same time. Whenever there was a feast in Jois's house, a packet of eatables was set apart for Razzak's mother. Razzak had never accompanied his mother, except perhaps as a child, when she may have brought him, perched on her waist.

So this was the first time Jois's wife was seeing him from this near and so surprised was she that she didn't know what to say.

Jois turned towards his wife and said in a teasing voice, "Tell me, have any of your sons ever been so spotlessly clean?"

She retorted, "The smell of fish suits him better than all that perfume he has poured on himself."

"Let her be," Jois said to Razzak. "She has no patience with anyone who is neat and clean. She wants the whole world to be full of good-for-nothings like her two sons."

Razzak did not know what to make of this banter between a woman who had never spoken to him before and the man who was the town's most respected person.

Jagali: The raised front verandah in a traditional South Indian house.

Razzak had been too young when his father died to have any memories of him. His mother had died within a year of his becoming a fishmonger. He had no one in the world to call his own, no one who bothered whether he was alive or dead, except perhaps Adram Byari. With all the others, his dealings were limited to the buying and selling of fish.

The daily fish trade in Muthuppadi was around six or seven thousand rupees. The supply came from Mangalore, forty miles away. A lorry arrived around noon every day, proclaiming its arrival with a very distinctive toot. This was the signal for the marketplace to come alive. On days when the catch was plentiful, a couple of cars followed the lorry. As soon as the horn was heard, fish-sellers got busy; they tucked up their lungis and came, pushing their bicycles as close to the lorry as possible. When the baskets were being unloaded from the lorry, urchins would dart to and fro to snatch any fish that slipped to the ground, out-manoeuvring the dogs which were there with the same intent. Razzak had mastered his trade as one of these light-footed boys who sold the fish they managed to lay hands on. Now he was an established fishmonger. And in a week he would have a car of his own.

"So, are you going to just stand there, staring at him or can you offer him at least a tumbler of milk?" Jois asked his wife. When she went inside, Jois turned to Razzak and said to him in a serious tone, "Listen to me, young man. When Adram Byari came to me yesterday, I told him that only a man who did not know his mind worried about the future. You are not one such. You are clear in your mind about what you want to do. I hear you have even paid an advance for the car. Suppose I consulted the cowrie shells and told you that the deal would not be profitable, would that stop you from buying the car?"

Razzak did not know what to say. The deal had been struck. An advance of two thousand rupees had been paid. All that remained now was to sign seven or eight documents at the office of Naik Finance the following Monday and the car would become his. It would not be very difficult to pay the monthly instalment of seven hundred rupees. There was no question of his going back on the transaction.

A smile played on Jois's face when he found Razzak at a loss for words. He got up, and so did Razzak. Just then Jois's wife came into the room with a tumbler of milk. Jois took it from her hand and, cupping it in both palms, offered it to Razzak, "Drink it before you go. May good fortune always be with you," he said.

Razzak took the tumbler in all solemnity, sat down on the floor and drank the milk. Jois's wife, who was watching this scene, broke the silence. She bent down and picked up the ten-rupee note which Razzak had placed at the edge of the mat, saying, "This money is mine, we have earned it." It was Jois's turn to be dumbfounded.

If Subraya Jois should ever say that the sun would not rise the next day, there was one man who would defend him with all conviction. That was Narayana Prabhu. His faith in Jois's predictions was total.

Prabhu was not only the sub-postmaster of the town of Muthuppadi but also one of the pillars of its society. It was he who had organised the very first Ganesh Festival in the Sahasra Lingeshwara Temple with much fanfare. And it was he who had persuaded Jois to give a discourse on the nature of dharma during the festival.

Normally Prabhu would not presume to question even one word that issued from Jois. But he was also a great believer in certain proprieties. He wondered whether it was proper for Jois to drag in the name of a Muslim fish-seller to illustrate the idea of dharma. With his vast knowledge of the Vedas, the Shastras and the Puranas, Jois could have come up with more suitable examples from our own tradition, if only he had given it a moment's thought. He could have spoken of Dharmaraja, of Hanuman, of Sabari. But he chose to mention Razzak, of all the people. What had come over him?

Not that Prabhu questioned the validity of what Jois had said about Razzak and his thoroughness. Why, Prabhu himself waited for the horn of Razzak's bicycle every afternoon to call out to his wife that it was time to make tea.

There was another reason why Prabhu was flustered. Ananta Bhatta was the most contrary man in town. No matter what was being discussed, he would start his argument with "It's not like that, swamy, but like this ..." As a consequence he had earned the nickname No-But Bhatt. Even he had agreed with Jois on this matter. "I just can't believe that this boy was born to a Moplah. What courtesy! What scrupulousness! If by any chance Razzak sees me on the road, he gets off his bicycle at once, moves to the edge of the road, and waits until I pass. If we ignored the fact that he goes to a mosque once a week, tell me in what respect is he inferior to us?" Bhatta had asked.

All this had happened two years ago and it came as a flash-back to Prabhu one afternoon.

He was locking up the post office for the day, when Adram Byari rushed panting up to him, saying, "I have to make an urgent call. I hear our Razzak has met with an accident."

The call went through to the Mangalore Hospital quickly enough. They learnt that Razzak's car had been hit by a lorry and had fallen into a ditch at a bend on the Bantwal road. Fortunately Razzak had not been seriously hurt. The car, however, was a wreck.

After Adram Byari left, Prabhu sat down on the doorstep, too dazed even to lock his office. Barely three months since Razzak had bought his car, and already an accident? Prabhu found it hard to believe that Subraya Jois had not known this would happen. If he had known it, why had he not warned Razzak, Razzak for whom he had such regard?

Adram Byari had told him all about how Razzak had gone to Jois for advice, how Jois, with not so much as a glance at the cowries, had sent off Razzak with the strange words, You do not need your future to be read. Prabhu had not attached much importance to it then. But, in retrospect, Jois's behaviour appeared inexplicable and out of character. What could be at the root of Jois's ambivalence? It was all a riddle to Prabhu.

He decided to go to Jois's house, carrying this bundle of doubts on his head. Even as he went up the steps he called out, "Have you heard, Jois-re? Our Radio Time, our Razzak, met with an accident this afternoon. The car is all smashed up."

Jois was just about to place a lighted agarbathi in front of the framed picture of a God. "What did you say?" he exclaimed and sat down heavily, as if his legs had given way beneath him.

Prabhu was alarmed. He sat next to Jois and, to make amends for the panic he had created, added, "But there's no need to worry, Jois-re. Adram Byari phoned Mangalore from my office. The boy's luck is as solid as a grindstone. He escaped with just a few scratches. They said he should be out of the hospital in a day or two. If anyone else had been in such an accident, it would have been difficult to recover a single bone. Adram Byari thinks the car will have to be sold off as scrap."

Jois sat motionless. He did not even look at Prabhu.

Prabhu was quiet for a few minutes. But he could not stop himself from asking, though with great hesitation, "I am told that those people do not believe in our astrology and things like that. But is it true that you sent him away when he came to see you?"

Jois sat unstirring like the trunk of a tree.

Prabhu moved closer to Jois and said, in a whisper, "Did you know all this would happen? Is that why you did not go through with consulting the cowries?"

Jois flinched as if he had been lashed by a whip. He stole a quick glance at Prabhu and was reassured to find no sarcasm on his countenance. "Oh my God," he murmured, covering his ears with his palms. Prabhu had known Jois for more than twenty years. Not once had he doubted Jois's integrity. What had driven him now to ask this question? "There must have been some error in my calculations. I must re-check," said Jois after a few moments and dragged himself back into his house.

Adram Byari was ready to stand before any dargah built for the glory of Allah the Merciful, and swear that if Subraya Jois had had any inkling whatsoever that Razzak's car would be smashed up within three months, he would have said so in so many words that afternoon Razzak had gone to him. So when Narayana Prabhu went to Adram Byari's house with Ananta Bhatta to tell him that Jois had not touched his cowries for more than a month now, he did not know what to make of the news.

Narayana Prabhu had heard rumours a week ago that Jois was no longer practising astrology because he was unwell. He had not made much of it. After all, when a man is on the wrong side of sixty, to be in poor health is not surprising. But now that a month had passed and people were talking about Jois refusing to even look at the cowries, Prabhu was deeply distressed. He was not the sort to share his inner thoughts with anyone else. But he had no doubt that Jois's practice had come to an abrupt end the day that he, Prabhu, had gone to him with the news of Razzak's accident. If anyone found that out, Prabhu would find it impossible to live in that town. He wondered if he should not go to Jois, fall at his feet and ask for forgiveness. If Jois forgave him, well and good. But if he didn't, it would be like giving a stick to a man and asking to be thrashed; it would be humiliating. The thought of the injustice he might have done to Jois tormented Prabhu day and night, robbing him of even his sleep.

Meanwhile Razzak had returned home after spending four or five days in hospital. He had dropped in to see Prabhu a couple of times to tell him of his troubles with the insurance people and with Naik Finance. These visits only deepened Prabhu's feeling of guilt. Once he almost asked, Have you met Jois, but managed to change the question at the last minute into "Have the insurance people promised to compensate you?"

"Partly. I think it might be more sensible to hand over the car to them than get it repaired. Luckily nothing happened to my hands and legs. I can get back to my business and one day perhaps buy a better car, maybe even two," Razzak replied, leaving Prabhu even more perturbed.

It was one of the longest months in Prabhu's life. He found it more and more difficult to bear the agony all by himself. Finally, he decided to take Ananta Bhatta into confidence.

No-But Bhatt heard him out patiently. Then he said, typically, "It's not like that, Prabhu-re. Let me tell you, the stars are the same whether one is a Hindu, a Muslim, or a Christian. Haven't the newspapers written about Americans consulting our astrologers before launching their rockets? If you think Jois deliberately chose not to consult his shells, that would amount to saying he knew what was in store for Razzak. There must be some other reason. But to me there seems to be no connection, as you choose to think, between the accident and his giving up astrology."

None of No-But Bhatt's arguments made any sense to Prabhu. It was like holding a lamp behind one to light one's way ahead.

"Look here, Bhatta-re," said Prabhu. "It's true I came to you and told you everything, but it was not so you could tell me what is right and what is wrong, but to see if you had any suggestions as to how I can go to Jois and apologise to him. Tomorrow is a Sunday. You must go with me to Jois's house. But there's one important point you must remember. Whatever I have told you today must remain between the two of us. If anyone ever gets to know about it, I will have recourse to one thing only – a rope."

Prabhu's tone showed he had come to a decision. To put him at ease, Bhatta said, "What do I lose by going with you? And what do I gain by broadcasting our discussion? I shall be at your house at lunchtime. We'll go after lunch. Elephants are not going to turn into horses in the meanwhile, are they?"

He was as good as his word, arriving at Prabhu's house at lunchtime. Consumed as he was by the confusion in his mind, Prabhu could barely force a couple of mouthfuls down his throat. But Bhatta enjoyed his meal, even asking for second helpings.

He finished his meal with a satsified burp.

Just as Bhatta stood up, saying, "Shall we leave?" Prabhu suggested, "Won't it be better if we took our friend Adram Byari of the cloth-shop along? After all it was Byari who sent Razzak to Jois. If he exculpates Jois of responsibility, that would make Jois feel better."

Ananta Bhatta, the "but" and "however" man, agreed at once. He was ready for anything that would lessen Prabhu's worry.

The two made their way to Byari's cloth shop.

Byari ordered two cups of tea for them from the adjoining Ganesh Vilas. After hearing Prabhu out, Byari said, "If Allah draws a line and says it shall be thus, nobody can alter that line even a little bit. Take it from me. The man who has lost his car has kept a cool head. Why are you behaving as if the sky has fallen on you?"

And he went on to say, "But I agree we – all three of us – should meet Jois. Today is as good a day as any."

No matter what god I swear by, my husband refuses to listen to me, Prabhu-re," Jois's wife said to them. "Now that you are all here, please try and persuade him," she said, giving the three guests some jaggery and water to quench their thirst. She sat down on the floor, leaning against the jamb of the inner door.

There was no sign of Jois.

"Is he resting?" asked Adram Byari.

Ananta Bhatta cut in, "It is this way, Akka. In this world most people think only of themselves. Our Jois is not like that. He is like the mother who always thinks of her children. There is a reason behind everything he does. As Lord Krishna said in the Bhagavad Gita ... "

"Whatever Lord Krishna might say, my lord and master says his horse has only three legs," Jois's wife said, matter-of-factly.

"Will you go in and tell him we are here?"

Jois's wife looked at the clock on the wall and replied, "There is no need for anyone to call him. When the clock strikes four, out he will come like a clockwork doll that has been wound up. Wait for just two more minutes and you will see for yourselves."

The three exchanged glances, not able to make out what Jois's wife meant.

A silence fell on the group. They sat there, gazing at the old clock, waiting for the minute hand to touch twelve. The tension broke when it chimed four times.

Jois's wife did not stir.

They saw the curtain of the inner door being pushed aside, and Jois's shrunken frame came into view. The three visitors who had been sitting on a bench in the front room, stood up.

Jois smiled vaguely at them without seeming to have really noticed them. Prabhu brought his hands together in a namaskara; Jois did not return the greeting. Instead, like a sleepwalker, he turned and walked towards the front door, crossed the threshold and went down the steps to sit on the last step. His eyes were rivetted on the road.

Ananta Bhatta rose, made a signal to Adram Byari with his eye, and followed Jois.

"No one, not even God can get a word out of him when he sits there," Jois's wife said, in a choked voice, beating her forehead with her palm. "He has had just one refrain since last month. Whatever I say, he silences me by putting a finger to his lips and saying, The fisherboy *will* come again. What can I say to his obsession?"

Suddenly, Adram Byari exclaimed loudly. "Yah Allah!"

The three others looked at him in alarm.

Adram Byari said in a ringing voice, "Jois is one hundred per cent right! Razzak *is* starting his business again. And look, he's starting today!"

Even before Adram Byari could complete his words, and as if to prove Jois's prediction, Razzak rode by, blowing the horn on his bicycle.

PRAKASH NARAYAN SANT

SHARADA SANGEET

TRANSLATED BY DHANANJAY KAPSE

NOMINATED BY G. N. DEVY

First published in Marathi as "Sharada Sangeet" in *Mauj*,
Diwali Issue, November 1993, Bombay.

On the way to school, just across the railway gate was the house with the green walls. On the ground floor were all sorts of shops. But they kept changing. One day a board with some mad name would go up, and some mad store or mart would open. The shopkeeper's first job was to shoo away children like us who, on our way to or from school, stopped to stare at all the goods in the store. His second job was to keep wiping the glass cupboards with that silly rag on his shoulder. And his third, to say "No!" to any question that started off with, "Do you have ..." These three tasks would tire him so much that he plopped down onto his stool and just sat there. He cleaned the glass cupboards less and less and then one day, the shop wouldn't open at all. Soon another board went up and another shopkeeper was there, shooing us away. Everything was the same, except that the shopkeeper now had a new face and a different voice.

While the shops on the ground floor kept changing, the board on the first floor, "Sharada Sangeet Vidyalaya," remained the same. Everyone called it just Sharada Sangeet. The name kept coming up in conversation, especially of the girls.

When I first heard the name, I couldn't figure out what exactly it was. Like the sun on a foggy day. You can't see it, but you know it is there. I longed to understand it.

The music school had nine windows looking out onto the road. Many different sounds flowed out of those nine windows. Some were familiar; others really strange. Every time I walked by the building, I felt as if waves of sounds crashed into me and I had this mad urge to climb the stairs and go in.

Then one day, I did just that.

The staircase led straight up from the street. Its walls were sky blue. Because it was slightly dark, it felt as if I was moving up through a lake that had parted for me. Right at the top of the

---

I thank Keerti Ramachandra for her help in translating this story - G.D.

The English word "mad" occurs often in the original Marathi; it approximates to the colloquial "weird." By and large, we have retained the word wherever it occurs in the original, or substituted "weird" or "silly" depending on the context.

stairs, just before I bumped my nose into a wall, I saw a left turn. I stepped over a high threshold to enter a big room.

To the left were four windows that opened onto the road. Each window began at knee-height and ended level with my head. They made me feel as if I had suddenly grown tall. The tiled roof rose from either side of the room to meet high above at the centre. There were forty-one different photographs on the walls; the Master was there in thirty-nine of them. In the centre of the wall was a coloured picture of the god, Sree Shankar. He looked really scary. Below the pictures were ranged wooden benches of different sizes. The smooth red-ochre floor felt nice and cool to walk on. Saraswati Kerur was to tell me later that it had been specially laid for the dance class because, when you learnt dancing, you had to stamp your feet hard.

In the centre of the far wall was a door which opened into another room. A blue durrie covered the entire floor. This room had five windows opening onto the street, and more benches along the walls. Students sat on the floor, the girls with their feet tucked under them, the boys as if for a meal, cross-legged. As soon as a student finished his or her turn at a harmonium, another came to take that place. There were eight harmoniums in a row, arranged from small to big. They divided the room into two. The first one almost touched the right wall. The last two had woollen covers on them.

The space beyond the line of harmoniums was as if reserved for Master. The first thing I noticed about him was his colour and his smile. He was very fair and had jet-black, curly hair. He was always smiling. On either side of him were many tablas, daggas and other musical instruments, kept in closed boxes. The porcelain bowls of a jal-tarang were arranged in a semi-circle in front of him. The mattress he sat on, the bolster, everything was spotlessly white. Behind him were two paintings of Laxmi and Saraswati, each five feet high, each in special gilt frames. A strange, yet familiar, scent filled the room. I had a mad feeling that I knew this place very well, that I had been there before.

Six girls sat with bowed heads behind the first six harmoniums, pressing the keys and moving the bellows earnestly. There was a confusion of sounds. To add to this, Master was tuning the jal-tarang.

I went and stood behind the girls playing the harmonium, holding the letter given to me by the Chief Guest at my school prize-distribution ceremony. The moment I held out the letter, Master raised his hand and all the harmoniums stopped playing. In the sudden silence, a bicycle rattling by on the road below startled me. Master read the letter. He closed his eyes and brought his palms together. Then he said, "Join the first batch from tomorrow. Bathe and put on clean clothes before you come to class. At seven o'clock sharp. You can go now."

It looked as if there were only girls in the class. I was beginning to get worried.

The next day I was up early and ready, and I reached Sharada Sangeet before anyone else. It was not yet open. I sat on one of the many logs lying in the vacant lot opposite the green house till Master arrived on his bicycle. He parked it, looked at me and said, "Shabash! You're early. Come in."

I went upstairs with him. At the top of the staircase, he bowed before the door, unlocked it and entered the room. He bowed again before entering the other room. He turned to me and said, "First, let's clean the place, then do puja; after that, your first lesson." He tied a big white handkerchief around his head, took a broom and briskly swept both rooms. Then he removed the handkerchief, lit an agarbatti before the pictures of Laxmi and Saraswati and said a small prayer. He dusted all the harmoniums with a yellow cloth. Then he sat down against the bolster.

I was standing near the window, watching him. Master looked at me and smiled. I suddenly felt as if we had known each other for a long time and I grinned back. He said, "The letter you brought yesterday was from my Guru's brother. It is his order that I teach you without taking any fees. So, what do you want to learn?"

I wanted to learn to sing, but there were so many harmoniums and I was dying to play one of them. I blurted out, "Harmonium!"

"Come," he said. "Sit at Number One." I looked puzzled. And he said, "Number One is the first harmonium on my left."

I went and sat down. Master sat opposite me, on the other side of the harmonium, and pointed out the black and white keys to me. He then played the swaras Sa Re Ga Ma Pa Dha Nee Sa from where he sat and asked me to repeat the first lesson.

Working the bellows, I pressed all the keys as best as I could. The sounds that came out were like a stream of happy, friendly sounds that flowed over me, drenching me completely. I was so caught up in the music that I didn't notice the girl who had come to stand behind me, till she said, "Ei boy, your time's up." I jumped to my feet. By then I had started feeling that my fingers, the keys of the harmonium and the sounds they made, were all one. Thus began my lessons at Sharada Sangeet.

I liked everything about Sharada Sangeet: the room, the master, the lessons. Within the first few days I had learnt all the scales and Master said, "Tomorrow we will start on raag Bhoop." By then the fingers on my right hand had gone totally crazy. Throughout the day they kept moving as if playing sargams. Tunes kept travelling from my fingers to my head and back again. I just couldn't wait for each morning to come so that I could go to class.

The next day, Master explained raag Bhoop. I did not understand what he was saying. I knew that the raag belonged to the puja room, that some people see gods and goddesses while singing it ... *Bhoop Roop Gambheer Shaant Rasa.* But as soon as Master sang it in his solemn voice, I suddenly understood it completely!

After Bhoop I learnt Durga. That raag I liked at once. Because Durga is my mother's name. I always saw her when I played it. Then Malkauns ... All around me were mango trees, full of blossoms, the air filled with their fragrance. Hidden somewhere in the leaves was a mad kokila, singing away ... That was Malkauns. After that came Yaman. Every time I played that raag, I imagined dusk falling over a vast, never-ending field. Then the skies turned gently dark to hang an enormous saffron moon over the edge of the field. After that it was raag Bhairav, and every time I played it, I saw a deep red sun, like a huge drop of blood. I always saw pictures like these while playing a raag.

One day I was staring out of the window, wondering whether the shadow of the opposite house was blue or purple when suddenly I felt as if I was standing beneath a tree and there was a wind blowing from nowhere, sprinkling many hundreds of drops of water on me.

I turned around. Master was running his fingers over the strings of an instrument. He said, "This is a sitar."

When I told him what I had felt on hearing him play it, he said softly, "You've come into this world with an innate understanding of swara." God knows what he meant. But after that, I started telling Master what I felt. He always listened to me with a smile.

By the time I was sitting at the sixth harmonium, Master and I had become good friends and gradually he started asking me to teach the scales to the beginners.

The new boys and girls thought it was easy to play the harmonium since Master had asked a little kid – me – to teach them. But before they knew what was happening, they would grow tired of pushing the bellows and thumping the keys, and weird sounds would emerge from the harmonium. Then they would look at me again and think, Oh, this is really difficult! This kid who teaches us must be great.

One day, after I had finished my lesson, I was arranging the tablas near Master's seat while he was getting ready to go out. He was putting on his coat, when a fair, really tall man came into the room. He was in a dhoti, a thick brown coat and a black cap. He had to stoop to come in through the low doorway. He came and stood in front of Master. Greeting him with a namaskar, he said, "I'm Jamkhandikar. I retired from government service recently. Now I want to spend my time learning the harmonium." They spoke for a while, then Master told him, "I have to go out on some important work. This boy here plays the harmonium very well. He will give you the first lesson. I will definitely be back before you finish."

By now I had got quite used to such things.

Jamkhandikar was going to sit at Number Seven. I waited till after Master had left, then said, "Come to Number One. We'll start your first lesson."

Jamkhandikar was surprised. But he immediately came to the first harmonium. He took his coat off , folded it neatly and placed it on the bench. "I'm ready," he said.

I explained the structure of the harmonium and showed him how to play the black and white keys and the bellows. All this I had memorised listening to Master. I gave him his first lesson. Then I told him, "Now repeat this lesson till you learn it well."

He repeated the lesson for some time but he had been pushing the bellows too fast and so much air had got trapped inside the harmonium that he was finding it difficult to move the bellows.

I said to him as if I were Master, "Easy! Don't press the bellows so much. Take your time."

But for some more time he continued as before.

I could see the house across the street. It had two staggered roofs, one for each floor. A man was placing a ladder on the ground to go to the first roof. After repairing the tiles there, he lifted the ladder up, found a flat space to stand it, then climbed to the second roof. After finishing his work there, he came down to the first, and then back to the ground. He had used only one ladder to go up and down. And I remembered Master's voice saying, "A sargam is a ladder of seven swaras. You should move up and down on it carefully."

I turned to Jamkhandikar again. As he played the harmonium, his tongue moved across his lips, following the movements of his fingers. Most boys and girls do just that and Jamkhandikar looked exactly like one of those kids to me. Seeing me, he stopped. Massaging his left wrist, he said, "Why is this one key always Sa? Why can't I start from any other?"

I heard myself telling him, "Sa Re Ga Ma Pa Dha Nee Sa is a ladder of swaras. You can keep the ladder anywhere. You can start the sargam on any key. But you need a flat space to rest the ladder and free space on top to climb to, just as ..."

I stopped, not knowing what to say next.

Jamkhandikar was staring at me. "Yes," he said, slowly. "You would need a firm base for the swara so that you have the freedom to climb up and down."

I didn't really understand him, yet I nodded my head. He kept looking at me. Then he smiled. With his palms together he said, "You are a real Guru," before he bent his head and started once again to go up and down the sargam. Sometimes he would land with a thud, then get up and climb again. Master had not yet come back when Jamkhandikar's lesson came to an end and he said to me, "Now, *you* play something!"

I sat at the second harmonium, the one next to his, and started to play a well-known tune Master had made me learn thoroughly for the competition. I had mastered it, taans and all. Jamkhandikar's eyes stayed closed right through. I thought he had fallen asleep. But when I finished, he patted me on my back and said, "Child, you are so little, but there is magic in your fingers. No matter what your real name is, I shall call you Guru."

He told Mhapsekar Master what had happened.

Master looked at me, smiled and said, "Jamkhandikar, it's true that this boy has magic in his fingers. He was born with it. In the world of music anyone can be anyone's teacher. The only thing that matters is the true note. He who possesses it is truly great. But we should be open enough to accept this."

After that Jamkhandikar started calling me Guru wherever we

met – on the road, in the market, in a shop. My friends found this really amusing.

One day, he came home to meet my grandfather. While leaving, he told my grandmother, "This grandson of yours is my Guru."

Ajji looked straight at him. "He may be your Guru, but for me, he's a real Shani," she said, dabbing her eyes with her pallav. But I could see she was smiling.

Jamkhandikar got used to the harmonium in time and his tongue had also stopped popping out of his mouth. One day he asked me, "Can I sit at Number Three?"

I wanted to say that I would ask Master, but I heard myself say, "I'll think it over and let you know." He burst out laughing, and I immediately realised what a mad thing I'd said. When I asked Master, he said, "Jamkhandikar Saheb, you can sit anywhere you like. A person like you ..."

'No, no, Master, rules are rules."

"All right, you may sit at Number Four," Master said, smiling.

Master was still addressing him as "Jamkhandikar Saheb" when I started calling him Jamkhandikar. Soon the girls in the class also started calling him by name.

Once Jamkhandikar was practising a complicated taan. But he kept making mistakes and his harmonium would stall. Champa Karajagikar, sitting at Number Five and practising the song, *Gharat padle aaj chandane*, also started making mistakes.

"Jamkhandikar!" she burst out. "What a racket! Look, because of you even *I* am making mistakes." Jamkhandikar stopped playing and said, "Okay baba, I have stopped my racket. Now will you please spread your moonlight?"

Shani: Saturn, a malevolent force in Hindu astrology; Guru or Jupiter is considered benevolent. Ajji is not only playing on the words but also warding off the evil eye here by calling her grandson "a real Shani."

"Gharat padle aaj chandane": It roughly translates into "Moonlight floods my house today ..."

Champa burst out laughing. Jamkhandikar smiled. "Yes," he said, "now it really feels as if moonlight has flooded this place."

Jamkhandikar did everything just like us.

He always came early. Sometimes he would be sitting on a log in front of the class even before I arrived. I could spot him from a distance by his sparkling white dhoti. He would start chatting as soon as I reached his side. He would tell me about his travels all over the world, about how he loved playing games, how naughty he was as a child ... He would keep talking till Master came and then he would follow Master and me up the stairs. He would wait till Master finished cleaning and then would begin practising on the harmonium.

Once it was Saraswati Kerur's turn after Jhamkhandikar's. She went and stood behind him but Jamkhandikar kept on playing even after his time was over. Saraswati said, "Do get up Jamkhandikar! You are eating into my time." But he didn't get up. So Saraswati picked the cap off his head, put it on the bench at the back of the class and said, "There, there's your cap. Now go and sit under it."

Jamkhandikar got up smiling. "All right, all right, I will go and sit under it," he chuckled.

As he was much taller than us, Jamkhandikar had to really bend forward when he was playing on Number One. But he continued to sit there till Master told him to move to a bigger harmonium. None of us ever felt that he was any different from us. And we certainly weren't afraid of him.

Once, I had finished my class early, so I was sitting on one of the benches at the back. Saraswati Kerur's brother, Srinivas, also collected stamps and I had brought some of my stamps to exchange with him. I had just taken them out of my pocket when I saw Jamkhandikar standing in front of me.

He said, "Guru, do you collect stamps?" I nodded. "I have some stamps, too. I'll give them to you as gurudakshina for the first lesson you gave me."

I was thrilled. I hadn't got any new stamps for a long time.

"When will you bring them?" I asked.

"I won't bring them. Gurudakshina has to be received at the student's house. We'll go to my house after class tomorrow. My house is a little far from here. So tell your people at home that you may be late getting back."

Ajji was very happy when I told her I was going to Jamkhandikar's place.

Next day I stood up as soon as the class ended and Jamkhandikar said, "Yes, let's go."

As we were coming down the stairs, I saw a huge black car parked right in front of it. Just when I was thinking that we would not be able to reach the street, a man in a white uniform and cap opened the door of the car. I was trying to see who was coming out when I heard Jamkhandikar say, "Guru, come, get into the car."

He had his hand on my back as I got into the car. I sat down. I felt as if I would sink through the seat, it was so soft. I had come prepared to go sitting on the front bar of a bicycle and here I was sitting in a car! We had never seen Jamkhandikar arriving in a car. I felt as if I were flying, as if there were feathers fluttering in my stomach.

After a long while, a huge white gate suddenly stood in front of the car. As soon as the horn sounded, a man came running, saluted us and opened the gate. Our car went in and stood in front of a bungalow. Three dogs, as big as calves, came bounding out from somewhere. Two of them stood up and put their front paws on Jamkhandikar's shoulders. The third saheb started going round me. He was almost as tall as I was.

Jamkhandikar patted the dog's back and said, "Guru, don't be afraid. He's your friend. He just wants to make friends with you. Stand still."

I couldn't have been more still. My legs were shaking so much, it was impossible to run. The second saheb was sniffing at my feet, breathing heavily, examining how my legs were shaking. Then he sat on his haunches and rested his head on my shoulder. My cheek and ear could feel the warmth of his big, fat head. His back sloped down from my shoulder like a slippery slide, ending in a nice big tail that wagged vigorously.

My fear vanished. I put my arms around him and he gave my face a big swipe with his tongue. There was a kind of sweet smell coming from him. Must be friendship, I thought.

Then Jamkhandikar shouted, "Go!" The dogs ran away barking, and we went into the house.

I had never seen such a beautiful house. Large windows, colourful paintings, a sofa-set, flowered curtains ... Jamkhandikar showed me around the whole house. Then we sat down on the sofa and a lady with greying hair came out. She said, "So, has your Guru arrived? Is this boy his grandson?"

"No, no, this is my Guru," said Jamkhandikar.

The lady was amused but she merely said,"Come inside."

There were so many things to eat. My stomach was really full. Afterwards, the lady gave me a cardboard box.

"Gurudakshina," said Jamkhandikar, pulling me close to him and patting my back. I felt so good! He said, "Child, always be happy like this."

I didn't realise how time passed in Jamkhandikar's house. Then he dropped me home in his car. Only after I had opened the gate, entered the courtyard and waved to him, did the car drive away. The smell of petrol filled the courtyard and house.

There were many, many stamps in the box. I didn't even know the names of many of those countries.

I had gone with Jamkhandikar to his house and spent so much time there, but I had not felt he was someone special. I still thought of him as Jamkhandikar of the first batch of Sharada Sangeet, the one who made mistakes and who stuck his tongue out, just like the other kids. It was only when, after his car left and I was describing everything to Ajji, that my heart started beating fast. It dawned on me for the first time that he must be a lot greater than I thought. I was really worried. Now how could I call him just Jamkhandikar? How should I talk to him?

The next day I went early to class. I saw from afar that Jamkhandikar was already there, but I felt odd going and sitting next to him.

The class began. When Champa came in, she saw Jamkhandikar sitting at Number Five.

"What is this Jamkhandikar, you have taken my place," Champa said. "You are really too much. Get up!"

"All right lady, I'm getting up." he said laughing, and moved to Number Seven. I was standing there. I immediately moved aside to make place for him. But Jamkhandikar said, "Oh oh, Number Seven is Guru's. I'll take Number Four."

Everyone laughed. The din started from all seven harmoniums and my sneaking fear of Jamkhandikar vanished.

A long time had gone by since I had joined Sharada Sangeet. I knew all the boys and girls in the morning batch. I could recognise even those who attended the evening class. I had started feeling that there were two kinds of boys and girls in the town – those who came to Sharada Sangeet and those who didn't.

None of us ever chatted in class. Of course, there was no such rule; no board saying Keep Silence, but everyone kept quiet anyway. It was as if we were all quite happy to either play the harmonium or gaze out of the window at the street. But as soon as class was over, we'd be chatting away even before we reached the staircase.

One day, Master taught me a song in raag Kedar and I was trying to play it on the harmonium. It felt really good to listen to it. I felt as if the child Krishna was running and his mother was trying to catch him. There were lots of trees with green-gold leaves and the path on which Krishna and his mother ran was twisted like a rope fallen on the ground. It was as if the notes of my Kedar tripped through a thick forest before coming out into the open. I thought I heard a voice behind me say, "Master, the fifth harmonium is playing beautifully!" I kept playing.

Suddenly, I realised that only my Number Five was playing.

I stopped.

Master was looking at somebody behind me. I turned around. A fair, curly-haired, soft-eyed girl was standing there. She was wearing a sari pleated so neatly, it looked as if it was moulded in wax. Her hands were clasped behind her back. She smiled at me. Her eyes flashed like fireflies in the darkness.

Bending down she said, "Wah! How well you played! Your fingers moved like a sheet of rain."

I kept looking at her, not knowing what to say.

"I felt as if I was travelling through a beautiful forest when I listened to your Kedar," she said. Then, she stepped right across the harmoniums into Master's space. Master smiled. "Sit down, Vasudha," he said. She sat, cross-legged, beside him. Looking at us, he signalled, and our din began again.

I took a liking to her at once.

While returning home that day, Saraswati Kerur told me that the girl's name was Vasudha Holekeri, that she played the harmonium extremely well and that she learnt it from Master. I was still amazed that she had felt the same as I did about raag Kedar.

She came the next day and the next ... and for many days after that. When she was there, Master would relax, leaning against his bolster. Sometimes he would even close his eyes. Vasudha Holekeri would sit cross-legged before each of our harmoniums in turn, and correct us in her silvery voice. Her fair fingers would point the right keys to us. We loved her lessons.

Champa Karajagikar told me that Vasudha was studying in college and that she had won many prizes for playing the harmonium. Champa's brother was Vasudha's classmate. He said that college boys hated such programmes and often made the artiste cry and stop halfway. But the previous year, when Vasudha Holekeri played the harmonium, it seemed the whole pandal was silent, and the boys clapped thunderously when she finished. Hearing this, all of us felt that Vasudha was indeed wonderful.

One day Saraswati Kerur said, "Aho Jamkhandikar, please ask Vasudha to play the harmonium for us, once."

Jamkhandikar said, "Oh, I forgot! I have already asked her. She's going to play for us here, this Sunday evening."

By 6 p.m. on Sunday, both halls of Sharada Sangeet were full. Everyone was there – students, their mothers, some important people. A lovely fragrance filled the hall. As the tamburas started, a feeling of excitement spread over my forearms and neck. I felt as if the lobes of my ears were floating in air. My eyes started watering. I was deeply moved.

Vasudha got up and touched Master's feet. Then she went onto the stage and sat behind the harmonium. She bent her head and joined her hands in prayer and one of her plaits swung elegantly forward. She closed her eyes and the sound of the harmonium filled the hall. Tears rolled down my cheeks. I looked at Master. There were tears in his eyes too; yet, he was smiling.

She played for two hours. I didn't even know how those two hours passed. I felt waves of something like happiness fill my chest. At times it was like trying to breathe while walking against a strong wind. Umesh Nagarkatti, who was accompanying Vasudha on the tabla, kept grinning throughout.

Some women started chatting as usual. Jamkhandikar saw three or four of them off to the staircase. Then he came and stood right behind the others. The women must have been in a real fix about what to do with their mouths!

The programme finished at half-past-eight. Finally Jamkhandikar made a speech, and gave a large bouquet to Vasudha. He said, "This girl, who is like a forest nymph, has lit up some moments in my life of sixty-one years. I am glad that I have lived to see this day."

We came home. What Jamkhandikar had said was true. I too felt as if our whole home had been illuminated. Some of the magic from Vasudha's fingers was locked up forever inside me.

From that day on, Vasudha started coming every morning to teach us. The girls in Sharada Sangeet were ecstatic about her saris, her beautiful hair in its two plaits, the big dot of kumkum on her forehead. But I could only remember Vasudha's fingers, running over the harmonium on the day of the programme, like ants scampering up and down the trunk of a tree. I wanted to play like that some day.

I was one of the children selected from our class to participate in the competition at Kalamandal. The competition took place in Radio Talkies one morning. A few people were seated here and there. Everything was so quiet, I started feeling nervous. I played exactly as Vasudha and I had practised but the sounds seemed to get scattered by the loudspeakers. They seemed to come from somewhere else. I felt as if my fingers were not mine but Vasudha's. Everyone clapped when I finished my piece. Vasudha was waiting for me. She put her hand on my shoulder and said, "I felt as if your music revealed a piece of my mind! There is sweetness in your fingers. Don't ever give up the harmonium."

After that day, Vasudha Holekeri would sit beside me at the harmonium every day, showing me how to play. Vasudha's voice always reminded me of tinkling silver coins. I would listen very carefully to everything she said.

One day Champa told me that Vasudha's wedding had been fixed. I wasn't at all happy.

At the time of her marriage, Master presented her a harmonium on behalf of our class.

It was Saraswati Kerur who told us that, after her marriage, Vasudha had gone away to Davanagere. Saraswati had even gone to the station to see her off.

Months passed. We had almost forgotten Vasudha.

One day after class, I was sitting on a bench, waiting for Therwadekar. Suddenly, above the racket created by the harmoniums, I thought I heard the clink of silver coins. I looked around. And there was Vasudha, walking into our class. Looking just the same as before; if anything, she looked fairer. She stopped to speak to everyone. When she came up to me she said, "So, you're still here, are you?"

Before I could reply, Master started talking to her. And he kept talking to her till it was time for her to leave. She had almost reached the door when she stopped near the eighth harmonium. Then she said,

"Master, I feel like playing for a little while. May I?"

All of us said, "Yes, yes! Play!"

Gently she took the woollen cloth off Number Eight, her eyes glistening with tears. The bellows of the harmonium started moving and Sharada Sangeet brimmed over with Vasudha's music. I only remember that its sadness touched the heart. Master who was leaning against the bolster, sat up straight, looking worried. We all sat, our eyes fixed on Vasudha's fingers, moving over the keys. After a long time, Vasudha stopped playing. Everyone was very quiet.

She sat there for a long while. Then she left without a word.

Two days later, a servant from Vasudha's house brought back the harmonium that we had given her. While returning home, Saraswati Kerur said, "Look at the life we girls lead. Vasudha's in-laws do not like her playing the harmonium, that's why it has been sent back."

Vasudha's harmonium was kept on a table in our class. While cleaning the rooms each morning, Master would dust it as well. But we never saw it being opened.

The first batch of Sharada Sangeet started at seven in the morning without fail. Till at least eight o'clock each night, sounds floated out of all its nine windows. Every morning, boys and girls who had got up early, without a complaint, and had got ready all by themselves, would sit on the wooden logs outside the class, waiting for Master to arrive.

Though everyone would be busy chattering, all eyes were on the railway gate. At exactly quarter-to-seven, Master would come down the road on his old but repeatedly-polished-to-a-shine bicycle, its bell tinkling.

By the time we jumped off the logs, and clambered up the stairs, Master would have opened the doors. And we would step into the familiar, pleasing fragrance of our classroom.

As usual, everything would be sparkling. Master's clothes were spotlessly white, his curly hair combed back, neat. Even his coat did not have a single crease when he hung it on the hanger. Each day, he swept and wiped the place carefully. Everything was spick-and-span, except for the smoke spiralling from the agarbatti. When his cycle moved away each night, we would see the rays of light reflected from the spokes of the wheels. So clean were they!

The sweet-smelling flowers in the girls' hair, the creams and powder they used, the agarbattis, the smell of harmoniums in their wooden boxes – all of these combined to produce a special smell – the Sharada Sangeet smell.

Though he could speak loud enough to be heard by a person sitting in the other hall, even when all the seven harmoniums and the tablas were playing, Master always spoke to us in a soft voice. Even while praying, his palms touched each other softly. Yet nobody missed class.

Every home had an aunt or a mother who was a "tigress for housework." Girls who skipped their chores were constantly threatened with just one sentence. "Wait! When *he* comes, I will tell *him* to stop your Sharada Sangeet." And the girls would whizz through their tasks.

But boys had a problem. Perhaps they felt that Sharada Sangeet was a girls' world and men like them had no business there. Boys who came to Sharada Sangeet were always teased mercilessly. Oh, they would say, you have a man who teaches music. To make matters worse, he teaches dance also, standing with his hands on his waist and saying, Tha Thei Thai Tat, while stamping his feet. Such things pricked boys' egos. And it was the same at home. If a boy asked, May I go to Sharada Sangeet?, his father or uncle, or whoever was the head of the house invariably asked, Why? So that you can dance with your hands on your waist?

But the girls, their mothers, or their aunts said nothing of the sort. They would constantly wander in and out of the class. Master was a man of few words, so they could not say all the things they wanted to. If he encountered a "tigress," Master would start all the seven harmoniums and the tablas simultaneously. But his white teeth would gleam in a smile and the tigress returned home, no longer angry.

Fathers and uncles normally never came to Sharada Sangeet. Maybe they thought, The person running this class is inferior to me, yet *I* have to come here for the sake of my daughter – or some such thing. But if one of them did come, he would smell the special Sharada Sangeet fragrance and see all the girls sitting quietly, the spotlessness of the place; maybe then, he felt that Master was someone special, for suddenly he would start to stumble and stammer. Then the harmoniums, which had stopped at a signal from Master, would start again, and the saheb would hastily leave.

Sharada Sangeet was never closed except on Sundays. One morning, after the Ganeshotsav programme, we went to the class early. As usual we planted ourselves on the logs, looking out for Master's bicycle. Master always rang his bell at the railway gate. Jamkhandikar arrived. Then Champa Karajagikar, Saraswati and Laxmi Kerur, Padma Pachchapurkar, Kamala Ghanti ... Then the girls of the second batch started arriving; then we all went home.

The class remained closed that day. The next day, we were sitting on the logs again, waiting for Master, when Laxmi and Saraswati Kerur arrived. They said, "Master's daughter is ill. He has sent the keys. We have been asked to practise."

Jamkhandikar opened the rooms. I took the broom and swept the place, just like Master. Saraswati wiped the harmoniums clean. Jamkhandikar garlanded the pictures and lit an agarbatti. The other girls arrived and Laxmi Kerur sat on Master's seat and started the lesson. That day, she was in charge.

In the evening she came to our house. "You and Jamkhandikar must conduct the morning classes," she said. "Ask Jamkhandikar to stay on till eleven o'clock. I will come at four o'clock. Tell Baburao to escort me home at eight-thirty."

Ajji, who was there said, "Don't worry, child. I'll send Baburao to the class tomorrow night, at quarter-past-eight."

From that day on, all of us had new responsibilities. We felt grown-up. Jamkhandikar would be there almost the whole day.

Two days later Laxmi told me, "Tomorrow and the day after are dance class days. Now that Master's not here, there's nobody to play the tabla. Go ask Umeshchandra Nagarkatti if he'll come. If he says No, then the dance class will have to stay closed for a while."

I knew Umeshchandra quite well. He usually played the tabla for all the programmes.

I went to his house.

It had three rooms in a row. If you stood at the front door, you could see right through to the back door which opened into the backyard. Umeshchandra was sitting against the wall in the front room and playing the tabla, every once in a while bursting into something like "Kattu Tunna Gidigidi Dha Dha!" His father sat on a chair near the opposite wall, wearing only pyjamas. His mother was in the kitchen. Somebody was sitting in the middle room, but I couldn't see who it was.

Just as I reached the door, Umesh's father suddenly got up from the chair, went to the kitchen door and let loose a long volley in Karwari. Umeshchandra's mother came out of the kitchen, and shaking the ladle in her hand, she let off an even

Karwari: Konkani is sometimes referred to thus by Marathi speakers.

longer volley. Then it was the father's turn again to shout and then Umesh's mother's ... Thus it continued.

I was afraid to talk to Umesh during such a war. I felt as if I had forgotten what I wanted to say. Just then Umesh's grandfather came out from the middle room. Looking at me, he said, "Umesh, didn't this boy win the music prize the other day?"

"Yes, he has won lots of prizes," said Umesh, not even looking up from his tabla. "He is a friend of mine."

"Shabash! Shabash!" his grandfather said.

Then, Umesh's grandmother came out of the middle room.

She started saying something to Umesh's grandfather. One would have thought from their voices that they were standing at least three miles away from each other. They also seemed to be quarrelling. Umesh's parents were still going on. Only, now they they were standing face to face, gesticulating wildly.

Finally, Umesh and I went onto the street. It was very quiet there. I said to Umesh,

"How can you even think of playing the tabla in all this noise?"

"Are you crazy? My people complain they can't hear a word because of the racket *I* create with my tabla! Right now, the quarrel is about whose idea it was to teach it to me!"

I gave him Laxmi's message. He promptly said, "I'll come."

And so the dance class also went on as usual.

One day, I was practising with the third batch. Six harmoniums were at it together, the boys and girls playing away happily. Jamkhandikar was reading the newspaper, sitting on a back bench. Suddenly a man wearing a pyjama, a green shirt, a brown coat, and a black cap, came in. He had a faded umbrella in his hand, although it was a year since the last rains.

I raised my hand and all the harmoniums stopped. The girls turned to look. Amalakka on Number Three, who always wore a blouse and long skirt made from a Dharwadi khan, suddenly

---

Dharwadi khan: A kind of woven material with a self design and a red border.

stood up, then sat down. It was Bendigiri Anna Saheb, Amalakka's father. He was so angry that he didn't even know whom to address. He looked around and then, staring at the picture of Saraswati, he said, "Is this a music class or a circus? We send our daughter here to learn something and what do I see here? A peanut-sized boy teaching the harmonium and a chilli-sized girl teaching dance. This is nothing but a game! On top of all this, there's no hope of winning a prize in the next competition. We ..."

"But Anna ..." Amalakka began.

Her father raised his umbrella and effectively shut her up. "No buts and ifs! Don't *you* start piping up now. It's enough that your mother talks back at home."

Jamkhandikar had put the newspaper down. Anna Saheb looked at him and continued, "I have paid ten rupees for the month. Only I know how much I have to sweat to earn that. I enrolled my daughter here because she kept pestering me. You tell me saheb, what should poor people like me do? Would you accept a small coconut in the market after paying for a big one?"

Jamkhandikar stood up. He went up to Anna and said, "Anna Saheb, you're right. You work hard so that you can pay the fees. Your daughter must receive the best education. But Master's six year old daughter, Sharada, is ill. She's fighting for her life. Master was going to close down this class, but these children have managed to keep it open. Your daughter, Amalakka, has been coming here everyday. It's true this boy is peanut-sized, but many grown ups are even smaller than that. They have even less intelligence than these children. Wouldn't you agree?"

Anna stood still for a long time. He shook his mad umbrella up and down. Then he said irritably, "So, you are saying I am just a pea. I ..." Jamkhandikar put an arm around his shoulder and took him towards the bench. Our six harmoniums resumed practice and Anna sat listening to them for a long while. Then, umbrella on his shoulder, he walked away. Amalakka was looking at me and laughing, her hand over her mouth.

At first, we couldn't have imagined a class without Master. But when the class continued for so long without him, I started feeling that everything was quite simple. You open the class, you keep it going and then you close it at night. The students will come and go. What was so difficult about that?

One morning we were waiting for Jamkhandikar. Saraswati Kerur was sitting beside me. But she wasn't saying anything. I was really surprised. Saraswati silent? Just then Laxmi Kerur arrived on her ladies' cycle. Her eyes were red.

Before I could say anything, Jamkhandikar arrived.He started saying, "Come on!" as usual, when he noticed Laxmi.

"Laxmi, what happened, child?" he asked.

Laxmi burst into tears. Jamkhandikar took her into the class. We were told to wait downstairs.

After what seemed like a long while, Laxmi came down. She rode off without speaking to any of us.

We went up to the class and started our din as usual.

When I was leaving for home, Jamkhandikar said to me, "A new girl will join the seven o'clock batch tomorrow morning. Sunanda Vengurlekar. She is from the evening batch. But from now on, she will come every morning. There's no question of teaching her anything. She'll practise what she wants and then leave. I will be there, of course."

I nodded my head. But I was puzzled. Why was she joining the morning batch?

I knew Sunanda. She was in the most senior class of the Balika Adarsh Shala. She sang beautifully and acted in plays, too. I had seen her at various competitions. She was pretty. She had curly hair that kept falling onto her forehead and cheeks constantly. She had won the first prize for Harmonium (Senior Group) in the Kalamandal competition last year.

Next morning, class began as usual. Then Sunanda came in. She started practising on Number Eight. She was playing so beautifully that I couldn't concentrate on anything. I was constantly distracted by her. "Lampu," she said, "pay attention to your work! Or I'll stop playing."

Pay attention to work while Sunanda's fingers are moving over the harmonium? It was like having to supervise a lazy servant while reading a beautiful story.

One day, the morning class was on when, above the sounds of the harmoniums, we heard noises from the street, as if people were fighting.

But we continued with our class. I was showing a boy the keys for teevra and komal nishadha when suddenly I felt a buzzing sound in my head. A large ball of paper fell on to the harmonium striking a strange note. There was a big stone wrapped in the paper. By the time I opened it, I felt something wet trickle down my forehead.

Blood!

The harmoniums had stopped playing.

I sat stunned, still holding the paper. Jamkhandikar got up and pressed his handkerchief to my forehead. It wasn't hurting or anything. I simply didn't know what had happened.

The paper just said: Sunanda, come down.

Telling Champa Karajagikar to press the handkerchief to my forehead, Jamkhandikar went down.

Again, another ball of paper came in from the window and hit Master's bolster. We were really scared. Saraswati Kerur bolted the door from inside.

At first there were at least four or five loud voices shouting from downstairs. Suddenly there was only one voice, drowning all the others. We were terrified by now. What had happened to Jamkhandikar? The voices downstairs ceased and it felt as if the owner of the loud voice was coming upstairs. Then the door rattled and Jamkhandikar's voice boomed.

"Lampu, Champa, open the door."

Cautiously, we opened the door. Jamkhandikar stood there, holding two boys by the scruff of their necks. He pushed them forward. Both of them fell flat on the ground. Jamkhandikar continued to stand at the door, his cap not even slightly askew.

There was a crowd behind Jamkhandikar. All the shopkeepers from the ground floor were there. Some others, too.

The shopkeeper who was right in front said, "Saheb, don't let these goondas go. They harrass the women who come to our shops. They say nasty things. And there is no way we can do anything about it. The father of one of these boys is a police officer. He can get us into trouble ... "

The boys lay still. I thought they were dead till the one on his stomach turned his head and looked at me.

"Girls come to the class in the evening and these boys say dirty things to them! You see, they've been after that girl for the last few days. The day before yesterday, she hit one of them with her chappal, but that's only made things worse. Please do something, saheb ..."

So! That's why Laxmi Kerur's eyes were red that morning, and Sunanda had started coming for the morning classes.

Another shopkeeper said, "There are two or three more boys in the gang. You caught this one, but the others have gone to fetch his father to file a case against you. Whatever you do, please don't involve us, saheb. Otherwise the police officer will be after us."

Jamkhandikar didn't say anything. He asked everyone to step out of the class.

Just then, there was the sound of motorcycles, immediately followed by the noise of heavy boots on the staircase.

A man entered the room with two or three people. He was as wide as the door and as black as coal, with blood-shot eyes. The Police Officer! Khaki clothes, a smart cap, three or four leather belts. He said as soon as he came in, "Where's the old rascal?"

Jamkhandikar was standing behind him, near the wall. He said, in an equally loud voice, "Here."

We had never heard that voice of Jamkhandikar's!

The police officer turned sharply on his heel, pulling his right hand out of his trouser pocket, as if ready to slap him, then his hand stopped in midair. He was staring at Jamkhandikar.

All of us were quaking with fear. What was going to happen? A fight? How could we get out of here?

Suddenly, what was meant to be a slap became a smart salute. The police officer said, respectfully, "Sir, you sir? *You* beat these two up, sir?"

"Yes," said, Jamkhandikar.

"You didn't kick them, sir?"

"No, I just slapped them."

"Good! Take this then," said the police officer, giving the two boys, in turn, a massive kick each. Both boys quickly sat up. A second kick had them flat on the floor again.

The policeman then stood erect in front of Jamkhandikar and said, "Sir, this one here is my brother's son, and that one is his friend. They keep raising hell, using my name. I had to straighten them out one day, anyway. I've done it now in front of you. Please forgive me, sir. I will do whatever you say, sir. You ask me to hit them ten times and I will. Let them die. Let them go to hell. You ask me to file a case against them, sir, and I will. Let them go to Hindalga jail."

Jamkhandikar didn't say anything. He merely stood there, running his fingers gently over my forehead. The blood had stopped flowing but my head was hurting.

"Ingerhalli."

I jumped as Jamkhandikar called to the police officer.

"Yes sir!"

"Don't do anything for the time being. Just arrange to put a plain-clothes policeman opposite this class for some days. And have a talk with these boys. I don't want to complain again."

"Yes, sir!"

The police officer saluted Jamkhandikar stiffly and all of them left. Everything became quiet.

Jamkhandikar was still standing in the same place. He was always tall. Now I felt as if his head reached the ceiling. There was one Jamkhandikar whom we saw every day, and now there was this other strange Jamkhandikar, whose head seemed to touch the ceiling.

"Come, back to your harmoniums," said the usual Jamkhandikar. We sat in our respective places and the racket started again.

By now I had realised that a class didn't run on its own. You need a Jamkhandikar in it.

On the tenth day of Master's absence, Laxmi told us that Master's Sharada was well and that soon, Master would start coming to class.

I was taking class for the third batch. We were practising a song in raag Bihag:

Piya ghar nahin, Kaise dheer dharun
Kya karun soojhata nahin
Jiyako kaise samajhaun

I was, as usual, feeling happy listening to the raag. I felt as if somebody had freed a lot of colourful birds into the sky and they were whirling round and round in the golden sunlight.

Seven harmoniums were in use. Jamkhandikar sat near Number Eight. His cap was off; his eyes closed.

Suddenly, Mhapsekar Master came in from the door, wearing his spotless white dhoti, brown checked coat, black cap set at an angle, and cycle-clips on both shins. A small girl stood holding his hand. She was fair, with two small plaits, wearing a beautiful white frock, a red coat and shoes. She stood close to him, holding his hand. Master's Sharada!

Master was smiling. I thought there were tears in his eyes.

I held up my hand just like Master. All the harmoniums stopped. The girls turned around. Jamkhandikar opened his eyes. "Ayya, Master!" said the entire row and stood up.

With one leap, I crossed the line of harmoniums and stood beside Master. Master put his hand on my shoulder and drew me close to him. It felt very nice. He kept looking at us and smiling. Finally he said, "I had to take Sharada to the doctor for a check up today. After it was done, I thought I should bring her here. I could hear all the seven harmoniums while coming up the stairs. My heart is filled with happiness and pride. Happiness because Sharada has recovered, and pride in all you children. I was about to close the class when I realised how seriously ill my Sharada was. But Saraswati, Laxmi, Lampu, you didn't let it happen. And Jamkhandikar Saheb, you have been a big officer, but you continued to come here. And to my humble home. Sharada was treated by a big doctor only because of you. What can I ..."

Stopping Master midway, Jamkhandikar said, "Master, don't say that. In our music you will hear the happiness that all of us feel in knowing you have got your Sharada back." Then, turning to us, Jamkhandikar said, "Come back to your places."

We sat down in our respective places. For the first time, Master sat on the bench at the back of the class. Sharada sat beside him, her arms around him.

"Guru, may I sit on Number Eight today?"

My eyes had been feeling heavy ever since Master entered the class. Struggling to keep them open, I said, just like Master, "Very well, but take it easy."

Everybody laughed, including Master. Then the song in raag Bihag started from all the eight harmoniums. Sharada was smiling. The music that filled the classroom overflowed with our joy.

That day I understood the true meaning of Sharada Sangeet.

MADHURANTHAKAM NARENDRA

RANGAMMA

TRANSLATED BY VIJAYA GHOSE
NOMINATED BY ALLAM RAJAIAH

First published in Telugu as "Nalugukalla Mantapam" in *India Today*, April 1993, Madras.

The moment the van carrying the English newspapers reached the four-pillared mandapam, the driver started blowing the horn and he kept at it, all the way to the Agent's, half a kilometre away. This was the morning alarm for the boys who delivered the newspapers and for Rangamma who slept at night in the shadow of the ancient walls of the mandapam.

Rangamma stretched wearily and sat up, rubbing her eyes. Strands of mist crept down to provide a backdrop for the monsoon insects which turned happy somersaults in the light of the sodium vapour lamps. Loud snores rose from a few human forms that sprawled on the cement benches under the tree. A rickshaw-puller huddled into the rickety seat of his stationary vehicle, and by his side, cows chewed cud and two fat pigs browsed in the stagnant drain.

Rangamma pulled herself out of the bondage of rags to shake awake the long bundle lying beside her. The "bundle" stirred – it was a woman – and so did the woman's infant girl who had fallen asleep, suckling.

Rangamma's stomach growled in hunger. Rubbing her stomach, she waited for Dayal, the boy who brought the morning tea. Unless that first cup of piping hot liquid went into her stomach, she wouldn't have the energy even to stir from her makeshift bed. Suddenly, a shrill bell shook her wide awake. It was a three-wheeler, belching clouds of kerosene fumes into her face, in a tearing hurry to get to the bus stop.

The four-pillared mandapam was a favourite haunt of the homeless, thought Rangamma, looking once again at the knots of people who slept there. An old man with a long nose lay near the chemist's shop under the trees, dead to the world. It was possible that he had come there when she had fallen asleep for a while soon after midnight. And there, closer to the oil depot, in the dust of the road, slept a man with a sacred namam on his forehead. He too, like the long-nosed man, had been coming here for a month or so. There were more people, in front of the photo studio next to the oil depot and near the tea-stall. On the other side of the mandapam lived the family of the beldari. As usual, no one slept near the Hanuman temple. No one had the courage to defile that place.

Rangamma felt an outburst of anger for all those who were still asleep. Had she eaten like the rest of them, she would be sleeping too. Just thinking of the single one-rupee coin tucked at her waist, made her livid. And she had this girl, Raji, to feed too. Rangamma shook her awake. "Wake up, Raji, wake up! It's time."

The day's work was beginning. A noisy truck came and stopped at the crossing. A boy clad only in shorts jumped out onto the road. He walked over to the people near the photo studio and shook them awake. He said something to them that made all of them clamber onto the lorry which left with great grunts and groans disturbing the morning quiet. The rickshaw-puller now shook himself awake, wrapped a towel around his head and made his way to the railway station.

"Wake up, you!" said Rangamma, in her loud voice. "Everyone's up and about, and you, still asleep!!"

Raji yawned, stretched and withdrew the breast the baby was suckling on. She hugged the little one, gave it a huge kiss, turned on her side and shut her eyes again.

Rangamma swilled some water in her mouth and spat it out. Then, pulling out a tobacco leaf from a small pouch, she tucked it deftly between her teeth, her gaze trained on a shadowy shape approaching the mandapam.

The black muffler wrapped around his face blended perfectly with the colour of his skin. He held a smouldering beedi between his fingers. Rangamma saw him stop at the crossroads and look around.

"So, Muniram Reddy," she called out, "how many people dc you want today?"

Beldari: A contractor.

Muniram Reddy walked towards her, saying, "Oh, you've seen me, have you, Rangamma Attha? Age may have turned your hair white but it certainly hasn't affected your eyesight! I need just four people today, but mind, none of your old fogeys. They must be tough and hardworking."

Rangamma turned round and squirted a mouthful of the tobacco on the stained walls of the mandapam. "If that's what you want, come later in the morning. Then I can identify the right ones. Now they all look like bundles of clothes. I only know the long-nosed man, the man with the namam and the beldari family. Everyone else is new to me. How can I make out in this poor light who is strong and who's not?"

"You called me here to tell me this?" muttered Muniram, turning to leave.

"Wait, wait, Muniram! One last word."

"Yes, what is it?"

"How is Jayalakshmi?"

"A fine woman you got me! I told her to get out but she stuck to me like glue till I parted with a hundred and twenty rupees." Rangamma couldn't make out if he was happy with the situation or not.

"So, Jayalakshmi is not with you now. Tell me, don't you want any more women workers? I have a young girl here."

"Enough Rangamma, I have no patience with you and your business deals. Do you think I'm foolish enough to fall for your ploys again? My master has asked me to get some marble from Rangampeta. If I don't turn up with it by ten o'clock, he'll fire me. Now don't pester me. I went through hell with Jayalakshmi. I'd be a fool to touch any of your women again."

"Don't talk rubbish. Just see the girl once," said Rangamma.

But Muniram refused to be tempted. Rangamma watched him disappear into the mist before she came back to sit next to Raji. The woman was still wrapped tight in a sheet.

"Prostitute!" Rangamma cursed as she squatted once again beside the sleeping woman.

Raji threw the sheet off her and looked around with fear.

"How will you survive if you keep sleeping all the time? And saddled with a baby, too. Don't you care what happens to you?"

Raji cowered, wondering what she had done wrong this time.

Rangamma spat out a wad of chewed tobacco and cleared her throat. "You know we've run out of money. What are we going to eat this afternoon? And you, when people come here looking for coolies, you are fast asleep. Go, at least wash your damn face and look like a human being. Otherwise how will people know you are available? Do you know who came this morning? Muniram Reddy. If you had listened to me and had been ready, he would have seen you. He has a hundred and one jobs. He would have really made your life for you."

This statement brought to mind Jayalakshmi. Rangamma lapsed into a long silence that was not broken even when Muniram went past them with four or five people in tow. It was only when she saw a man come by, carrying an iron bucket-stove and a bucket of water, that she perked up. "Dayal Anna, it was you I was looking for. Come, pour me some tea!"

Dayal put down his stove and the bucket of water. He washed two glasses and poured out the hot tea. "Seems like there are very few people here today," he said, looking around him.

Two of the people lying in front of the medical store had come to life and were puffing away at their beedis. Two other men sat huddled before a bonfire of old tyres. Gandhi Market was slowly coming to life.

The hot glass of tea warmed Rangamma's hands. She stopped talking as she sipped the tea.

Dayal extended another glass of tea to Raji. The thought of having to pay for Raji's tea also, made Rangamma furious, but she swallowed her anger and fell silent once again.

The man with the namam came and squatted next to them. "One tea," he ordered. He looked like a small, peeled coconut.

"What Rangamma, who is this new girl that I've been seeing with you these last few days?" he asked.

"My fate, what else? I had gone to the government hospital the other day," said Rangamma, reluctantly parting with the sole rupee she had with her. "A girl I knew was having a baby. The delivery proved to be a difficult one and the girl had to spend two nights in the hospital. Her people asked me to look after her and I did. Mind you, it was not free. They paid me ten rupees a night. It was then that I heard a terrible commotion at the gate. When I went to investigate, I found this girl with her infant in her hands being manhandled by someone who I suspect was not her husband. If it had been her husband, she would surely not have kept falling at his feet; she would have gone back to him, just as a cow returns to the stake it is always tied to. When I asked her if he was her husband, she said nothing."

The man with the namam looked at Raji. Raji was staring into space as if Rangamma's story had no connection with her at all.

"Apparently the man had slipped into the ward at midnight, after bribing a watchman. When he was asked to leave, she wouldn't let him go. He promised to come in the morning, but she wouldn't hear of it. Finally the watchman came and dragged him off saying the doctors would sack him if he let a newborn baby and mother out of the hospital. The man pushed off and Raji remained with me. I thought, She is young. If I show her around, we may find a way to survive. After all, if we hide what belongs to us, how will anyone come to know of it? But for the last three days we have been wandering around with not a paisa in hand. She refuses to cooperate."

The man with the namam returned the empty glass to Dayal and turned to Rangamma again as Dayal slung his blue bag on his shoulder and went off, calling out, "Tea, te–a!"

"You don't have to elaborate further, Rangamma. I was born and brought up here. The railway station and the bus stop and the shopping centres all came up before my eyes. Everything has changed ... but I don't think I have ever found it as difficult to eke out a living as I do now. Just see how people from the nearby villages flock to this place. As if there are jobs going a-begging!

Even a coolie's job is hard to find. And as for other jobs ... If everyone wants only those who are as strong as bulls, what on earth will happen to weaker people? The people of Gandhi Nagar colony get their water from the Railway colony. But, no matter how good the rainfall, there is never any water for us. Who cares for dharma or religion? It limps along like most of us!" The man with the namam sighed deeply and left in search of work.

In the feeble light of morning, the lamp-post stood like an emaciated shadow. The wings of the night insects that littered the ground were stirred up into eddies by an errant breeze. A lorry was being unloaded in the distance. Gradually, the square filled with people. A bald-headed man came along now, selling neem twigs. He wore a saffron lungi. His hair stuck to his forehead like small twigs. The broken frame of his spectacles was tied with a thread to his ears. Rangamma took the two neem twigs he held out, gave one to Raji, who had depended on her for everything since the last two days. Then said, "Old man, I'll pay you tomorrow."

Not even reacting to her, the man moved on.

Rangamma chewed on the neem stick and spat the bitter juice out on the walls of the court house. "I wish there were more people like this man," she mumbled. "No matter how hard up he is, he never pressurises you. He must have broken the twigs from the tree, so he accepts money from those who pay him. Those who don't, he leaves alone."

The street lights were now switched off. A man in a red T-shirt was washing glasses close by. Groups of men – wrapped in the stale smell of beedis, wearing buttonless shirts, torn dhotis, crumpled vests – and some cattle began their morning rounds. The piglets near the drain had already gone off to forage elsewhere.

Rangamma was in a contemplative mood, not knowing how to get Raji to work for a living. Suddenly she saw a man wearing an oversized shirt over very short pyjamas.

"Mastan, come here, will you," she called out.

"Rangamma," said Mastan. "I have no time for small jobs."

But suddenly his eyes fell on Raji and he stopped short. Still staring at Raji, he said, "I need female coolies. Not one or two, but six. Our Subbarami has got a large contract. The lorry will bring the materials. We have to lay four roads. Twenty days' work to start with. But tell me, whose baby is that?"

Raji quickly covered the baby with a cloth. "Don't look at her as the mother of an infant," said Rangamma. "She is hardy. She gave birth to this baby of hers without a problem."

"So you say. But the work I have is back-breaking. People faint in the hot sun. And hospital bills ... that is not part of the bargain. Tell me when the baby's six months old. I'll find some work for her then. As for you, I can't and won't get you any work. You work for a few minutes and then you take an hour off."

When Mastan had gone, Rangamma looked at Raji once again. A slim, young body, she was obviously used to hardship, eating when and what she could. It was her youth that made her glow. Who wouldn't be attracted to her? If she couldn't get customers now ...

Rangamma suddenly grew enormously confident. "Ai Raji," she called out. "How long will you chew on that stick? Go wash your face at the bore-well and look presentable. I have got work for so many people, it shouldn't be difficult to fix you up, too."

The city centre was humming with activity. Motorcycles, buses, vans and trucks thundered past men and women who stood waiting to be hired. Every once in a while, a contractor would come along, choose three or four people, haggle over the rates, and walk off with them. Rangamma walked up to two people who were standing near the optician's with unshaven faces, torn dhotis, sacred thread hanging loosely over thin, hungry bodies.

"Swami, is it a good day today?" asked Rangamma.

"It's Ashtami. Not a good day for any work to start."

"Where were you yesterday, Rangamma? I couldn't find you,"

said one of the old men. "There was a taddinam in Bhawani Nagar. It was a grand death anniversary that they performed. They gave me fifty rupees to conduct the ceremony."

"Never mind what happened yesterday. What about today? Maybe you know of someone who needs the services of a brahmin," said the other old man hopefully.

"Don't trust these two," said Rangamma in a low voice to Raji who had reappeared, her face washed and hair combed. "If they were really as good as they claim, they wouldn't come to poor people like us. They can quietly make you part with anything."

Mastan Sahib went past with five women labourers he had chosen.

"See the audacity of Mastan sahib! Here I am, an old hand at this trade, and he goes and picks up some new women. I remember the time when he and his whole family came to live here. When he was living from hand to mouth, who do you think gave him courage? I! And that Muniram Reddy. Do you think he was any better off? Look at him now! Does he even think of those days when he came from Kottur, a greenhorn trying to eke out a living? Learn from the world, Raji. Look about you. Do something while you are still young and have the courage and the strength to do it. Or you'll end up just like me."

There was no response from Raji. It was as if Rangamma had not spoken at all. Turning her face away, Rangamma sulked.

When she next looked up, the man with the long nose was squatting by her side. "Rangamma ..." he asked in an ingratiating voice. "Can you give me a wad of tobacco?" Rangamma took out a small stick from her cloth pouch. Looking up at the sky, he said, "It's a dull morning. Looks like it is going to rain."

Rangamma looked to the east. Black clouds had gathered in the distance. "In this city of sin even the rains are hesitant. A few drops in the morning are enough to frighten everyone into stopping work. If it rains, how will she get some work that will bring in enough to fill my stomach?" grumbled Rangamma, cursing herself for having parted with her tobacco to a man she hardly knew.

'Rangamma, who is this new girl?" someone called out. It was Kuppuswamy, a small dark person who had hitched up his lungi, above his chequered drawers.

Rangamma jumped up. "Come, Kuppuswamy," she said. "I have been waiting for you since the morning."

"Don't spin tall yarns, Rangamma," said Kuppuswamy. "You only turn to me when you have exhausted everyone else."

"I know why you are angry. It's because I didn't show you Rahmat's wife, isn't it? I had to hide for three days from Manigaru. But never mind. How about today?"

"Well, there are some flats coming up. There's enough work for six months and they need a lot of labour. But a woman with a small baby? What can she do?" Then turning to Raji, he said, "Ai you girl, what is your name?"

Rangamma came and stood before him. "Oh, she knows how to talk all right. Now tell us, will you give us work or not?"

Kuppuswamy laughed. "Let's see. I'll first have to hire some people who look strong and healthy. Then I'll see if I can slip you in somehow."

The mist gave way to sunshine. The roadside shops opened. A traffic policeman stood in front of the tea-stall, lighting a cigarette. Now a blue scooter that was driven by a large man, dark as a drum of tar, came and stopped in front of the man with the long nose.

"What's the work, ayyagaru?" asked the man with the long nose.

"You won't do," said the man and turning to the wiry bricklayer, he said, "Ai you. Coming? Whitewashing job. Two-storeyed house. If you want a helper, take one. But the work must be finished in two days."

"No ayyagaru, I don't need anyone. My son and wife will get the work done in two days," said the thin chap.

"Don't take on any of your family. Is that your son? Look at him! His legs are like sticks. I need someone strong. If you can find someone, bring him along. I'll pay thirty a day. It's the house next to the Ramnagar post office."

"Thirty is too little," said the bricklayer. "The chuna corrodes the body."

"Thirty-five. That's my last offer. Take it or leave it," said the dark man.

"Ayyagaru, give us at least forty."

"No bargaining. Thirty-five. That's the last word."

Rangamma, in the meanwhile was busy hatching her own schemes. "Raji, sit here," she said. "I see Kuppuswamy."

The traffic policeman had by now made his way to the centre of the square, the red "stop" sign in his hand. Women were moving around purposefully, their mouths chewing paan incessantly as they transported baskets full of wares on their heads. Dayal, the tea vendor, was washing his cups and things at the tube-well. Kuppuswamy was talking to some labourers. When he finished with them, he turned to Rangamma. "So, who's this girl you have enticed this time?" he asked.

"You have seen her, haven't you? She's a tough, independent girl. If you can't offer her work, rest assured she'll find something on her own," said Rangamma.

"You know very well that is not what I am asking about. Who is she? What is her identity? What if she has a husband who decides to set the police on me? I won't take a risk, remember?"

"Her family comes from a place near Burrakayala Kota. During the drought last year, they were driven to find work here. She seems to have met a scoundrel who was already married. When her folks found she was carrying a child, they threw her out. And the man also ditched her. She is absolutely alone with the baby. Give her some work. You will be doing her a favour."

"I wish I could help her. But I can't feed a young, nursing mother. I need hardy people," said Kuppuswamy.

By this time they had reached the mandapam where Raji was

sitting. Without a glance in her direction, he turned to the bricklayer's wife saying, "I have some construction work. If you work hard, I can promise you work for four months at least."

"You know that construction is what we are best at," said the bricklayer's wife. "My son, too, enjoys working on a construction site. You'll have no problem with us."

"Then come to the railway station. We'll fix your wage there."

Rangamma was annoyed. "Kuppuswamy, what about us?"

"Later, Rangamma, later," he said, walking away.

The day wore on. Raji held her baby to her and squeezed herself into the shade. There seemed to be no end to the rush. Well-dressed people wandered in and out of the shops.

Rangamma sat cursing Kuppuswamy. But it didn't seem to bother Raji. She sat as if nothing in the world could touch her. Just then, the bricklayer's wife came back to the mandapam. She looked around as if she was searching for something.

"So," asked Rangamma,"has Kuppuswamy let you down too?"

The bricklayer's wife didn't reply. She went to Raji and began to whisper in her ears.

Rangamma strained forward. "What message have you come with from that wretched fellow?" Rangamma shouted. "If you have something to say, say it openly, you cowardly woman!"

"Why should I tell you anything? Don't we all know how wily you are?" asked the bricklayer's wife.

Before long the discussion turned into an ugly brawl.

"You want to hire out the girl and live off her earnings. Kuppuswamy asked me to tell Raji about you. He also said that he would give her employment if she came alone. Don't tag along. He'll break your legs, he says," crowed the bricklayer's wife as she walked off.

Rangamma looked at the scratches she had received during the scuffle. "Don't pay any attention to her, Raji," she said. "That wretched fellow only wants to create trouble for us. After all, haven't I looked after you like my own child? Haven't I shared everything I had with you?"

Raji was wrapping the baby in some old clothes.

"Raji, Raji," shouted Rangamma. "Where are you going? You'll see once you get there, he'll take advantage of you. He's not only a wife-beater but he also beats up his mother."

Raji was moving away.

Rangamma grabbed her by the elbow. "Don't go, Raji," she pleaded. But Raji, with new-found courage, pushed her against the wall and walked away towards the railway station.

Rangamma's sorrow and anger spilled forth. "I curse you," she screamed, tears welling up in her eyes. "I curse you and your child. May you never find happiness. You ate my salt and you have betrayed me!"

Suddenly, she saw the policeman and she darted across to him. "Ayyagaru, help me. Please stop her running away from me. She has robbed me of everything, Ayyagaru ... "

But the policeman did not even waste one glance on her. "Go away you old hag" he said, shaking her away. "I've work to do."

Rangamma staggered back. Losing her balance, she fell into the gutter that ran alongside the road. Grime-smeared and trembling with fear, she sat there for a long time. What do I do next? she wondered, hunger gnawing at her stomach once again. Where can I go? How can I get Raji back?

Dusk descended on the city. And the clouded skies which had made the whole city look like a faded water-colour sketch, suddenly parted, suffusing the surroundings with the glow of an oil painting. Rangamma remembered something. It's Ashtami today, she told herself. A bad day. But tomorrow ... something would surely turn up tomorrow.

The thought gave her courage. Her steps not even faltering, Rangamma walked back home to the four-pillared mandapam.

SURENDRA PRAKASH

AAGHORI

TRANSLATED BY C. REVATHI
NOMINATED BY ANISUR RAHMAN

First published in Urdu as "Aaghori" in *Zehn-e-Jadeed*,
February 1993, New Delhi.

My father had a weakness for amruti, besan laddu and chitriwala kela. Once we – my father, Bawaji and I – were walking past Chelaram Halwai's shop when his feet suddenly stopped. The sweets were tastefully decorated and arranged in huge trays. Chelaram, dressed in clean, neat clothes, was being his usual attentive self, deftly weighing the sweets for his customers. On his left, his assistant was frying the amruti in a shallow frying pan.

My father's nostrils began to twitch. Without uttering a single word, he went and stood in front of Chelaram.

"Come bauji," Chelaram said, a faint smile on his lips, "what can I serve you?"

"Give me one quarter seer of steaming hot amruti," my father said, and looking at us he added, "And yes, one quarter seer of besan laddu. Now, what will you have, Bawaji?"

But Bawaji was not paying attention.

"And you Bawaji?" My father asked again.

"Nazar Suwalli," murmured Bawaji. "No, nothing, I don't care much for these things." He was pushing an exploratory finger into his right nostril.

"But still ... something?" You could see from his face that my father's mouth had begun to water.

"All right then, get me a quarter seer of raw bhindi, Nazar Suwalli," Bawaji answered with utmost indifference.

Chelaram placed the packet of amruti and besan laddu in my father's hands. We paid him and started walking towards the vegetable shop. There were all kinds of vegetables there, freshly sprinkled with water and glistening. At my father's request, the vendor chose small, tender bhindi, weighed them and gave them to Bawaji. He tied them up in one corner of the chadar that was wrapped around his shoulders. We started on

---

I thank Shri Dhian Singh Chawla for his help in editing this translation – G.D.

Aaghori: A group of sants who reject society and any identity bestowed on them by society. **Amruti:** Also known as imarti and as jangri. **Chitriwala kela:** Special plaintains that are speckled when ripe and very sweet. **Nazar suwalli**: May the benevolent eye be on you!

the laddu and amruti while Bawaji ate the raw bhindi as we walked towards the graveyard.

The graveyard had many small and big graves. Grass had grown wildly on some, some had raised platforms, while a few others had headstones. We stopped near one which was bigger than most and had a plastered platform. On the headstone was engraved:

BABA FAKIR SHAH, SON OF ...

DATE OF BIRTH ...

DATE OF DEATH: 15 AUGUST, 1947.

The three of us fell silent for a moment, our eyes fixed on the grave. Taking a deep breath, Bawaji spoke, his voice so strange that the hair on my body bristled.

"Arre Kirpa Ram, ask for whatever you want. You are in Baba Khizr Shah's durbar."

My father had always wanted enough money that would buy him certain conveniences – a two or three-storied house with six rooms, which, no doubt, would have a municipal water connection but there would also be a hand-pump, in case of an emergency. In one corner of the large courtyard in front, there would be two or three plantain trees with huge bunches of long chitriwala plantains which, on plucking, would become speckled and have just the right sweetness. There would be a guest-house just off the courtyard – always filled with guests – and a huge verandah with comfortable cane chairs. During summer, the courtyard would be sprinkled with water and charpais would be brought out. Sitting on these charpais, everyone would feast on piping hot amrutis, washing them down with cold lassi. The safe would be stacked with money and the keys to it would hang at my mother's waist.

My father looked at Bawaji, amazement flooding his face. "Baba Khizr Shah is dead?" he asked. "But I thought he was immortal. How can such a man die?"

"Nazar Suwalli," said Bawaji, kindly. "This is not that Khizr, child. This Khizr was my fellow-disciple. We were followers of the same saint. He is dead. And I am about to die. He was older than me and attained eminence in his life. He now stands in the presence of the Holy Cherisher. I have seen him in my dreams several times, sweeping the durbar. Go ahead, don't hesitate, your wishes are sure to be fulfilled."

My father removed his footwear and fell to his knees. He spread out both his hands and started muttering something. Presumably, he was praying for his dreams to come true.

On our way back, a thought suddenly struck me. The year was 1945. The month, April. I was still a fifteen-year-old. Why did the tombstone on Baba Khizr Shah's grave show 1947 as the date of his death?

When I asked my father, the look on his face changed as if an unexpected tragedy had befallen him. He remained dumbstruck for a minute and then he asked, "Now Bawaji, what is all this?"

Bawaji looked evasive. "Nazar Suwalli," he murmured again. "What does this slave know about the ways of the Invisible?"

Where was the time for my father's wishes to be fufilled? In just two years the Partition took place and we moved over to this side; my father died a few years later.

When we returned after performing his last rites, I saw my brother open his diary. He put his right hand over his eyes. Tears flowed down his cheeks and into his beard, as he picked up his pen.

"What are you writing, Bhapaji?" The words tumbled out of my mouth before I could stop them.

"Bauji's date of death." The words choked in his throat.

"Then write, Kirpa Ram, son of Attar Singh; date of death: 15 August, 1947."

My brother just stared at me with tear-filled eyes.

But then these are matters about days that are no more. What's the use of remembering them, I asked myself. Except that ... Bawaji was still on my mind.

Bawaji (whose name was Dayal Das), belonged to the town of Jhang where the grave of Waris Shah, the well-known poet of Punjab, is situated. The grave has neither fence nor roof. Yet, it is said that, during the monsoons, not a drop of rain falls on it. Some say that the grave is Mai Heer's. Maybe Waris Shah, Heer and Ranjha, all lie buried in the same grave, though there's no headstone declaring that – but such things are of no consequence, really.

Bawaji. The man with a shaven head, a broad forehead, large eyes, a round, lustrous face and a short, stocky body. Whenever we asked him, "Bawaji, who are you? Where do you come from? What is your caste?" He would reply with a smile, "Me? Oh, I'm a mad, mixed-up man, neither a Hindu nor a Mussalman. I am a native of Jhang."

The astonishing thing about him was that, when he was in deep thought, his face had a striking resemblance to a hooded snake. He had lost both his parents when he was a child. He had joined a group of Aaghori sadhus and had later become a disciple of a Sufi saint. Thus was his life spent ... but was this how his life was spent?

I asked him once, "Bawaji, who are the Aaghori?"

"Nazar Suwalli," he said, after a long, meditative moment. "You are a child, just a child, and you wish to plumb the depths of the sea by jumping into it?"

All I could gather was that these people wish to live with only one identity, that of an Aaghori, casting aside every other identity bestowed upon them by society. But it is a lifelong struggle.

Waris Shah (1730 - 1790): One of the greatest poets of Punjab. No Punjabi poet has translated its deepest desires and dreams into verse as well as he has. The story of the legendary lovers, Heer and Ranjha, had already acquired fame by the time Waris Shah wrote his famous poem in 1766. He became so possessed by the characters, especially Heer, that he wrote very little else.

I am seated in my room when someone suddenly emerges from within me and sits down on the sofa by my side.

"Who are you?" I ask.

He says he does not yet have an answer to that question. He's still trying to understand himself. And at that moment, he's in the process of effacing the identity bestowed on him by society.

I don't know him, don't recognise his voice. There's a strangeness about him that fills me with dread. My heart is thumping as I get up and quickly walk out, leaving him behind.

The lane from my house leads to the main road with its continuous stream of scooters and cars and trucks. These things are mightier than man, they are made of metal that is much stronger, and the speed at which they run can smash a human to smithereens if he gets in their way. The one lesson I have learnt in my life is: Follow all the rules of the road conscientiously, otherwise ...

I turn right. There is the huge forensic laboratory that belongs to the government – a place where tools used in crimes and the fingerprints of criminals are identified. It has a compound wall behind which everything lies hidden. Huge gates open out onto a bridge that spans a dirty drain. One or two people are always sitting on the broad parapets on either side of the bridge. When I walk past, I see a man whose face resembles a hooded serpent. His large eyes seem to bore into me. The man I thought I had left behind in my room is here. He becomes one with the crowd and loses his strange identity.

I feel a tingling in my feet. My heart beats louder, my mind seems possessed as I walk on. The road I'm travelling on dissolves into another, which merges into a third and that in turn into another ... endlessly.

What is your destination? I ask myself.

But then, no one has a true destination. At some point in time, we all start on our life's journey but later lose ourselves in something or other. The identity bestowed on us by society disappears. I now understand the meaning of Baba Dayal Das's words of long ago: Every human being's struggle throughout his life is to establish an identity for himself which will continue to live even after his death.

The road which I have taken is coming to an end. I have reached the main road. Darkness has set in. Street lamps glow on either side.

In spite of the darkness, our flight continued. Was the first flight the one made from Canaan to Egypt? Or was it the one from Mathura to Dwaraka? Or the one from Mecca to Medina?

No, people have been fleeing for countless years, but those who fled during those early days had no special identity of their own. Their stomachs were empty and their throats parched. They all lie buried in graves around Baba Khizr Shah's tomb. And once a year when the moon is full, they rise from their graves, to narrate the story of their flight to each other. They relate the hardships they faced before they acquired an identity and the oppression that was their lot afterwards.

Now I understand it all. When Baba Dayal Das and my father returned after praying at Baba Khizr's grave, one half of me had stayed behind while the other had walked with them. While the former self witnessed the narration of the corpses, and later became one with the dead in their graves, the latter self witnessed the untimely death of my father's wishes.

It was a time when gods and goddesses were not born and we were a group with no identity. What was our strength then? I have no idea. I only know that thunder, rain and storm filled us with terror; our hair was matted, our beards unkempt. There were some amongst us who did not have hair on their faces, whose bodies were soft and exuded a strange warmth and they carried our children in their arms ...

When I return home after the long journey, I see that he's still there in my room. He raises his head and asks, "Is it raining outside?"

I am puzzled. "What makes you think so?" I ask.

"You are thoroughly drenched."

Arre, what is this? I *am* drenched to the skin. When did it rain? And where?

I feel very foolish. I have been unaware of a significant reality in my life. There I have been, out in the rain, I have got wet and yet, I am totally unaware of it.

To hide my embarrassment, I say the first thing that comes to mind. "Did you have tea?"

"No, I was waiting for you."

He speaks as if we are well acquainted. But why, why is he acting so familiar? Who is he? Why is he here? In what way is he related to me? These and other questions jostle for attention within me. Time itself seems to come to a standstill while I'm waiting for answers.

But nothing, nothing comes to my rescue.

My wife comes in with tea.

What is this? When did I ask for tea?

"Will you have something to eat?" my wife asks.

"Yes, yes please – something light," he says, then turning to me, he asks, with the familiarity he had adopted earlier, "What would you prefer? Sweet or salted?"

I'm taken aback. Who's the master of the house, he or I?

"Who the hell are you?" I demand.

"Arre, don't you recognise me? I am the master of the house," he says, chuckling.

"Then who am I?" I shout, pounding my chest with both my fists, each word dripping poison.

"You are the self I left behind when Baba Dayal Das took us to visit Baba Khizr Shah's grave," he explains patiently.

I am stupefied. I suddenly remember words once heard from Baba Dayal Das: Such experiences are inevitable when one is in the process of moving from a state of identity to one of non-identity.

I have to accept the fact that I am that self which had stayed behind in the graveyard. And now, after a long journey, had reached here in search of its other half.

We have tea and snacks together and then he says, "Tell me, what brings you here?"

"I have come all the way to narrate the story of my flight."

"What do you mean?"

"I mean this: Once upon a time I had an identity which was bestowed on me by Him. Then there came a day when He could not tolerate that identity of mine. He ordered all of us, that is, all those who had that identity, to flee – and I ..."

"Mmm ..." He slips into deep thought and for some time keeps staring at the empty teacups. Then all of a sudden, he says, "Listen!"

I look at him, all attention.

"Was the tomb really Baba Khizr Shah's?"

"That's what we were told by Bawaji."

"Was there not someone called Hazrat Khizr who showed the way to misguided travellers?"

"Yes, I remember! Bauji had also asked the same question that night when we were at Baba Khizr's tomb: How can death have any effect on him?"

"Where was he, then? When you were forced to flee, did you not ask Hazrat Khizr, Where should we go?"

"Such a thought never occured to us. All of us gathered on a full-moon night around Baba Khizr Shah's grave and prayed and lamented for a long time."

"Did Baba Khizr listen? Were your prayers accepted?"

"How can one know the ways of the Invisible?"

"No. But how long can such things remain concealed? When God's creatures are in peril, when people of one identity compel those of another to flee, then it becomes the duty of Khizr – whether he is Hazrat Khizr or Baba Khizr – to tear the veil of duality and show the right path to misguided travellers. Allah has made this task obligatory on him."

"Perhaps you are right. We belong to the race which has been guided by Khizr."

"Then come, let us pray and plead for guidance."

We embrace each other and weep bitterly for long, till the moon disappears from the sky and the Universe envelopes itself in darkness.

And in the stillness of the night, all of us who were bound together by a common identity, lay fast asleep. We had left our houses and gathered in an open place, waiting for Hazrat Khizr ..."

Who had started the narration? He or I? I experience a moment which is drowned in silence. I look around me with a great sense of uncertainty. The room has a cot, a centre-table, and shelves filled with books. Standing next to the books is a statue of a half-naked black woman, holding a small black child in her arms.

I've seen the statue several times before. The black woman has always looked sorrowful, while the child's face is devoid of any expression. But, but what is this! Today, her face wears that curious expression which appears just before laughter bursts out. Already the whole place echoes with her laughter.

Once I had imagined that she was the Holy Virgin and that the little child was Christ. Why can't this be so? Can't the Messiah be black? But then, with blacks all over the world awaiting their sacrifice on the altar of identity, wasn't it a time for great sorrow rather than for mirth?

The sound of her laughter fills me with dread and a scream dies within me. For God's sake, revert to your sorrowful state, the look of a mother is what befits you ...

Suddenly he, who is my other half, speaks softly.

"Where have your thoughts strayed? Why have you stopped the story of your flight?"

"Yes, yes," I say, shaken out of my reverie. "It's a story ... but remember there is a story within a story and that in turn leads to another story. Grasping the identity of the story, finding the essence of that which is a figment of the imagination, is your business. This story is such that it cannot be put into words."

The words I speak come out as if from a void. I start narrating the events of the night once again.

"When the sky was moonless and the world was in complete darkness, those of us who had been bestowed the same identity, awaited Hazrat Khizr. We spotted in the distance, the dim flare of a torch moving towards us. Those of us who were not asleep, woke the rest. We looked towards the approaching light. There was not just one torch out there, but many."

Someone asked, "Do these lights which brighten the Universe herald the arrival of Hazrat Khizr?"

"Maybe," someone else said. "Though our forefathers have been guided by this light, it is the first time this has happened in our lives."

And then the sound of slogans rent the air – there seemed to be many voices.

Was Hazrat Khizr accompanied by his army?

"Yes," said a voice. "They are for our protection. Now rest assured that our long wait has ended and we shall soon begin our journey towards our destination."

The last words of the speaker were drowned in the deafening sound of slogans. Then we heard screaming and shouting from one side.

Perhaps ... perhaps it's Hazrat Khizr?

Ha, Ha, Ha! Sounds of hysterical laughing. The voices reached a crescendo.

I was startled. The smile on the face of the Black Virgin vanished abruptly. I looked around. There were many people there, confronting us with guns in their hands. They wore huge turbans, one end of the cloth covering their faces. We could not make out whether they were laughing or crying. Then all of a sudden their guns started spitting fire, and one by one our people fell to the ground.

But we were saved! My black mother had shielded me.

"We are safe, aren't we Mother?" I asked.

"Yes, my son," she said, softly. "Because we are idols of clay."

At this moment, a man appeared in front of us with a gun in his hand. He asked, "Who are you people?"

Looking towards me, my mother replied.

"We," she said in her soft voice, "do not have an identity."

"All right then, we will grant you one," he said and rituals were performed which bestowed us with an identity.

We were thrilled. They started dancing with joy. Then, suddenly they stopped and turned to us.

"We know who you are!" one of them said, "You belong to the same group of people whose corpses lie scattered all around!"

"Maybe," my black mother murmured.

But this mild answer only provoked a volley of shots.

We stood there, amazed.

"Why don't you fall down and die?" they asked in unison.

"We don't know. Perhaps because our identity is self-made," my mother replied.

They stared at each other in silence and spoke to each other in gestures. The fire they had lit had spread and was about to reach the place where we stood. They seemed to be in some sort of a hurry.

One of them removed a sword from the cloth tied around his waist and moved towards my mother.

Everyone watched him with bated breath.

Grabbing the left breast of my mother, the man swung his sword. The next moment, my mother's breast was in his hand.

Now, he attacked the other breast.

My mother's chest was soaked with blood.

She stood there in silence, watching, while I struggled to find the meaning behind this madness. The black child's eyes continued to be expressionless.

We stared at each other, astonishment growing on our faces. The man stood up. He snatched the child from its mother and started walking away.

"Stop!" I shouted. "What is your intention? Why are you separating a child from its mother?"

"I do not know the reason behind the commands of the Invisible. I am merely following an order to separate the child from the black mother after her breasts are severed."

"But where are you taking the child?" I asked.

"To Baba Khizr Shah's tomb. He accepts everyone's prayers," he said. "I want this child to give up that identity which can be killed."

Tongue-tied, I watched him as he disappeared from sight.

I turned round and saw the black woman. She still stood on the book shelf, bleeding profusely. She no longer held the black child with the expressionless face. But the face of the black woman now reflected a myriad emotions.

MITHRA VENKATRAJ

THERE WAS A MESSAGE . . .

TRANSLATED BY C. N. RAMACHANDRAN
NOMINATED BY RAMACHANDRA SHARMA

First published in Kannada as "Ondu Osage Oyyuvudittu" in *Udayavani*, November 1993, Manipal.

There was a time when Jalaja Chikkamma meant everything to Narmada. But then, isn't it true of all children? When they are young they give freely of themselves to anyone who loves and indulges them. It is only as they grow older and they come under the pressure of one person's comments, another's orders, a third person's confidences that natural feelings get heavily coloured. So it was with Narmada. As she grew older, she developed an aversion for Jalaja Chikkamma. But now, after so many years, she was on her way to Jalaja Chikkamma's place once again, carrying the weight of Appanna Chikkappayya's message, struggling to sort out the welter of emotions surging within her.

Jalaja Chikkamma's house was just a fifteen-minute walk away. But if you took the shortcut and ran all the way, you reached there in barely five minutes. As a child, Narmada was always running to Chikkamma's house, because she was bored or she had holidays ... And she would come back, depending on her whims, after two hours, or after two days. This was true, not only of her and her sister but of all children in their family. In fact, Nagu her cousin, once stayed there for so many days that his mother had to come, cane in hand, to take him home.

Not that there were many people in Chikkamma's house. In that huge, old house – called the House of Pillars, maybe because of its two big teak pillars at the centre – there lived just two people: Jalaja Chikkamma and Appanna Chikkappayya. Both of them adored children, and the children were drawn to them as if to a magnet.

Even from a distance, through the woods, the railings of the jagali could be seen. Beyond this were the two giant pillars and beyond that, the squarish inner courtyard. From this central point flowed the house, spreading aimlessly till it touched the

---

The story makes many references to secondary relationships which are important to the storyline. We have kept them in Kannada since there are no equivalent words for them in English. **Appanna Chikkapayya:** Narmada's father's sister's husband. **Jalaja Chikkamma:** Chikkappayya's cousin's wife.

Jagali: The raised front verandah in a traditional south Indian house.

woods at the back. To the right of the woods, down a few steps, stood the paddy fields and the pond. If you proceeded along the edge of the fields and turned right, you were, suddenly, at the bank of the river.

Narmada remembered the time when, with great enthusiasm, she had agreed to get into the pond – a coir rope around her waist giving her courage – but the moment she touched water, there she was, screaming, "Ayyo Chikkamma, *please!* I don't want to learn swimming or anything!" and struggling to scramble out. Jalaja Chikkamma had grabbed her, pulled her back into the water, and, holding her up firmly, said, "Come, come, what's there to be scared of? Now beat your arms and legs."

Children couldn't resist Jalaja Chikkamma. No matter how many guests were in the house, she would finish her chores quickly and then she was all set to entertain the children. She would weave a colourful web of anticipation. "Let's go to the river," she would say. Or, "Let's go to the grove today. We'll carry some snacks." Or, "I'll talk to the boatman. Tomorrow we'll go boating!"

Chikkappayya wasn't different from her. As a matter of fact, she used to joke that he became at least ten years younger when he was with children. Whether he had to go supervise the picking of coconuts or the servicing of the water pump, he took the kids along, the little ones riding on his shoulders. Early each morning, Chikkamma would get the children ready to go swimming. Chikkappayya would shout, "Oi, shall I come, too?" And Chikkamma would ask, pretending to be angry, "You? What will *you* do?" and she would chase him away. Tying a coir rope to each child, she would start the lessons. But in no time at all, Chikkappayya would appear amidst them and then any game would become more exciting.

As soon as he scooped the water in his cupped hands and splashed Chikkamma, the whole pond would be filled with commotion. The children would fall into two groups, and start splashing water on each other. "You're the one who gets the children into bad habits," she'd say, but this fell on deaf ears.

On such occasions, Narmada would wonder why elders seemed to disapprove of those whom children adored.

Many people made disparaging remarks about Chikkamma, but always behind her back. Narmada's Dodda-atthe couldn't stand the sight of Jalaja. "What a woman! She doesn't have the slightest notion of shame or honour," she would rail, as she sat on the jagali, massaging one leg, the other tucked under her. "Why did that Jalaja turn up at the last minute at Raghu's upanayana? Would anyone have missed her?"

Dodda-atthe's sister, Rukmini, rolled her eyes dramatically as she said, "It seems that boy said, Jalaja Atthe, if you are not there, I won't go through the ceremony."

"Oh? Then why didn't they welcome her with an aarti?" Dodda-atthe asked.

It was difficult to understand the reason for such contempt. Jalaja was a slim, good-looking woman. Her voice could draw any stranger into conversation, almost effortlessly. She never forgot what she was told once. She would remember that Sheenappa was allergic to badnekai even if they were to meet after ten years. "Sheenappa, I know badnekai does not agree with you. I have prepared a special southekai huli for you," she would say. Even during the hustle and bustle of a wedding, she would remember that Ajja suffered from acidity and would serve him milk before he started his meal. Or she would remind her sister, "Lakshmi, your husband doesn't take coffee; he only likes tea," and, despite Lakshmi's nonchalant response, "He won't die if he took coffee once in a while," Jalaja would make sure tea was served to him. And if the wedding was in a friend's house, she would rush in and make the tea herself. But, of course, those who didn't like her said dismissively, "Oh this soft-soaping! We can't stand it."

As a matter of fact, the very people who found fault with

Dodda-atthe: The eldest paternal aunt. **Putta-atthe:** A younger aunt. **Badnekai:** Brinjal. **Southekai huli:** A dish made with a kind of cucumber. **Ajja** : Grandfather

Jalaja, were ready to accept her help, when the need arose. Mumbling, "We're not capable of such fawning; only Jalaja's clever enough for that," they would let Jalaja attend to their every comfort. Jalaja would say, "You needn't go all the way to the well; it is so slippery. I'll get the water for you," and they would happily wait for her to carry the water to them. If someone had to visit the Ganesha temple nearby, either to fulfil a vow or to take part in a festival, and didn't have anyone to go with, Jalaja would impulsively say, "Akka, if you like, I can take you. Let me see, eighth is Monday, ninth Tuesday. Let's go on Wednesday. If we leave early in the morning, we can return by sunset."

Jalaja's jackfruit happla, her ragi sandige and her mango pickles were in great demand. It was quite normal for even Dodda-atthe, who raged at the very mention of Jalaja's name, to say, "Jalaja, do you have any happla? I couldn't make them this year, what with my arthritis ... " and Jalaja would happily pack some in a plastic bag for her.

Chikkappayya kept himself away from all this. A man with neither high ambitions nor serious regrets, he was content merely to attend to his work. However, once he opened up, he could be delightful company. Sitting cross-legged, his mouth full of betel, he could talk at length on the puranas, metaphysics and current politics. He was of medium height. He wore a dhoti and a banian, occasionally a loose jubba; a shawl would be added on special occasions like a marriage or a festival.

When Narmada pondered over the sudden changes that took place in her relationship with those in the House of Pillars, she remembered some half-heard words that had passed between her mother and Dodda-atthe: "Poor Appanna! She has totally bewitched him. She'll sell our family honour for a song. You are stupid, Rama. Listen to me. Don't let your daughters go there. Think of what people might say about them."

That was it! Children could no longer fly at will to Chikkamma's house. The grown-ups retained some contact but children were curtly told to keep off! Once Jalaja had come to visit Narmada's mother. On hearing her voice, Narmada had come running down the stairs to meet her but she was given a sound scolding by her mother and sent on an errand. And poor Jalaja had come there only to ask if Rama needed help in getting the rice ground.

It was never clear to Narmada whether Chikkamma couldn't understand how she was treated or didn't care about it. Jalaja continued to be the same, even after others were rude to her. When her sister-in-law, Rukmini, who used to constantly criticise her, fell ill, it was Jalaja who looked after her for months together. What really touched Narmada, even surprised her, was that in spite of all their derision and slander, Jalaja didn't quarrel with anyone or lose her temper, even once.

Narmada knew intuitively that an integral part of their childhood fun in the House of Pillars was the presence of Jalaja Chikkamma and Chikkappayya. Even today, when Narmada looks back, she cannot give a name to the affection that existed between Jalaja Chikkamma and Chikkappayya. If Chikkappayya said, "Look, I have to catch the first bus to Mangalore tomorrow," Jalaja would be up at four, get the hot water ready for his bath, and prepare dosai and chutney for breakfast. If Chikkappayya protested that a cup of coffee was enough, she would say, "So, do I have a mountain to break?" And when he returned, Jalaja would have warm water ready for his wash. Everything would be just right in the puja room before he entered it each morning. And hardly would he have washed his hands after a meal when a beeda made of the tenderest betel leaves would be waiting for him. She could tell by just looking at his face if he had a headache; she could make out from the way he walked if he needed a cup of coffee.

Anyone could see that Chikkappayya cared as much for Chikkamma. Every once in a while he would call out, "Jalaja, Jalajakshi ..." affection spilling out with the words. He would come to her, pretending to have a backache so that she could apply ointment and massage him; if she refused to sit on the swing after dinner, he would sulk till she agreed. He could do nothing without consulting her. Returning from the garden, he would say, "What do you say to planting some twenty more coconut plants this year, Jalaja?" or, "Venkatesh promised to bring his lorry. Should it be this week or the next?"

Not that they didn't disagree, but even their arguments were amusing. When the house was full of children and Chikkamma was busy with them, Chikkappayya would mope around, muttering, "Nobody cares for me anymore. I am sure I will be kicked out of this house one day."

"My God, what melodrama! What have these poor children done to you? Look, you can have Sadu, Giri, and Sathi. They'll be with you upstairs; the others will be with me here."

Whenever shamige was to be made, Chikkappayya would come "to help" Chikkamma. Their arguments then, coupled with the shouts of the children, would send the whole house roaring! On such occasions, Narmada would wonder why her parents also were not like them.

Narmada's feelings toward Jalaja Chikkamma may have begun to change the day she overheard Latthi's mother talking to Putta-atthe. Putta-atthe was fuming, "My elder sister Kamakshi – bless her soul! – is no more. But when I think of the scandalous things happening in her house, I feel as if a sword is being plunged into my heart ... My father had told Appanna Bhavayya to marry again – if only to look after the child. But did he listen? And what is going on now? At least, shouldn't that widow have some sense in her?"

Narmada, playing gajige with Latthi, could not understand a word. She looked up questioningly at Latthi. "Don't you know?" whispered Latthi. "It seems Jalaja Chikkamma and Appanna Chikkappayya went out together yesterday, to see a film."

Shamige: Fresh vermicelli made of boiled rice. **Gajige**: A popular game played with five stones, usually by girls. There are variations of this game in practically every part of the country.

"So?"

"You are an ass," declared Latthi, tapping Narmada's forehead with her pebble. "They are not husband and wife, are they, to go to a film together?" She tossed one pebble up with the superior air of an elder sister, and resumed the game.

It was Latthi again who explained to a bewildered Narmada all the subtleties of man-woman relationships. And Narmada had broken into sobs listening to the story of those two, in whose house she had played since she was a little girl, as if it were a tale about strangers. The relationship that had given her so much happiness suddenly began to look ugly.

"I'd never have believed that Jalaja Chikkamma was such a wicked woman," Narmada said, her heart hardening.

"I didn't either. No one really knew. But I stopped going there a long time ago. You also don't go there, Nammu," advised Latthi, as if she wasn't four but forty years older than Narmada.

Then what about Jalaja Chikkamma's affection and concern? Was that too a pretence? Why didn't she meet a sudden death, like all those evil women did in films? My God, what a hypocrite! In the wake of the surging anger and rage, Narmada felt a stab of pain.

"If what you say is true, what about the kumkuma on her forehead?"

"Oh, that! That's only a tattoo!"

In the pretty round face, exactly between the eyebrows was a grain-sized tattoo. Narmada suddenly remembered an incident during Pammi Akka's wedding. Sheela Akka was in charge and she had told Narmada to offer kumkuma to all the women, while she herself distributed the flowers. Narmada had offered the kumkuma to Jalaja Chikkamma before offering it to the sumangalis. It didn't strike her that Chikkamma was a widow and widows were not supposed to be offered kumkuma. As soon as Sheela Akka saw this, she came running, snatched the kumkuma from Narmada and asked her to fan the guests instead.

As Narmada grew up, she learnt that Chikkappayya had been married a long time ago to Kamakshi, Putta-atthe's sister. When his wife died giving birth to a child, Appanna was only twenty-six years old. But he refused all advice to marry again. His mother, Seshamma, worried so much about this that she finally became bed-ridden.

Appanna was the younger of two brothers. His elder brother had settled in Bangalore and just Appanna and his cousin, Venkappa, lived in the ancestral home. Even while Appanna's father was alive, the house had been partitioned; and with the girls getting married and the boys going away in search of jobs, the house which once bustled with people had slowly drifted into emptiness. Finally, only Appanna and Venkappa remained in the two separate wings of the house. At the time of Appanna's marriage, Venkappa was also married off to Jalajakshi. But just two years later, Venkappa died suddenly and Jalajakshi was left all alone.

Jalajakshi had lost both her parents when she was a child. Now there was no one she could turn to. Though she had four brothers, they were so wrapped up in their own lives that Jalaja despaired of finding a niche for herself amongst them. She decided to stay in her own home, the eastern wing of the House of Pillars, going each day to the western wing to look after Appanna's young son, Keshava, and Seshamma.

Seshamma never stopped talking about the once-thriving House of Pillars. "It's the evil eye," the old woman would lament, describing in detail the countless guests who would congregate in the house for lunch or dinner. Jalajakshi sympathised with Seshamma, but she could do nothing to comfort her. In course of time, Seshamma, consoling and being consoled by Jalaja, breathed her last. Even before her death, the wall between the two wings of the house had lost its relevance and Seshamma had seen to it that there was only one kitchen. And this arrangement happened to be convenient for the widower, Appanna, after Seshamma's death.

When Kesava grew up, he went to live with Appanna's brother in Bangalore where there were better schools. After his studies, he found a job there and his ties with his native village gradually weakened. He would visit his father occasionally, but stayed only for a day or two. Thus it was only Appanna and Jalajakshi who lived in the big house; and an unusual relationship developed between the two.

After the "enlightening" conversation with Latthi, Narmada did not visit Jalaja Chikkamma again. Even when she met her by chance, she would turn away, strangely embarrassed.

Narmada had settled down in Bangalore after her marriage. Though she came home once a year, she found no occasion to visit Jalaja Chikkamma. You find an opportunity only when you want to. But now, after so many years, she had decided that she would meet Jalaja Chikkamma before she returned to Bangalore: She had recently seen Chikkappayya, lying alone in a well-furnished room in Kesava's house in Bangalore, staring with vacant eyes at the ceiling.

When Appanna had fallen ill, Kesava had come and taken him to Bangalore. Everyone understood how difficult it was for him to come all the way from Bangalore to look after his father. Besides, he couldn't afford to have people say that in spite of being well-placed, the son didn't take care of his old father.

The day Narmada had gone to see Chikkappayya, Pramila, Keshava's wife, had confided in her. "He must be past seventy, right? Still, he doesn't have an iota of shame. Two days ago, would you believe it, he wanted to know if Jalaja could be brought here. The old man is senile. I said, Nothing doing! Then he started pleading with his son to send him back to his home, saying that Bangalore didn't agree with him. Now, listen. We look after his comforts so meticulously – milk, food, medicines – all at the appointed hour. But, of course, *she* isn't here; and that's his problem."

As Pramila's voice rose, Narmada felt more and more ill at ease. What if Chikkappayya were to hear her? But Pramila was intent on proving how conscientious she was. In a way, she was right. There was no cause for complaint. Chikkappayya's room was airy and well-lit. He had clean, white bedsheets, and within reach, a waterjug with a tumbler, a pocket radio, and a calling bell. There was a big clock on the wall. Nurses came at regular intervals to change his sheets and give him a sponge bath and a doctor came twice a day to examine him. Everyone declared that the arrangements were perfect. But ...

Are physical comforts alone enough for a man in his last days? Can they satisfy him? Narmada wondered.

When Appanna saw her, he made a sign for her to come and sit near him. Pramila left her at the door – probably because it was not the "appointed hour."

Sitting beside him, who lay like a long bamboo pole on the bed, Narmada racked her brains for the right words. And as if she had just remembered, she said, "I am going home next week. The children have their holidays."

"Going home, child? Jalaja ... " Before he could say anything more, he began to cough horribly. Unable to speak, he tried to tell her of many things, through exaggerated gestures. "This cough will be the end of me," was all she could make out.

Just before leaving for home, Narmada went to see Latthi. She lived in Mysore. They sat chatting for a long while till, finally, the discussion turned to Jalaja Chikkamma. Latthi said how, the last time she had visited Chikkappayya, he had told her that his back was full of bed sores, and Latthi couldn't help thinking that if only Jalaja Chikkamma had been there, she would have massaged his back and made him comfortable.

"What do you think, Nammu?" Latthi had asked, sighing deeply. "Chikkamma there and Chikkappayya here ... He looked like a helpless orphan to me. Of course, Keshava looks after him well, and even Pramila is all right. But ... " she paused, and then, finding the right words for her vague thoughts, she said, "They were always together; they never stayed away from each other even for a day. Tell me, how many real husbands and wives have shared as much? Do you remember ..."

She brought back to life all those old memories.

It was then that Narmada's resolve to meet Chikkamma became firmer; and, the very next day after she reached her mother's house, she went to see Jalaja Chikkamma.

Her sari tucked up, Jalaja Chikkamma was dragging a dry coconut frond along the path, when she saw somebody in the distance. She stopped in her tracks and quickly untucking her sari, she shaded her eyes with her palm, to see better.

"Who is it? Isn't it Nammu?"

Jalaja Chikkamma has grown so frail, Narmada thought.

Childhood memories came rushing back to Narmada as she saw the familiar tulsi within its brick enclosure, the jasmine creeper, the flowering parijatha, the spreading mango tree behind it – once again she felt she was sitting on the rope-swing tied to one of the branches of the mango tree, reaching out to touch the clouds. Her face lit up.

"Come, come in, child. You came all the way to see this Chikkamma, didn't you?" The same endearing smile, the same rush of words. "Are these your children? What are their names? What will you have? Wait, I'll give you some warm milk."

She placed the milk vessel on the mud stove, reached up for a tin of homemade laddus, and putting them on a plate, "Children, come, eat," she said. "How fast they grow! I saw your son on his namakarana, a long time ago. I know. You come home only for a few days, and you have so many people to visit ... Wait, children. I'll give you something to drink, and then take you around." She still instinctively knew what children liked.

Glasses of milk in their hands, the children followed Jalaja Chikkamma into the back-garden. "Be careful," she cautioned telling them how Narmada had slipped while jumping down those steps and lost a tooth.

"What a memory!" thought Narmada, her feelings tinged with sadness.

Chikkamma took them to the cowshed, and showed them how to feed hay to the cattle. "You aren't in a hurry, are you? You must have your lunch here. Give me a minute, no, nothing special, just mango curry and rice."

She ran into the kitchen.

Narmada felt her throat choke. She feared that the minute she opened her mouth, she would start crying. Here was her Chikkamma, busy cooking her favourite dish, and she had carried on a struggle all these years, to resist this overflowing affection.

Jalaja Chikkamma called Narmada into the kitchen and made her sit beside her, as she cooked.

"I had been to Keshava's house."

At last, the words were out.

Chikkamma's busy hands froze. "How is your Chikkappayya, Nammu?" Her whole body turned into a question mark. Her gaze was expectant, penetrating, searching for something in Narmada's eyes.

"He is bedridden." Narmada's voice broke.

Pretending to stoke the fire, Jalaja Chikkamma bent her head. "This is the problem with raw fire-wood," she muttered. "There's always more smoke than fire." Blaming the non-existent smoke, she turned aside and wiped her eyes with the end of her sari. Tears welled up in Narmada's eyes too.

The flame in the stove leaped high. Narmada got up and walked away. She wandered through the house where she had once laughed and played and run all over. Though the old house hadn't changed, it looked quite desolate. The base of the huge pillars had cracked, and the bamboo poles placed around them for support, appeared fragile. The roof at the back had collapsed.

By the time Narmada and her children came back from the garden, food was waiting for them. Jalaja Chikkamma sat down to eat after they had finished. She was up in no time, fussing around, working as usual.

"You didn't eat anything at all!" Narmada scolded gently.

"I don't have any hunger, child. You know my age, don't you? After your Chikkappayya left for Bangalore..." Jalaja Chikkamma explained that being alone, she sometimes didn't cook for days together. Often she felt lost, benumbed. She had cooked the breadfruit today, because there were children. "Your Chikkappayya used to love it," she murmured. Then, with great earnestness, "Shall I give you some breadfruit to carry to Bangalore?"

Narmada swallowed hard. Chikkappayya had been on a liquid diet for quite some time.

"Forget it, child. I'm crazy!" Chikkamma checked herself.

When evening came Narmada got ready to leave. Jalaja Chikkamma had picked the jasmine flowers from the creeper at the back of the house, strung them together, and tucked them into Narmada's plait.

Narmada was almost out of the gate when Jalaja Chikkamma called out to her, came running up, and said,

"Tell Chikkappayya ... "

She grasped Narmada's hand and fell silent. Narmada could feel the words floating up to her lips and getting imprisoned there. The silence grew ...

"Shall I go then?" asked Narmada, as if they had had a long conversation.

Jalaja Chikkamma slowly let go of Narmada's hand.

Narmada had another message to carry. To Bangalore this time. But what had Jalaja Chikkamma wanted her to say? At that instant, another thought struck her. And Chikkappayya's message? Did I give it at all?

VANDANA BIST

THE WEIGHT

NOMINATED BY RUKMINI BHAYA NAIR

From the top of her large pearl nose-ring, Nima could see the louse crawling out of the cropped, but still matted, hair of the woman on the bed. Her eyes followed it along the entire length of the cot until it slid out of view, before she turned back to the rice she was cleaning. Her husband would be back soon and the rice had to be just the right temperature when he sat down to eat. She hoped he would be a little more cheerful today. The rich Thakurs in the neighbourhood had had a third son and, once again, Pandit Bhairon Dutt Joshi had been called upon to perform the naming ceremony.

A "long-dhoti" pandit (claiming his descent from the region somewhere between Brahma's neck and head), he was pretty far up in the hierarchy of Kumaoni pandits, and fiercely proud of the fact that one of his clearly traceable ancestors had been a diwan in the court of the Chand rajas. Bhairon Dutt was known for his unrelenting belief in ceremonies. "Not a word short, or you can call another," he had often threatened his patrons. Even after fifteen years of marriage, Nima was still scared of her husband's piercing eyes. Every morning before his prayers, when he combed his hair back from his broad forehead, the face of a stranger would emerge, a stranger Nima was destined to spend her life with.

"Nima! Oh Nimuli!"

The dry rasping voice of the woman on the bed broke into Nima's thoughts. She hurriedly poured some water from the brass pot into the rice and began washing it, draining off the husk and the little black insects that floated to the top.

"Hurry up Nima! Take me out, quickly!"

"I'm coming Bubu! Just let me put the rice on for him! You know his temper, don't you?"

The woman on the bed became quiet.

Long-dhoti Pandits: Pandits from Maharashtra and Jhusi (U.P.) came and settled in Kumaon between the 9th and 11th centuries. Some of them managed to become priests of the Chand rajas. These pandits wore long dhotis and were considered to have a better knowledge of the vedas.

Nima put the rice to boil, and wiping her forehead with her pallav hurried out of the kitchen. The woman on the bed was restless. Nima pulled back the smelly quilt. The woman's petticoat had risen above her legs, that she now held clenched together, and her wrinkled belly. Under the pale, tired skin, Nima could see the stark blue veins that sketched a frightening design. Nima brusquely pulled the woman's petticoat down.

"Come on now!" Nima helped her to her feet and supporting the old woman's arm on her shoulders, took her out into the aangan. The woman huddled inside the tiny urinal and the liquid gushed out sharply from within her, making a loud clatter as it fell into the tin kept there.

Each time Nima took the old woman out to ease herself, two words, sieved out from a secret her mother had told her, surfaced and frolicked in her ears, blocking out every other thought – virgin-whistle, virgin-whistle. Then, at other times, there were other words which hovered around this woman like obstinate flies. Nima listened silently whenever the woman spoke. She never questioned. And the woman talked on and on about her miserable childhood, a beleaguered youth and the endless suffering of old age. Her nephew, Bhairon Dutt, was the hero of many of these tales. But words, detached from these leaden tales, were all that remained in Nima's mind. Crisp dead words, like dry leaves fallen from trees, full-of-sound words – child-widow, cholera, vomiting, no dolls, no tomatoes, tamasik and chastity, moksha and karma and vaikuntha. Bubu talked only half as much as she did when Nima was newly married. Yet the words had been repeated so often that they were imprinted on Nima's mind, and every time the old woman opened her vacant mouth, Nima wished she would shut up.

Outside, the line of mountains was temporarily obliterated by a thin mist. Clouds covered the sun and a chill spread instantly. Nima hurried the woman across the cold stone aangan and pushed her into the bed roughly.

The woman pulled the quilt over herself, groaning loudly.

How did the naamkaran go?" Nima asked her husband that night, as she unrolled her mattress on the floor, next to her sons who were fast asleep. She sat down to massage the cracked soles of her feet with the tips of her fingers.

"Quite well," he replied, without turning towards her.

"And the horoscope? Must be good. A Thakur's son after all!"

Nima's husband covered himself with his blanket. "Ha! Thakur's son, indeed. A child cursed by Shani! They should be happy if he sees his sixteenth birthday."

Nima's hand instinctively reached out to caress her son. Stupid ominous things, horoscopes. Pronouncements that mesmerised you into proving them. *She will have a good husband and will bear him sons. A major obstacle will create unhappiness in the first few years of marriage.* Nima's horoscope had worried her father. But there were the rectifying ceremonies and after her marriage to a tree (the walnut tree in their field), Nima's marriage to Bhairon Dutt had taken place. Well, she had proved at least two of the predictions right – a good husband, sons ...

Nima looked at the man lying on the bed.

"Bubu had fever again today."

He turned and looked at her. "Did you call the Dakshaiv?" The concern in his voice irked Nima but she also felt a certain satisfaction at having caught her husband's brief interest. It was only at times such as these that Nima felt she should be grateful for the old woman's presence in the house.

"Hari got the medicines, the same as before. The man at the shop wanted the money by tomorrow."

She revelled in the authority in her voice.

"I'll give it to him tomorrow."

Her husband's back was turned to her again.

Nima was sure that if she measured the distance between her mattress and the bed, it would be exactly four steps even

Dakshaiv: A corrupt form of "doctor saab"; the usual Kumaoni way of addressing a doctor.

today ... Four steps ahead he had walked on the curving mountain path, the weight of an umbrella bending his back; and she, still in her bridal dress, her long, sequinned ghaghar flapping heavily against her legs and slowing her down considerably. The unfettered rays of the mountain sun had beaten down on her. It had melted the raw colours of the magenta and yellow pichchaura that covered her, sending rivulets of orange perspiration trickling down her neck and between her breasts. On her head she had carried her belongings in a large aluminium trunk ... On just two nights in these fifteen years, that distance had disappeared for a few brief seconds, in a blur of frenzied hands, groping fingers, heaves and guttural sounds, before the room was engulfed in an embarrassed silence. Even through the opaque darkness, Nima had made out that he had risen and moved away from the bed, as quickly as he had come to it, to walk out of the room.

On that first night, Nima had lain awake for a long time and those muffled sounds had swirled around her in a ceaseless whirpool, till her eyes had closed in sheer exhaustion. She didn't know when or whether her husband returned to the room that night.

The next morning, she had seen him sitting in a corner of the stone aangan, muttering to himself. He was scrubbing his dhoti with soap and beating it on the stone to rid it of its stains.

Now, Nima's gaze lingered on the man's sleeping body for a while. Then turning towards the products of those two nights, she closed her eyes.

Hai! I'm dying! Bhairon! Oh Nimuli! I'm dying! I don't want to die on a bed. Put me down, Nimuli."

"What's happened, Bubu?"

Before Nima could get up, her husband hopped over her and the children to switch on the light in the old woman's room. Nima lay there, her eyes determinedly shut. This had happened three times in the past twenty days. Eyes rolled back, breath stuck in her throat, she had screamed. The same words – Hai Ram! I'm dying! Put me down!

The last time they had been so sure Bubu's end was near, that Nima had sent the boys away to her mother's house and her husband had waited by the doctor's side, ready with Ganga-jal and the Bhagavad Gita. But after three anxious, unsure days, the old woman had given the hopeful, waiting Yama, a solid kick on his rump and risen. Back to her smelly bed. Back into Nima's life ... The horoscope had been correct. Time would prove if these fifteen years were indeed "the first few years of her marriage."

Nima's eyes remained shut. The old woman had quietened down. Pacifying and cajoling sounds in her husband's warm voice floated out of the room and stung Nima's ears. Words began to rise within her. From the pit of her stomach. From somewhere even lower: Tough old hag ... lice-ridden parasite. More words rose wildly now, probably from the cracks and fissures within Nima, from those dark holes in her household where the old woman had made her home for years – hunger, sore feet, empty rice tins, school fees. Words now abandoned by their meanings surged upwards: horoscope ... good woman ... dharma ... patience ... fate ... future. They churned and convulsed inside her and banged their empty weights against Nima's temple. Hard, round words. Words she could hold with her fingers, like the lice she had picked from the clumps of grey matted hair, like the stones and husk she had weeded from the thali of rice every day for fifteen years.

Nima became hot and breathless. She felt her soft breasts shrivel, her teeth loosen, her throat going dry. Sweat formed on her forehead.

Nima's eyes flew open. Her husband was back in the room.

"Did something happen to Bubu?"

Her husband seemed to notice the innocence in her eyes. He nodded.

Nima got up and moved towards the door.

"It's all right now. She's sleeping."

Stupid things, horoscopes.

Eight days later, Bhairon Dutt's Bubu had a convulsion and lost consciousness. It was Mahashivratri and Bhairon Dutt had gone to the temple, to help the priest there with the surging crowds and their offerings.

It began as it usually did. Nima was in the aangan, scrubbing the large brass parat with ash and lime. It was one of the few utensils still with her, from the boxful that her father had given her when she got married.

"Hai! I'm dying! Oh Nimuli!"

Nima scrubbed harder. The two dekchis had been given away for her first sister-in-law's marriage and the younger one took away the three thalis. All this on the old woman's orders. Nima had cursed her through clenched teeth as her husband had looked on helplessly.

"Hai! Today I won't survive! Call Bhairon! Oh Nimuli! Come here woman!"

The parat shone like gold as Nima washed it slowly. And her anger ebbed just as slowly. She carried the pile of utensils into the kitchen. The groans and wails continued. Then there was an unexpected silence. When Nima saw the old woman, fallen half out of the bed with her arms dangling to the ground, and the white of her eyes bulging, she screamed.

The neighbours rushed out. "She's dead! Bubu's dead!" somebody shrieked. "No! No! She's still breathing!"

"Hurry up and call him!" Nima yelled to Kishna, her husband's cousin who lived across the courtyard.

Nima's husband brought Mahesh Pant with him, the doctor's slow steps in complete contrast to Bhairon's agitated strides. Mahesh Pant's narrow topi, balanced at a precarious angle, the oblong, vermilion pitha on his forehead and the elbow-patched tweed coat that had lived on him for years made a curious combination. Anyone who knew Mahesh Pant knew that it was as inseparable from him as was the incident that led to this prize acquisition. That was the day he had excised a painful boil from the armpit of an Irish member of the local seminary. And the coat was the priest's grateful gift to the "Doctor." That was the day Mahesh Pant had happily traded the antiquity of his existing title of Vaid-ju for a more suave Dakshaiv.

And it was Pant Dakshaiv who sat next to the unconscious woman now. From the depths of an ancient leather bag he pulled out a worn-out stethoscope, pressed it to the woman's chest. Poking her with a careless finger, he rolled his eyeballs under closed lids. Lines formed on his forehead, breaking the vermilion pitha into several smaller segments. Then he pursed his lips and said, "Can't do much Bhairon-da, it all depends on Him now," pointing the same careless finger to the heavens above.

The old woman was put back on the bed. There was an awkward, unearthly quiet in the house after that. As wobbly and unsure as the thread on which hung the old woman's life. Every time Nima looked at the inert form in the corner, she felt an uncomfortable tightness inside her as if something was trying to push itself out. It was a feeling Nima couldn't identify. Sorrow? The woman wasn't dead yet. Anger? Irritation? She hadn't heard those demanding tones for three days now, though she still picked lice from the old woman's head, still wiped and changed her, and washed her soiled and stinking bed clothes. No, it wasn't guilt. Maybe it was something Nima did not feel at all. The ambiguity of the disquiet confused Nima as the tightness inside her grew. She was waiting for release as probably the old woman was, too.

Two days later, when the old woman's breathing became perceptibly irregular, the fear and panic that had lain dormant in the household, surged into a storm. Neighbours rushed in again. But Mahesh Pant had shaken his head and refused to come.

Bhairon Dutt sat with his head in his hands, as the old

woman on the bed hovered between two worlds.

"Don't just sit there Bhairon, do some thing!" Kakhi, Kishna's mother, urged. She had been sitting in the room since the previous night.

"What should I do?"

"Put her down on the floor and put some weight on her chest. Her time has come, son. Stop that breathing!"

There was a sudden silence among the neighbours who had gathered there.

Bhairon jerked his head up and looked at Kakhi.

"Help her to get deliverance from this damned world!"

Bhairon Dutt knew that somewhere inside one of his innumerable yellowing books, there lurked a wayward paragraph which did permit him such benevolence. But he still sat motionless.

Kakhi turned towards Nima.

"Go get some rice from your kitchen."

Nima went into the kitchen. Her husband followed her. And, as she stretched up to bring down the rice tin, his voice stilled her.

"Nima!"

It pierced her, a sharp needle on soft flesh. Alien, yet exciting, full of promise. She stood frozen for a second. But then, as though with rehearsed ease, Nima replied, "Mm?"

Her husband stood close. "Should I do as Kakhi says?"

Everything around her suddenly seemed so different. Totally vincible. On another plane of existence, Nima had lived this moment innumerable times ... The tiny rice tin in her large palms; those dwarfed men and women gathered around the semi-corpse, whispering to each other ... She had explored this moment over and over again in all its dimensions of time and space and now Nima's limbs moved with the ease of practice, like a performer in his moment of triumph before a thousand eyes.

And the words came, moulded and flawless. "Bubu is suffering, but of course, you know best." Nima did not stay the light, gliding movement of her hand as she handed him a brass bowl, with the last two measures of rice from the tin.

Bhairon Dutt walked out with the bowl.

With the help of the other men, he carried his still unconscious Bubu and laid her down on the cold, stone courtyard.

Nima sat down on the kitchen floor. Waiting.

Words began to rise within her. Murderess ... hell ... Nima pushed them back, back deep into their pit. She didn't want their weight to fill the pleasant emptiness of this moment.

Outside, the weight of the two measures of rice on that frail chest did its work in a short time.

"Hai! Bubu's gone!"

The wails emanated one at a time, then streamed out in a torrent, searing across the aangan to rise to the rubescent evening sky.

Nima rushed out.

It was a curious sight. Her husband sat with his head bent. On the ground beside him lay the lifeless body of his Bubu, the child-widow, his aunt, she who had lived in that corner of the room ever since he could remember. And balanced on her inert chest was the brass bowl, brimming with rice grains.

Nima sat down beside her husband. The same hand that had handed him the last two measures of rice, touched his taut, bare arm. "What was to happen, has happened. It was her fate."

Perfectly moulded words again. Pristine and unblemished.

Pandit Bhairon Dutt looked at his wife. Nima did not remove her hand from the warm flesh of his arm. This pulsating moment, in complete isolation from the rest of time was hers; this fragment of infinity belonged only to her. Like those two vagrant nights in fifteen years.

"Go in and light a diya."

On the thirteenth day after his Bubu's death, the aangan of Bhairon Dutt's house filled up again. The pandit served the rice, repaying his debt to all those who had borne the burden of the dead woman. And in the kitchen Nima rolled out the puris.

The words rose again. Only this time it was from the mouths of those men and women in the aangan. Full and pregnant words, precious and pure. They fell, like the petals of delicate flowers and floated on a gentle wind towards her, caressing her sweat-flushed skin lovingly: patience ... good wife ... moksha ... dharma ... vaikuntha.

After everybody left, Nima picked up the brass bowl kept under the tulsi plant and, with a carefree swing of her hands, scattered the rice grains for the waiting birds.

ꝺh

GAURI DESHPANDE

INSY WINSY SPIDER

TRANSLATED BY THE AUTHOR
NOMINATED BY G.N. DEVY

First published in Marathi as "Bhijat Bhijat Koli" in *Saptahik Sakal*, November 1993, Pune.

What are 'we' when we are 'we'? It is easy enough to answer this question in the negative. For instance, 'we' are not 'they' or 'he' or 'she'; nor are 'we' that book, bedsheet, shirt, bicycle, crow, dog or cat. But this is still not an answer to the question. Psychologists say that in the beginning, a baby cannot differentiate between itself and its mother (or any other person in the place of a mother), but when it slowly begins to perceive this difference, the idea of its own self also starts to take shape in its mind.

In my own case, perhaps this process did not follow quite so smoothly, for my mother died giving birth to me, and my father quickly dumped me on his sister's lap and went his way. The world had not progressed far enough then (not that it has now) for fathers to consider caring for their babies. My poor aunt did the best she could for me even while caring for her own children and family; but I think, when at the age of a few days – or maybe it was a week – I realised that no one had the time to run to feed me, or to change my sodden diaper even after I had been yelling lustily for a considerable time, I began to perceive quite quickly, that there was an 'I' in this world and there were the 'they', who mostly ignored me. It may have been due to this early indoctrination that the picture I had of 'myself' was strong and definite, its outlines dark and bold. I knew exactly where 'I' ended and 'others' began.

But maybe this was an illusion and I did not really know myself. For if I did, I would have followed, like so many other women in my situation, a course of studies that finished quickly and earned me a job. Instead, I went for higher education in philosophy. My father, who used to visit me on holidays and festival days, found this a puzzling development. He wanted my aunt to find me a husband after I got my BA. When I said I was going on to do an MA in Philosophy, he looked at me, obviously wondering, Who is this creature who has been masquerading as my daughter all these years? and asked, "But why Philosophy,

Vishalakshi?" (Oh yes, I forgot to tell you my name, undoubtedly a contributing factor to my strong sense of self: Vishalakshi Sethumadhavan. Now, isn't that a name! Of course, all but my father call me Vishu.) I answered with a superior air, "I wish to study Buddhist philosophy." He raised his eyebrows a little and asked, "Hinayana or Mahayana?" I was stumped for an answer, but thought, Even a busy physician apparently seems to find time to read about these arcane matters when not saddled with wife and children! Not expecting an answer, he went on, "I think you have already burdened your aunt enough. You can go on with your studies only if you get hostel accommodation. Otherwise, it's marriage for you, young woman!" Not allowing my aunt to utter a few feeble protests, I answered proudly, "Right." With a first in BA, I was quite sure of getting a place in the University hostel.

The HOD of Philosophy was an interminable bore. The whole class used to fall asleep – with their eyes closed or open – the moment he entered. But I, who soon grasped the philosophical truth that to get where you want to be, you have first to get into the good books of the HOD, was an exception to this rule. Even when my mind was fast sleep I tutored my large eyes (those very eyes which had earned me my name, presumably) to fix themselves with serious intensity upon his face. This tactic paid off and he was soon convinced that I was an earnest, hard-working, intelligent student. After this it followed, inevitably, that I should make myself visible to visiting professors (especially foreign), be always eagerly underfoot during departmental seminars and such, and begin to be mentioned in footnotes of thanks for research assistance in the HOD's papers.

Even when I was busily engaged in all these activities, my aunt persisted in finding "suitable boys" for me; but when I, in turn, persisted in rudely asking some poor engineer or doctor or accountant to explain the difference between the Heraclitan and Platonic concepts of Truth, she gave up; and so did my father. If he had again brought up the question of Hinayana or Mahayana,

I would have told him unhesitatingly, "Hinayana." For, by then, my M.Phil. dissertation on "Some Problems about the Concept of Self in Hinayana Philosophy" had received rather distinguished notice from the right quarters.

It also followed, inevitably, that I should then begin to teach Philosophy and fall in love with another teacher of Philosophy whom I met at some seminar or other. Here I wish to note that we never asked each other such philosophical questions as "What is the Meaning of Love?" I am also tempted to assert that in our life together we hardly said a word that did not pertain to philosophy (well, maybe just an occasional loving remark). But in truth, our marriage was no different from that of any other couple's. To the usual struggles about the daily dal-and-rice, mopping up, washing up, various shortages and how to meet them, we added the stresses and strains of our professional rivalries and ups and downs. I cannot say that my refusal to give in to my husband's demands – that I pay a little more attention to the above-mentioned daily strifes, and a little less to Philosophy – added to our happiness. What we did add to our life together was my daughter. In order to help her on her way to greatness, we named her Maitreyi. (All but her mother call her Mittu.) Also, in order to guard her from any confusion in her mind regarding 'self' and 'others,' I kept her on a tight schedule since birth. I am sure that the demarcating lines between her 'self' yelling with hunger; her mother, waiting for the clock to strike three before giving her the bottle; and her father, shouting in the background, "Will you stop that brat! I have to finish this paper today," became quite clear in her mind at a very early age.

The funny thing was she became most attached to my father, who had retired prematurely on account of a heart attack, around the time of her birth, and who was a frequent guest in our house thereafter. To tell you the truth, he more or less brought her up. I was sure that he was not telling her bedtime stories about the difference between the Hinayana and Mahayana philosophies, but most of the time I ignored their childish chatter. Also ignored remarks she made at the age of twelve – actually quite shocking – such as, "Must make a separate garlic seasoning for the ambadi bhaji, you know." And then, at the age of eighteen, even before she got her BA, she declared she was going to marry the son of one of our colleagues.

It was not possible to ignore that announcement. It cast a deathly pall over the house. Whatever else my husband and I disagreed upon, we were perfectly in accord about the great future we foresaw for our daughter. He pushed away his dinner uneaten and yelled, "What! Getting married? And who is going to do your BA? And MA?" I objected to his premise that women cannot do anything after marriage, and said, "She will do her BA and MA after her marriage. Won't you Maitreyi?" She said, "I am not interested in further studies." Now I too pushed away my plate. In one corner of my mind I whined about the timing of familial strifes which always seemed to take place at the dinner table. Even if my dinners were just about edible, I still wanted people to eat them since I had gone to the trouble of cooking them. But aloud, I said, "Oh great! What are you interested in, if not in studying? Become man-mad, have you? They say its natural at this age, so let's leave that. But tell me, do you mean to do anything else in life at all?" Her father didn't give her time to answer and growled again, "What the hell do you mean, not interested in studies? You tell me! The poor, the lame, the blind, and the unlettered are struggling, panting for an education. And here's you who's got it all on a platter, not interested! I don't believe this!"

Now my father entered the "discussion" and said, "Well, if those not interested in education are out of it, those who want it will have more space, won't they?"

Oh, now I got it. A grandfather–grand-daughter conspiracy. I turned to him, breathing fire, and he too pushed away his plate saying, "Why do you always make potatoes or doodhi?" From the corner of my eye I saw the slight nod my husband gave. It blew my temper to smithereens. I said through gritted teeth, "I don't have time to pick over finicky, dainty vegetables. Why don't *you* take over the cooking? You haven't anything else to do anyway." My husband was taken aback by this rudeness and half-said, "Vishu!" but Maitreyi forestalled him and said, "I don't want to do anything else, Aai. I just want to get married and look after my home and family."

That night I wept with anger and sorrow and what do you think my husband said to console me? "It was a mistake to have stopped after only one child. If we had had another, we could have tried to bring it to our point of view and you wouldn't have felt so bad!" I pushed him away and turned to the wall, but kept on asking myself, "Where did I go wrong?"

The next day I wiped my mind clean and sat down determinedly to write the paper I was to read in Bangalore: If the 'self' is posited as 'non-continuous' and does not journey from birth to birth, then the question arises, What is that entity that keeps awake my awareness of 'liberation' and directs my steps towards nirvana through many births? And then suddenly I threw down the pen and stared at Maitreyi who was chopping onions. It was a revelation.

The psychologists were all wrong. It is true that when a baby slowly begins to grasp the difference between itself and its mother, its awareness of its 'self' also gradually becomes stronger. But when does a *mother* begin to differentiate between herself and her baby? It was necessary to begin all over again. To ask, What are 'we' when we are 'we'? It is easy enough to answer this question in the negative: 'I' am not this Maitreyi.

THANJAI PRAKAASH

THE BLAZING COCONUT TREE

TRANSLATED BY LAKSHMI KANNAN
NOMINATED BY GNANI

First published in Tamil as "Patri Erinda Thennaimaram" in *Subhamangala*, January 1993, Madras.

It was around three a.m. when Lochana found herself suddenly wide awake. She could have sworn that it was three o'clock, the hour that had been chasing her relentlessly for the past ten days. Even the fact that he had not come to the island troubled her less than the unbearable agony of waking up exactly at three o'clock every night. She would sit there remembering the way he had brought her to this village with its clusters of bamboo and tamarind trees as far as the eye could see and, surrounding it, the brimming, bountiful Kaveri. Even today, it was like something that happened in a dream. Why did he choose this particular village? Was it only so that she could wake up night after night, to start the long lidless vigil for daybreak? Each day had been spent in the anticipation of his arrival till, well past midnight she would fall into a heavy sleep. Yet three a.m. stabbed her awake, as if opening up specially for her enquiries. She would keep gazing at the river for hours on end. There was nothing else to do but to sit around asking, Will he come? just as this river and its waters had nothing else to do but to flow on and on.

Lochana had known him since she was eight years old. From that day on she had also known that she was going to marry him and none other. The marriage kept getting postponed. But no one was worried. What was there to worry about? Who stopped him when he hovered around her all the time? Not her father, mother, uncle, or aunt. Did any of them protest or say that it was "not proper"? Right from the time when they were in school together, he would pinch her cheeks and even the teachers did not stop him. The whole street knew that the two of them were going to "pair up"; the whole town knew just who Lochana was; and the whole world knew what kind of a person he was.

Everything happened in a most predictable and auspicious way. Even when she gained admission into college at Thanjavur and a bullock cart would take her all the way there – the two oxen as sprightly as a pair of horses – her classmates would call out to him – "Raghavan!" – as soon as she entered the college gate. How the sound would reverberate within her cart! And as it pulled to a stop, its brass accessories gleaming, Raghavan's blue Ambassador would greet her from the car park.

Those were wonderful days.

She had never desired anything. And the reason? She needed nothing. What can one give to a queen? What could she possibly want? Was there anything she did not have? All that the girls around her could do was to sigh longingly – What a girl! – their eyes growing wide. The creamy fairness of her complexion with its hint of gold-pink, the curves of her figure visible through the diaphanous silks she wore, the fragrance of her soft flowers, the restrained radiance of her diamond jewellery and her eyes that were deep as the sea – everything about her was marvellous.

At first Lochana didn't understand why they reacted like this, almost falling at her feet in obeisance as it were ... but she had eventually got used to it.

Now, her only relationship was with a village on an island that opened up like a verdant eyelet along the river Kaveri, far off on the western end of Kollidam. It was a village called Anjini. If you looked out from the village, you would see the waters gush on both sides, much like a sea. But the Kaveri would not desire her. It would not marry her. It would not fawn at her feet nor load her with jewels. And it would not desert her like he had. Even if it did, it would not return. And should it return, she would not feel that it had ever gone away.

She had accepted things as they were when she came here. The sand dunes, the sprawling tamarind trees that stood staring at her, and, at a distance, the speck that was Anjini, with nettilingam trees dotting its fringe, its nights lit by crores of glow-worms. It made her feel as if there was no one else except her on this island on the Kaveri.

What did she do the whole day? What was there to do, anyway? Hers was a tiny cottage surrounded by the fresh-leaved kiluvai hedge. Spreading over this was the thorny thuthuvalai creeper with its purple flowers and entwining it, the kovai vine with its pendant red fruits. And then there was the rambling rose on one side, spreading out like a veritable wall, fresh and green. Nurtured by her, the garden flourished. Vines displayed green fruit, mango trees their fruit; huge jackfruit hung from leafy trees. She bought soothing shades of distemper from the market in Thiruvaiyaru and colour-washed the rooms. She whitewashed the outside of the cottage and painted the windows that overlooked the river. She did everything without anyone's help.

He came to visit her once. 'For how long should I stay here?" Lochana asked him. He laughed but was silent for some time. Then he said, "I don't really know. Everybody is frightened of you! They don't want you. Three years have already rolled by. And you ... you say you're a great artist and keep painting things all over your body! Even your mother says, But how will we ever get to know if she has been cured? Must this girl paint lotuses, leaves and vegetables all over her hands, legs, face ... But you just don't listen to her. You refuse to do anything according to advice. All of us believed that you're rid of this thing. At least listen to me now. I've asked you a thousand times to give up this disgusting habit of painting your body. Everyone in Anjini, from the farmers' streets to the agraharam, asks me if you're mad. They say, Who'll live so far from the city, near a cremation ground that's deep inside a bamboo grove, and that too all by herself in a house she's built? It's five years since you came away on your own from the Leprosy Hospital and you haven't changed a bit. I know only too well that you've no wish to lead a normal life like everyone else. You think you're some big martyr or something! Do you at least have a thought for me? Have you told me even once that you wish to see your child? I bring her on my own initiative and you gape at her as if she is an alien." Raghavan had held forth.

Agraharam: The brahmin quarters in a traditional south Indian village.

She despised him. Even felt like spitting on his face. Raghavan looked just the way he did eight years ago. The same princely look. He earned a handsome salary. But he spent cautiously. People were all praise for the way he brought up their daughter.

Her daughter. Was this the same child she gave birth to? It was this child who, as soon as she was born, had brought about an irritation all over Lochana's skin. The itching would start the very moment she touched her child. She had a raging puerperal fever. The doctors had asked her not to breast-feed her baby because of the rashes that erupted not only all over her body but on that of her baby as well. Angry red inflammation surfaced; some of them looked like ugly welts. They consulted doctors from Thanjavur, Madras and Delhi and all of them agreed that this was a case of Mother Allergy. People were astounded when they heard about this strange disease.

That was the first curtain to fall between mother and child.

When they asked her to suggest a name for the child, she said, Maitreyi. But nobody liked her suggestion. They called her Susheela; Raghavan called her Mahalakshmi; while her name in school was Anjana. The child never came anywhere near her mother. She was not allowed to, for her mother's body would protest immediately. Yet, wouldn't a child rush to her mother, hug her and call her Amma?

There was a time when Lochana longed to call out Maitreyi, to taste the full sweetness of her name. But if she happened to touch her daughter, even by mistake, the child would yell, "Don't touch me! I'll also get Mother Allergy. I'll become breathless and blisters will break out on my body, too!"

Raghavan. Lochana could never understand him. It was when she was kept in bed all the time, with everyone whispering amongst themselves about her disease that Lochana the queen, realised that she was, in fact, no queen. Her breasts were heavy with milk. She would go to the back of the house and squeeze it out over the broken brick wall near the cow-shed, the fear that pressed upon her heart flowing out with the milk. She felt as if she was dying when she tied her nipples with a string of jasmines in order to sour the milk. She could hear the broken bricks of the wall in the back courtyard crying out in anguish. She was left with only one thing now. A sense of shame.

Raghavan had asked her one day, "Why the hell do you need another child? Isn't it enough to bring up our Mahalakshmi properly?"

Lochana languished in bed, her face to the wall. But for how long can one sleep? Nobody allowed her to do any work. She scratched the freshly-limed wall with her nails till the surface peeled and crumbled, frightening Raghavan.

"What are you up to? Just look at what you've gone and done on the wall. You've drawn two eyes that are staring out, look!" exclaimed Raghavan.

Only then did Lochana look at what she had done. It was true! There were two bloodshot eyes on the wall – the eyes of Kali – that gazed back at her, blinking every once in a while. Did she scratch these eyes on the wall? Who coloured them? Why were they wet with tears as they continued to stare at her? There was life in those eyes. Lochana was surprised to see that.

On that day, she too got her own life back again.

The allergy had spread over her entire body, islands of white and pink patches. Leprosy had begun to caress her. She went to Thiruvaiyaru and bought herself several bottles of paints. She painted leaves and fruits on her arms, her legs, her body. She painted the edges of her shrinking nails gold.

The news swept through the agraharam and beyond. When the pink-white leprosy spread to the forehead and the scalp, people turned their faces away. She was discarded by the world. Her mother-in-law, the other daughters-in-law, her sister-in-law and the wives of her brothers scurried away in different directions, seeking refuge in their own houses. Her parents too kept their distance, repelled and sickened.

And Raghavan? He refused to come anywhere near her. Food was now served to her in an aluminium plate. Water in a tin tumbler. And a mat served as her bed. She lived in a hut behind the house. But all these arrangements were made at the insistence of Lochana, the queen. Nobody had asked her to keep a distance; they had merely withdrawn. The queen kept driving them away. Only Maitreyi asked, "When will you be cured, Amma?" when she saw Lochana dressed in coarse cloth – often this was no more than the gunny sacks she found in the backyard – painted with startling images of Kali in white and blue and black, although no one had taught her how to paint.

The doctors insisted that leprosy was not infectious. They said it was not the result of one's karma. They gave her injections. The medical treatment was excellent but that did not stop Lochana from roaming around with flora painted all over herself. She was in and out of the Muthupillai Mandapam Hospital at Kumbakonam. She took to going to the hospital without Raghavan or any other escort. And she unloaded the inexplicable burden that she carried onto the gunny cloth.

Gradually, the colours on her body, the shine, the swellings subsided. The Mother Superior of that missionary hospital asked her, "Why do you still paint your body? Don't hide yourself behind colours. It's only an illusion. Do you understand what you're doing?" And Lochana said, softly, "No." But when Mother Superior saw a couple of her paintings, she was amazed. "Oh, now I understand you. But, don't hide yourself *behind* yourself. Come out. Enjoy yourself. What's happened to you is not an act of injustice. Your society rejected you. But you've got even; you've rejected it, too!"

That day Lochana's gunny clothes started talking to her. Her Kalis laughed merrily and played with her, entwining her arms in theirs. Her unborn children tore through her womb; they rushed to her and hugged her, sending the blood coursing through her bosom; they put life into her veins. And Lochana decided to set off by herself. Raghavan and his parents and sister, her parents, her child and her brother-in-law, all of them tried to stop her but Lochana was adamant.

One evening when the sky had smiled like a dream and then, suddenly roared, she headed for Anjini on the Kaveri. It was the queen who laughed when Raghavan tried to stop her.

That night, the Kaveri resounded with the croaking of frogs as Lochana reached it, clutching a bundle of her belongings. The boatmen whispered amongst themselves: "Just look. It's the lady from that brahmin household. She has come here all alone!"

"I want to go to Anjini," Lochana said, politely.

"There are strong currents in the river, Amma. Besides, the water's rising."

"I have to go to the agraharam. I'll pay you well."

"It's not a question of money, Amma. Aren't you from the Vella Aiyer family? The force of the water is too strong now. Let it subside a little. I sat all night without a wink of a sleep, on the steps leading to the river. Then I saw the red monster climbing up the sky in the east and the river, the sea, and the mountains, they all came rolling in. All the tamarind trees of Anjini stood in water. The boatmen have turned their flat-bottomed punts upside down and are squatting on them. In the morning sun, we saw the torn thatches of huts from God knows where, floating with the flood waters ..."

The boatman held forth trying hard to stop her, but Lochana merely stepped into the river, her bundle poised on her head.

The boatman came running after her, jumping down the steps to the river, crying out, "What will we do, Amma, if Aiyer asks us tomorrow, Tell me, where's that lady from the house of Vella Aiyer? What'll we tell him?"

Who can argue with the queen? If Lochana decided to do something, she just went ahead and did it! When Raghavan had protested, "Everybody is getting scared of you," Lochana decided to leave, and nothing would make her change her mind. "Let us take you to a specialist in Madras," begged her father. "We'll go in for a more sophisticated treatment. Don't go to Anjini! What's there in that godforsaken place? Who'll look after you there? If you insist on staying on here, alone, like a ghost, you'll finallly have no place to take refuge in but a tamarind tree! Listen to what we say, child."

But the more he talked, the more adamant the queen became. It was her mind that was sick. But then, any sickness begins in the mind before it reaches the body. What could Lochana do when her body began to talk back to her? Lochana was convinced that the disease that had burrowed into her heart and sprawled all over her skin in white and pink patches was her daughter Maitreyi!

Who can understand that it is not a malady I battle against but Maitreyi? thought Lochana as she struggled to keep swimming between the two swarthy boatmen, her bundle perched precariously on her shoulder. Her leprosy could have been treated by specialists in Madras or in Delhi. But what about Maitreyi? Lochana's brain was all afire; her body was filled with an urgency that could not be tamed with medicines or treatment. And what did Raghavan do? No, Raghavan did not discard her, he only ran away from her. What else could she do but spurn everybody?

The tumultuous waters gushed, overflowing the banks as far as eyes could see. "Amma! Be careful, watch out for whirlpools! Stand still. Plant your foot in firmly, oh Amma from the Aiyer house! Let the force of the currents subside!" shouted Chamban and Kaliyan.

Suddenly two whirlpools opened their cavernous mouths. The bundle was snatched from her head and scattered as if caught by a flying wheel. "Ayyo!" cried out Chamban. Kaliyan was not to be seen. The turbulent waters heaved and pirouetted, surging up from what seemed to be the wide-open mouth of a hippopotamus. When the waters finally calmed down, Lochana was nowhere to be seen.

It is a common superstition in Tamilnadu, that ghosts live on tamarind trees. There are similar beliefs in other parts of the country also.

The villagers gathered to watch the fiendish fury of the waves, the frothing waters that rose like the towers of a temple. Everything floated on the waters – the tin roofs of houses, corpses of men and dogs, uprooted trees, assorted junk.

The people of Anjini were too scared to come anywhere near Lochana. They refused to accept her because she camouflaged the colour of leprosy by other colours painted all over her body. Yet, knowing her family as well as they did, they could not interfere with any of her actions. "How can a woman stay all alone inside a bamboo grove? The ghost-hermit with the seven swords there will surely strike you," they warned, trying to dissuade her. "What a hideous sight," exclaimed the women of Anjini. "Pictures in green and red all over her body!"

No one knew that the only cure for this was Raghavan.

But when days and then years rolled by, they began to understand Lochana. The once-deserted bamboo grove had visitors now. The woman who sold milk and the one who sold curds went into the bamboo grove specially for Lochana. The women from Chaliya Street who sold greens went into the grove every day, to give Lochana a few bunches of freshly-plucked keerai. The women who washed clothes and the men who mended fences sought her company. When she raised a mud wall with her own hands, the carpenters and masons wondered aloud: "Just look at the fate of a woman from no less a family than that of Aiyer's! She wears herself out with all kinds of work. What has befallen her that she should come and stay in this godforsaken place?"

Raghavan was a decent person. He had not approached her for eight years. It's the disease, you see, people said. He tolerates all her wild ways. They thought he was sacrificing so much for her whenever he drove up to the bamboo grove in a car with doctors, pleading with her to take treatment. She would look like a picture of modesty then, following her husband decorously

Everyone wondered if she was the same woman that people talked about as "a leper" or "a mad woman." But Raghavan never liked the pale colours of her sarees. He said her paintings scared him. Raghavan and the queen had nothing to talk about when they were alone with each other. The queen would lift her head just once to look at him. There was nothing more to say. And as one by one, five years went by, it struck Lochana that she understood Raghavan's sacrifice.

The village was awed by the way he had renounced the very idea of marrying again; Lochana was merely apprehensive. She went to Kumbakonam only to get over this fear but her parents and sisters-in-law said that she had gone there for treatment. Everybody felt sorry for Raghavan. At his age, with his wealth, good looks and professional standing, where was the need for him to be alone? But it was only Lochana who knew his secret. She would, however, not speak about it. She would accept nothing. She would not beg him for anything. The weird, solitary woman who roamed the nooks and corners of that village did not need anybody. She was not related to anyone. She was not a mother. Or anybody's sister. Or wife. She was a mere woman. For five or six years she had been one amongst the many men and women who moved around there as the sons and daughters of the soil. She broke stones, baked large bricks and built a house that was as weird as she was, as wild and rough and uncaring.

Lochana grew a variety of spurges around the house, and on the sand dunes the round cactii. Green and blue flowers pushed their way through the thorns of exotic-looking cactii. The house had many openings and they were all wide open. There were no doors. She had skilfully sculpted the doorways that now looked like the entrances to a temple. There was a pond right in front of her house, its waters reflecting the blue of the skies. The peasants had helped her dig it.

Who would like such things? But then, who should approve of them? The valaiyars who were fishermen and the keedhars who herded sheep liked her immensely. They liked the spicy tea she brewed, the lime juice laced with salt, and the sambar, made with an assortment of vegetables, that she served with the rice. They could not see any disease in the leprous woman. The washer-women brought white cloth on which she worked out striking batik designs.

The pictures of Kali that she had drawn over the walls of the house now wore a serene smile. On one of his visits her father asked her, "What's all this, my child? You've ruined this nice place. Look at all the cactii you've crowded the place with. All the thorny plants that can be found in the village are here! What the hell is happening? Doesn't Raghavan say anything at all? But he's a patient man. Let's you have your own way. He is indeed great. You're very fortunate to have got a husband like him. Just look at the way he keeps you fulfilled in every way, even in this diseased state."

"Who is diseased, Appa?" hissed the queen.

"You, who else?"

"I'm *not* diseased. It's you and your son-in-law who are. I was cured two years ago."

"You still have these pink patches. Are you really cured?"

"I'm not saying that, Appa. It's the doctors who say that."

"Everyone says the same thing. But who believes it? Even Raghavan said so. If that is so, why do you still paint your face with leaves and flowers? To conceal the patches? Or to camouflage yourself?"

"I'm not camouflaging anything. It's both of you who're concealing things. In fact, it's the world that conceals things. We're all just the same for you, we women, the cattle, the beasts. We should eat properly, breed, not be deviant in any way. Even if I'm cured, you're not going to accept the fact. I've languished like this for eight full years. If any other woman had been in my position, the grass would have grown over her by now. All of you have families, a hearth and home, everything you want. But I've been all alone for eight years. Yet I haven't become a wreck because I've created a complete universe around myself. I still have a lifetime of work. What would have happened if I'd just retreated into a corner?"

"I don't know. It's you who says you're all right. Is this any life at all, without people, without any social contact? You might as well have stayed in a nursing home."

"Oh yes. That's a fine place to dump a person!"

"Indeed! Why the devil are you like this, Lochana? Why can't you be like anyone else?"

"But you don't want me to be like everyone else, Appa. That's why you've dumped me here!"

The sky was darkening. Clouds billowed, gathering in dense clusters. The memories of her life with Raghavan slowly blossomed again ... Won't he touch her, even once? Wouldn't he press her small but full lips with his own? But she could never bring herself to ask him. And Raghavan? He would just sit there and watch her, placid and composed, compassion personified.

It was only Lochana's mother who burst into sobs every time she visited her. Her younger sisters pitied her from a safe distance. The brothers-in-law decorously brought gifts of fruits. How wonderful! The world really conducts itself in a fair, orderly manner. Wherever she looked, there were these sterling qualities of compassion and justice! Lochana had partaken of the isolation of eight years and had eaten, little by little, the poison inside the ambrosia.

"Lochana, my darling girl, look, I got these jalebis for you."

'My daughter, here's a box of paints that I bought for you."

"Dear Amma! Here, let me give you a kiss."

"Lochana, child, are you cured now?"

Has anybody given her the gift of two drops of tears? Do they know that these are the only real gifts anyone could give? But they are all people who have made sacrifices. They have a great sense of justice and they are the protectors of the world.

It started raining. Lochana stood amid the various spurges and the thorny cactii. She stood on the swampy ground, making beds around each of the plants. She peered into the distant horizon. Raghavan was nowhere in sight. The queen may be a queen, but her mind longed for a king.

But then she asked herself, So what if Raghavan was not there? These last eight years everyone had lavished compassion on her from a distance. Even her mother had distanced herself. But neither the nomadic kuravas nor the fishermen had shrunk from Lochana. One day a shepherd asked her, "These things on your body , isn't it leprosy?"

"Yes," she replied.

His face registered no change of expression.

"The tips of my wife's fingers have become deformed, wasted, with this disease. Will that happen to you, too?"

"Where's your wife now?"

"I don't know."

"She's your wife and yet you don't know where she is?"

"We are shepherds. To us our sheep mean everything. I came here herding my flock. She must be herding hers, wandering somewhere in the south. For about nine months every year we roam from one village to another, in search of green fields."

Lochana was astounded. At that moment, the winds of freedom blew strongly. They left her gasping. She looked at the statuesque body of the shepherd, jet-black, as if carved out of ebony.

"But you said she had this disease. Do you know that it can be cured? Take her to a hospital. After all, she's your wife."

"She lives with another shepherd these days," he said, sipping her tea. "Ah ... good tea!"

"Does he know that she has leprosy? Will he love her, keep her well?"

"What do you mean by love, Amma? He keeps her only because he likes her."

There was a crash of thunder. Flashes of lightning. The Kaveri was covered by a sheet of rain. The skies turned dark and the cactii quivered in the downpour. Lochana, stood, soaked to the skin, waiting for Raghavan though she knew she was being foolish. The humiliation of her body, the degradation of her mind – these were all hers. She was painfully aware of all that she had gone through yet ...

The rain continued to lash down.

She was washed clean of all the colours on her body. Her face and fingers emerged, cool and clean. Healthy tissues pushed their way up and spread over her body.

She was not a leper any more! She inhaled freedom once again. She knew there was no need to stay in Anjini any longer.

A great radiance rose from her mind, tearing the sky in two.

Now, another flash of lightning, followed by thunder. It must have struck the coconut tree that stood on the other side of the river. The coconut tree caught fire. Foliate flames fanned out as the tree crackled and burned in a blazing fire even in the pouring rain. Glowing cinders scattered, coconuts burst open, and were flung in all directions.

Lochana shouted in joy: I'm not a lone woman. Not any more. The coconut tree had caught fire from my smouldering mind.

When she simmered down, there was no more storm, no more rain, no more thundersquall. The wind had subsided, opening up a way for her.

She went out, clad in her wet saree. She took nothing with her. She went down the entrance of her house, the entrance that she had constructed with her own hands. She walked briskly towards the river. There were no boatmen on the flight of steps leading to the water.

The river raged. Lochana plunged into the water and started swimming towards the opposite bank, whirlpools on either side of her. Lochana dodged them, flung out her arms vigorously and swam on. The rain gathered all its force and furiously lashed about her, flinging a shower of pearls onto the surface of the river.

Lochana swam for nearly forty-five minutes before she reached the opposite bank, exultant, knowing she was not alone. She was just like anyone else, one amongst the teeming millions of the world. Even if the universe quaked, she would not turn a hair. She stood there, enjoying the breath of freedom, all alone, becoming one with the universe. Lochana had finally given up everything. To become everything.

MANOJ KUMAR GOSWAMI

THE RETURN

TRANSLATED BY JAYEETA SHARMA
NOMINATED BY PANKAJ THAKUR

First published in Assamese as "Samiran Barua Aahi Aase" by Journal Emporium, November 1993, Nalbari.

Barman lifted the receiver off its cradle. At the other end was D.I.G. Har Datta – each of his words reverberating with tension.

"Yes *sir*," said Barman, his voice properly respectful. "I have made all arrangements as per your directives, sir. Two Inspectors have been stationed at Saukidingi outpost. I myself am going on inspection. All the police thanas have already been put on alert. The latest IB report is with me."

More staccato instructions followed, terse and brief, the telephone cable trembling under their impact.

Barman knew the facts only too well. The man was a dangerous character, the leader of an insurgent group. He had been involved in a series of crimes. Seven years ago, he had been captured after much effort, but had soon slipped out of police custody. Despite the redoubled efforts of the police and the Intelligence, he had managed to escape their dragnet. Many of his associates had been arrested; others had negotiated terms with the government and surrendered. The backbone of the group had been broken. It was perhaps because of these developments that he was coming back. People said he had received training across the border in the latest and most sophisticated weaponry; that he was bringing across deadly ammunition.

"Yes, *sir*," Barman replied in smart monosyllables. Ananta Barman had become an S.P. at a very young age, superseding many of his seniors. He knew the qualities that built careers: the devotion of a hound to its master, the swiftness of a hyena, the alertness of a hare, the hunting instinct of a wolf. His ambition knew no limits. But to rise any further, *this* man had to be caught. Even if it meant taking risks. It was an opportunity not to be missed ... Barman certainly had to think a lot about his career.

'Thank you, sir!" he said as he replaced the receiver.

Drops of sweat trickled down his face.

The layout of the first page seemed to be to the chief editor's liking. He took his glasses off, thought for a moment and said, "Yes, the headline is fine. It will sell. But we must have that man's photo. That's essential."

"But sir," remonstrated the staff reporter, "there is no way we could manage a photo. Goswami and Lahkar have tried their best. Even the police files don't have one."

The chief editor lit his cigarette, a new one from a fresh pack.

"All right then. Goswami, you keep in touch with the police thana. Lahkar will have to do the rest on his own. Make daily box items of whatever information you get from our sources. If he is arrested, the first photograph should be in our paper. Our readers have to know everything about this case. Remember this man's name sells."

The teleprinter was spewing out words in the next room – bits and pieces of news from various places. Muted sounds of traffic from the street below. A telephone rang in another room. The sub-editor and Goswami bustled out.

Lahkar hitched his chair a little closer to the editor's table. He looked around carefully and then said, "We could do one thing, sir. As far as I can see, we don't have much chance of meeting him. The police haven't found any trace of him. How would it be if we ... set up a false interview?"

The editor reached out for an ashtray, his eyes staying glued to Lahkar. "You mean, one of us is taken blindfolded to a hide-out used by these insurgents. There we meet our man, speak to him about his future plans, his experiences across the border, his views on the present government ... "

"We could have a blurred photo to go with the article," Lahkar finished enthusiastically.

The editor stubbed out his cigarette. "No," he said, his long years of experience coming to the fore. "That will cause trouble, Lahkar. Police interrogations, cross-examinations ... and if later it leaks out that it was all a cooked-up interview ... the paper's image will take a battering, all for nothing."

Neela was combing her hair, the huge dressing table mirror before her. It was a still afternoon. Music – a song by Cliff Richard – was playing softly in the background. The servant boy was out – for a matinee, he had said. There was no possibility of her husband, Neelam Mahanta, returning before half-past four.

The emptiness of that enormous house was getting to her. From the window, she could see the afternoon street; deserted, except for the rare vehicle that sped by. She got up abruptly and flung herself onto the bed. The wall clock relentlessly sloughed off the afternoon hours. The curtains rustled in the light breeze. Suddenly the harsh ring of the telephone made her jump. She was too frightened to even look towards it. What should she do? Pick up the receiver? Or not?

The telephone continued to ring. The house seemed to shake with the persistent ringing.

She approached the instrument hesitantly. What if she picked up the receiver and heard his voice at the other end? That grave, deep, well-remembered voice?

"Hello?" She could hardly recognise her own voice.

"What's up, Neela? Aren't you well?"

Oh! It was her husband. Even so, her heart continued to thud for a few more seconds.

"Neela? Is something wrong?"

"No, nothing. I had dozed off, that's all."

"Let's see a film today. There's a good one at the Spielberg. Get dressed. I'll be there in fifteen minutes. Don't we have to go to Bhatt's place this evening, for his son's birthday party?"

Neela shut her eyes. She tried to immerse herself in the comforting tones of Neelam's voice. It seemed to be the only possible refuge. "Not today," she said. "This Anil has also gone off somewhere. See if you can come home a little early. I'm feeling quite lonely today."

Neela walked up and down the large room. The softly yielding carpet underfoot, the expensive furniture, the refrigerator in a corner, standing like a huge block of ice, the colour TV reflecting off the Belgian mirror. Neela drew the curtain back. She could see the garage beyond the lush green lawn from where her husband, only a few hours ago, had driven their blood-red Maruti to his company office. Her heart started racing again. She wondered, would she be able to give up all this without a pang? Would he allow her to continue the carefree life she led here, in the midst of all this abundance? One day, on one such afternoon perhaps, she would open the door to the insistent summons of the calling bell, and find him waiting there.

"How are you, Neelie?" he would ask, that cruel, slightly enigmatic smile on his face. Unruly hair, stubble on his chin, clothes dishevelled and hanging loosely on his frame, a vein throbbing blood-red on his arm. Perhaps he would slip into the room, to disgustedly survey the prosperity of her home. Perhaps he would look her straight in the face for a few moments, and say in his slow, calm voice, "Come back, Neelie. Come back to me."

Neela sighed. One day he would be back. That was certain. He would never forget her. Nothing would deter him – not even the prospect of death. And now, after having lived for seven years with wild beasts and wilder men, he must be that much more fearless.

She felt disgusted with herself. Ten years ago, she had been in love with him. Love ... the very word repulsed her now. But it would be because of that, that he would return to her. She had never been in love with Neelam, yet, surrounded by all his possessions – the fridge, the TV, the car, the house – she had lived a happy enough existence. All of it could disintegrate, now that he had returned.

Her cheek against a bar, Neela stared out of the window. Yes, he was on his way.

Someone had opened a fresh bottle of whisky, a glass dropped and rolled on the floor, there was the sound of liquid being poured, and a voice could be heard singing, "*It's been a hard day's night, I should be sleeping like a log* ...," very off-key. The room was filled with cigarette smoke. In the dim light of the zero-watt bulb could be seen a few scattered chairs, tables, a bed, and some young men: Bipul, Ajit, Dul, Bagen, Rafiul.

Ajit got up and opened the window, letting the night breeze into the stuffy room. Turning, he recited in a solemn voice:

We drink the whole night through
A cocktail of darkness and wine ...
for we are the ones who have to see
the morning in

Ajit was considered to be an upcoming poet.

"Shut up, fool!" said Bagen. "*This*" – an obscene gesture followed – "is what I think of your poetry."

The room seemed to rock with Dul's laughter. "Why do you say that, comrade? It's through such poems that he makes such a name, has gamochas draped on him, gets mobbed by beautiful girls begging him to sign autographs. Remember, it's poetry that helps him lead so many of those girls on ..." Dul's words faded away into an indistinct mutter.

"What good does my poetry do?" Ajit asked sombrely. "Damn it, each word in my poems rises to mock me. The number of times I've taken them to interview boards, shown off magazines which had published them – I tried so hard for that job of a publicity officer. But what happened? Someone appeared from nowhere and just walked into the job."

A motorcycle stopped outside. They knew it was Ishwar. He had got a scholarship to an American University. He was treating them to drinks that day.

"Hello," said Ishwar as he entered.

"Are you leaving us, young man?" someone asked.

"Sure, I'm leaving you!" declared Ishwar, draining a peg. "You guys must come to the airport in the morning."

Rafiul walked unsteadily towards him. He put a hand on Ishwar's shoulder, "And what will you send us from America, bhai? Some good brand of liquor, pictures of sunbathing American blondes, some hot porn ..."

"And real juicy stuff," finished Ajit.

"Promise, you bastard, promise," shouted Bipul.

"I promise," said Ishwar, solemnly.

"Go, saala. Go," Dul muttered. "And when you come back after five years, you'll find everything changed here. A quintal of rice for twenty bucks, a bottle of whisky for five, free fags, and girls queueing up to marry loafers like us, money blowing in the wind ... Our Ramrajya. Because we have heard that ... "

"Achha, I'll be off," Ishwar announced briskly. "I have to drop in at a couple of more places. I haven't even been to Neelie's yet. I'll meet you guys at the airport in the morning."

"Goodbye, young man. Wish you all the best," someone said from a dark corner. "We've had some fun at your expense, but forget that. After all, you've had your share of amusement, too. Revolution, changing the entire system – we don't mind that you used to speak of all that. They should be shot, strung up the nearest telegraph post – that's what you'd say about all black-marketeers, corrupt officials, MLAs, faithless mistresses ... "

Ishwar smiled thinly, "I have shut the door on yesterday, and thrown the key away. Good night."

He walked out. They could hear the motorcycle revving up and then its sound fading into the distance.

Bagen made his way unsteadily towards the open window, his hoarse voice raised in song – "Lying in someone's arms ..."

Suddenly, Dul shouted, "All right, saala. We'll shoot them. We'll hang them all ... blackmarketeers, ministers, MLAs, corrupt officials, unfaithful mistresses." He crawled on all four towards the centre of the room in his underpants. "Don't worry, brothers," he drawled out. "Everything will be fine. We'll take up sten guns and grenades ... Oh, you want to know who'll give them to us? Don't worry. You know our Samiran Barua is on his way back. *He'll* lead us to heaven." Dul let out a cackle of laughter. He stopped abruptly and was sick all over the floor.

The flickering flame of the kerosene lamp failed to light up the verandah. The woman holding the lamp seemed even more emaciated in its light. The man opened the gate. He crossed the threshold and entered the house without uttering a word. The lamp followed his every movement. An extraordinarily calm face, framed by an untidy mass of hair. He unbuttoned his shirt and threw it on the bed. Then he sank onto the bed himself.

"It seems he's come back. Everyone says so."

The wick flickered – as did the shadow on the man's face. "Why has he come back?" he murmured, as if carrying on a monologue. " To me he was as good as dead. Did he ever send a single paisa to me, his old father? Now his three sisters have to be married off – will his being here bring that about?" His voice shook with suppressed emotion. "Why did he not die? So many wild beasts ... guns ... bombs ... how did he survive all that?"

The woman clutched the lamp. "All I know is that he's coming back," she said, speaking for the first time that night.

They were five people sitting around a huge, ornate table. Strewn across it were newspapers and magazines, an ashtray, a cigarette packet, plates of dry fruit, glasses of sherbet. A stocky man asked, tentatively, "So Phukanda, you should know Samiran Barua pretty well?"

"Certainly, I know him. I know him well," answered the old man. He was one of the most experienced of politicians. He sat ensconced in his chair, silver-framed glasses upon his nose, two golden buttons glinting on his kurta, his walking stick propped against the table. "His father and I were in jail together. We were friends. After Independence, I became a Minister and we completely lost touch – I don't know where he went. He was a very self-sufficient person, very proud. He was just not meant for politics. After many years, I met him in a village where I was to address a meeting. He was the headmaster there. He hailed me cheerfully and introduced the small boy by his side as his son. The lad greeted me, calling me Khura. That evening, I had tea at their house. Yes. Of course I know him."

"Then why don't you tell him, Phukanda? Make him understand that our party will be the best platform from which to oppose the present government."

The old man's lips puckered into a faint smile.

"You must get hold of him. By whatever means possible. We'll get you all the information about him. Phukanda, you know that the only way for our party to make its political presence felt right now is through him. If we lose him, there's no hope left."

"Ah, that I can manage. It will need some fast talking, some persuasion, but that I can do," the old man declared, fingering the tip of his stick, his voice dropping almost to a whisper. "I've reached such a position that I have left my own concerns far behind. I can't even hear my own voice any more. I no longer feel the need to look after my interests."

"The old fool must have tippled a bit too much."

"I will speak to him. I will put my hand on his shoulder, and in a voice glowing with pain and compassion, I will say, Sameer, you must return to a normal life. What will you get from all this? The path you have chosen is not fit for someone from our world. Give it up, son. Come with me. You can work with our party, for the people. Sameer, stay with me. You know how long your father and I have … "

He had reached the cinema hall at the crossroads; a huge building, new paint still shining on its walls. Samiran remembered this spot. This was where Kusha Master's house used to be. But where were all the houses, the people? All that remained was this monstrous edifice of a cinema hall.

He had come into the city two days ago, after many years. There were changes everywhere; not a single familiar face on the streets; no one to recognise him. There used to be a huge banyan tree at this very corner ... it had probably been cut down. Now there were more shops, many more cars and buses, and hundreds of busy people on the streets. The shouts of the truck drivers and others, the blare of bus horns, all added up to a scene pulsating with incessant noise and motion. Samiran went into a nearby tea-shop. There were only a few people inside. He took an inconspicuous corner-table and sat facing the door. He hadn't dared to spend the last couple of nights at any hotel. His own home was out of the question. And he hadn't had the courage to seek shelter with any of his old friends. He realised that the police knew he was in the city. He had barely managed to escape the police cordon at Saukidingi; at the Lumding rail station too, there were several suspicious characters, possibly from the IB.

Two fire-engines rushed past, their sirens wailing. He gave a start, looked all about him. No, there was only the clang of dishes, the manager's stentorian voice, a Hindi film song coming from a tape recorder. Everything else was drowned by those humdrum sounds.

So he had returned. Empty-handed. The little money that he had was almost exhausted. He had managed some ammunition which was supposed to arrive within the next few months – but this hinged entirely on trust. And, increasingly, he was beginning to doubt whether he could depend on something so fragile. From what he had seen till now, most of his old comrades had drifted away. Pinaki Mahanta was in a cushy job; Dipen Phukan was a prosperous contractor; Ramen had become an MLA and he had seen, a couple of nights ago, a minister's car parked outside the home of his best friend, Dwigen. What was he to do now? Where could he go?

A marriage procession went past him – cars decorated with cascading flowers and bright lights, a hired band, clarinet and drum resounding, young men dancing – noise and lights filled the street. Samiran passed a group of young men aimlessly loitering outside a paan shop. They shouted obscene remarks at some girls who were walking past them. A crowd shuffled and strained to watch the TV that was in the showcase outside a shop – a cricket match was on. A running commentary could be heard from the crowd – "*Another* wicket down! Ravi Shastri is bowling extremely well!"

Yes, thought Samiran Barua, he was definitely back in the city. People swarmed the street outside a cinema hall. A show must have just ended. On the wall in front of him were garishly-coloured posters: a hero lifting the heroine off her feet; a musical nite sponsored by a cigarette company; a family-planning advertisement; a hoarding extolling the undergarments in Ramlal Sevadutta's cloth shop. The city sprawled uncaringly before him, its inhabitants walking past him without even a second glance. A sudden gust of sound reached Samiran. It came from two buses with blaring loudspeakers, filled with youngsters. Perhaps a picnic party.

He trudged on wearily away from the uproar. Near a saloon was a man selling peanuts. He stopped and bought two rupees worth of the nuts. A furtive glance – no, there was nobody who had an eye on him – and then he stood there, shelling the peanuts, eating them one by one. From time to time, fragments of noise, light and dust from the road reached him. He caught sight of his face in the saloon's mirror – clean-shaven cheeks, longish hair, spectacles. A gaunt, tired-looking face, the cheek-bones sticking out.

For whom had he returned? Why had he stayed away so long? What had forced him to give up his own youthful dreams? For whom had he done so? These people, didn't they want anything more? He had thought that people would be awaiting him, their saviour, like victims trapped in a rail carriage after an accident.

But nobody seemed to need him here. Everything seemed to be running smoothly, effortlessly, with an abundance of money and happiness. Did he have any relevance in the midst of all this? If he was to stop and declare at that street corner – *I am Samiran Barua* – would anyone reach his side, apart from the police?

"Should I give you some more?" The old groundnut seller asked him, his trembling fingers raking the roasted nuts. His pushcart had a decrepit stove burning on it, the small heat from the quivering flame hardly making a difference to the cool air. The smell of fresh, roasted peanuts wafted in the breeze. Samiran bought some more. "Did you sell enough today?" he asked as he took the small paper bag from him.

The old man smiled, displaying toothless gums. "Just enough, just enough," he said, "it's the same every day."

Samiran continued to stand there. Should he go back to where he had come from? Or go to his mother? Should he surrender himself to the police? Or should he go to some distant city, begin once again, a law-abiding, secure citizen?

Samiran walked slowly on. The city was still bustling with life, noise and light from numerous spotlighted advertisements. Under the steady yellow glow of a halogen streetlight, Samiran took the last nut out of the packet. He was about to throw the wrapping away when something on that scrap of newspaper caught his eye. Printed on it in bold letters was the headline – **SAMIRAN BARUA RETURNS!**

He stood there, clutching it tightly, growing cold inside.

A stream of vehicles and people flowed past him. Laughter, gaiety, music. Young women walked by in their colourful dresses, some older women, a bunch of small children, a few elderly men. The gossipers at the paan shop had broken up; he could see the young men coming along the road.

He let go of the scrap of paper.

SAMIRAN BARUA RETURNS – this significant bit of news was picked up by the wind and blown along, to be trampled by the crowds of bustling feet in the city.

SETHU

WHITE HERMITAGE

TRANSLATED BY NIVEDITA MENON
NOMINATED BY K. SATCHIDANANDAN

First published in Malayalam as "Velutha Koodarangal" in *Kala Kaumudi*, Onam Special, September 1993, Trivandrum.

There's yet another reminder from Meledath Amma that two, three months have gone by without a letter. Urmila replies: You needn't get so worried. Writing letters is such boring business. After a couple of lines I start yawning. I scratch my head. Crack my knuckles. And before I know it, I'm through with the thing. In any case, what am I to write about? The news from here? Didn't I write and let you know when I got a job immediately on passing my exams? What do you want me to write now? Gossip from my newspaper office? The exploits of the girls from my hostel? But you're not really interested in all that. I promise that when we meet we'll sit and chat for ages, and without the mediation of bits of paper. But a letter, no! Now, if it were palm leaves of old, holding the quill straight up, scoring marks along the lines in an ancient script, it might have been fun. Anyway, how can you possibly think that regular correspondence alone can maintain a relationship? I remember the long-winded letters of Abu Dhabi Achchan ...

Abu Dhabi Achchan. Meledath Amma. That's how Urmila has always referred to them. From as far back as she can remember her mother's been at Meledath, and her father in Abu Dhabi. A blue father, borne regularly to them on blue writing paper in neat blue envelopes. The sky-blue Lord. And then he would arrive, every two years, bearing blue dresses.

I started detesting blue at that time. Is this the only colour available in Abu Dhabi, I asked once. He laughed, his pot-belly quivering. And inside him quivered the whisky and soda.

Blue is the colour of the sky, my child, he had said. The colour with the greatest depth. He had followed this with a couple of lines of trite verse, some utterly boring school stuff.

Are these the only lines you can recite, Abu Dhabi Achchan? You mustn't call him that, child, corrects Meledath Amma from somewhere behind me. Call him Achchan. Or Daddy.

Remembering, Urmila bursts out with laughter. I can only call him that. It's too old a habit. Impossible to change the habits of a lifetime. Like singing in the bathroom. Tapping unconsciously to the rhythm of a moving train or to a melody which floats into one's mind. Like swallowing part of every sentence as the next one comes tumbling out.

I wish I could change these habits of yours, my child, says Abu Dhabi Achchan sadly.

Every little thing I do either entertains him enormously or fills him with sorrow. But then, that's me.

I realised that my calling her Meledath Amma bothered her when on the first day of my vacations I returned after a visit to Kizhedath Cheriamma.

Down the hill, across the fields, through a narrow bumpy lane, the fifth house is Kizhedath Cheriamma's little place. A white, sanded front yard. Guarding it, a dog that doesn't bark. That dog has a strangely calm expression in its eyes, a look of detachment. It approaches slowly, wagging its tail. Licks my feet. Comes up close against me, rubbing its face on my legs. Hearing my voice, Kizhedath Cheriamma comes running out. Hugs me close. Strokes my forehead. Tries to give me a kiss. Her eyes fill with tears. For a long time she is unable to speak.

That day Meledath Amma flew into a fury. It was as if a fierce demon had made its way through her insides and was glaring out of her face. A stranger's voice roared from her throat. Everyone felt the razor-sharp edge of her tongue – Abu Dhabi Achchan, Kizhedath Cheriamma, Urmila. The demon inside her dragged them out one by one and slashed them to pieces. When she swept the bottles of paint off the table, smashing them, Urmila's half-finished painting of Kizhedath Cheriamma was completely smudged. Her white robes were stained. Red paint all over everything.

It was much later that Meledath Amma calmed down. Then she lay face down on her bed and cried all night. Her sobs reached Urmila in her room.

By morning the table had been cleaned. The smashed bottles of paint had disappeared. So had the smudged, half-finished painting of Kizhedath Cheriamma. It was as if nothing had happened. Everything was as before. As usual she woke Urmila with a cup of tea. As usual, she had bathed at dawn. The familiar dot of chandanam on her forehead lent her a spurious air of calm, but last night's demon seemed to lie dormant in her pale skin. She looked exhausted. Her face looked ravaged, like a field after a battle.

Urmila couldn't meet her eyes. She waited in terror for her body to break into uncontrolled shivering, for her face to swell up, become distorted, for those strange forces of darkness to start roaring from her throat.

What is it child, are you angry with Amma?

She comes to sit by Urmila. She runs her fingers through Urmila's hair. She tries to draw her close, but Urmila turns her head away and shakes herself free.

I'm not angry with you, Meledath Amma, she says. Nor am I angry with the old grandmother at Cherunkavu. Nor with the milestone at Kalatthiparambu. Nor with the little puppy shivering with cold in the April heat, nor with the pond boiling in the cold of winter.

Her mother is silenced.

Urmila thought of writing to Abu Dhabi Achchan. Come back, come running back to this vale of lava, come and feel yourself melt in it. Half-burnt, half-cooked, throw your burning body into the river, there to be squeezed to death by the monster serpent that lurks in the waters. But she did not write. Her laziness was the only reason.

Years later, after a boring day at office, when she relates this to Ashwin as they linger in the Coffee House, he laughs several times during her narration. What a nutcase, he says. Looks like a case of heredity. This illness.

He may be right. It's quite a possibility. For all I know, my chief may be thinking the same. But to be fair to Ashwin, he sits listening with real interest. Stroking his chin, taking off his spectacles once in a while and wiping the lenses, nodding slowly, hmm-ing in agreement.

Suddenly, irrationally, Urmila asks, If you just go "Hm," will Meledath Amma's illness be cured?

Nonsense.

If you say "Nonsense," will it be cured?

Stop it. Don't bore me.

If you say "Don't bore me," will it be cured? She relentlessly continues to revert to an infuriating childhood game.

Stop it, I say. Ashwin's face turns red.

Falling silent, Urmila gulps down her coffee. It has gone cold.

After a while Ashwin asks, Does Kizhedath Cheriamma write to you?

Yes.

And do you reply?

Yes, regularly.

How's that? You're overcome with laziness when it comes to writing to your own mother, then how do you manage this?

God knows.

You can't get away with an answer like that. There must be a specific reason. Tell me, do you love that woman more than you love your mother?

A fly has drowned in the coffee at the bottom of her cup. There is no one else now in their corner of the Coffee House.

She takes a long time to understand his question. She has never ever thought of it this way.

I can't do it, Ashwin, I can't assess my likes so accurately, she manages to say after a long while. Somehow it just comes easy, writing to Kizhedath Cheriamma. I don't yawn then, or crack my knuckles with boredom, or scratch my head. It just comes pouring out without a break.

Do you feel this Cheriamma loves you more than your mother does?

Urmila is now in the witness-box. The bespectacled, bearded, bore of a lawyer comes at her with his probing questions. No way out but to answer. After all, she had entered the witness-box willingly. So she replies, Chhi. I've never thought of it like that. She nibbles at her finger, pensive. How impertinent the lawyer's questions are. How can one possibly know exactly how much one is loved by someone else? Some people are able to show their love. Others aren't. It would be stupid to think that love is only what one can see. No, these questions are not relevant here.

Then?

I only know the moment I get her letter, I feel I must reply immediately, without wasting a single moment, catch the very next post.

But why? Is it sympathy? Empathy? The fool of a lawyer continues his cross-examination.

I don't know. Urmila is overwhelmed with a sense of helplessness. I only know this, she says. When I'm with Kizhedath Cheriamma, relaxed, my legs stretched out, I am absolutely at ease. My mind is calm. No tensions at all. No other thoughts. Just she and I in a world of our own. Her thickly whitewashed walls. Pure white curtains. White sheets. Dazzling white her clothes. It is as if their whiteness permeates my whole being. I brim over with a deep sense of peace. Like sitting before one's guru, cross-legged. Inside me rises the hum of shanti mantras. I am absolutely at peace with myself, and you know how difficult that is for me. So often have I imagined the cold solitude, the stillness during the ultimate state of meditation ... Drops of dew falling on my head, making their way through my hair, over my face, just flowing ... Close by, a small river of melting snow.

Ashwin listens, stroking his chin. His eyes are unusually bright.

But – and here Urmila's voice breaks – I have never been so lucky. My mind is constantly rocked by waves. Even the smallest things rattle me. Once when I was a student, I was filled with rage and smashed all the crockery in the hostel mess. They should have expelled me, sent me to a lunatic asylum, perhaps. But they did nothing of the sort. There comes a call from Abu Dhabi Achchan. At Mother Superior's growl he bends over in obeisance. Offers to send as much money as is required to meet the cost of new crockery. And then, apologetic explanations. She's an only child, Mother, I've spoilt her a little. The fault is mine. But what can I do, living across the seas. You people are all she has now. And as I watched Mother Superior's face clear and rise like the full moon, my rage grew. But the moon was to reach its height of glory only when the draft arrived from Abu Dhabi. Then she had nothing but the greatest of admiration for me. All over the shelves new crockery was laid out for me to break whenever the mood should take me. And a warning to the other students not to provoke me unnecessarily ...

A big grin grows beneath Ashwin's beard.

What's so funny?

It has just struck me that you're more like your mother than you know. I mean, there she is, with a demon ready to possess her at a moment's notice. And here you are, in search of conveniently placed crockery to break!

I don't think it's funny, says Urmila, frowning. It's difficult for people who are similar in temperament to be close. That may be why I feel closer to Kizhedath Cheriamma.

They leave the restaurant and start walking towards the YWCA. The path around the maidan is damp with dew. Ashwin tucks his hands into his pockets and walks, leaning to one side. His hair is thinning at the back of his head. Urmila doesn't chatter about her office. Nor does Ashwin narrate the inane incidents that happened in his PG class. Kizhedath Cheriamma absorbs her thoughts totally.

Ashwin must have realised this and maybe that was why he said, a little sharply: Stop it! Stop it, I say!

It had become dark. Ashwin stood still by a lamp post, holding on to the fence at the southern end of the maidan.

That's enough! he repeats. Stop it right there.

Why, asks Urmila.

It's better for all of you to stop it right there. For you, for your mother, for your father, for your aunt.

But why, why?

Look, you mustn't glamourise unconventional relationships on the basis of some random, uncharted memories. Just think this over quietly in your room. You're mature, you're reasonably experienced. Control your mind, meditate for a while on your guru. Things will become clearer. There are certain things that one can realise only by oneself in the solitude of meditation.

When I meditate, it's always the face of a yogini that comes to my mind. All in white, the bhasmam on her forehead, a sanyasini. And she has the face of Kizhedath Cheriamma.

Stupid! I never thought you could be such a fool. How do those Marwari bosses of yours tolerate you?

Oh yes, you men can say things like this. What do you know of the depth of such relationships?

You're right. Maybe unconventional relationships do have more depth. All right, before we leave, just one more question: This aunt of yours, how exactly is she related to you?

Kizhedath Cheriamma? Mother, elder sister, playmate, guru, yogini. And so much, so much more.

Stupid! growls Ashwin. That's the biggest swear word he can use. From that alone Urmila can tell he is very angry.

I'd better go. It's getting late.

Yes, that would be best. Don't make me angrier. All day, the stupidity in class and now this!

Urmila does not say anything. They part at the crossroad.

Lying back in her chair, Urmila reflects for a long while on what Ashwin had said. She can't quite put her finger on it. What is it about Kizhedath Cheriamma that makes him so angry? He says, You must not glamourise unconventional relationships on the basis of some random, uncharted memories.

She searches for the latest blue cover from Abu Dhabi Achchan. A flood of love on blue writing paper. Words of endearment. Advice. The whole garnished with some lines of third-rate poetry. A young man's bravado.

Once, to one such letter, she had dashed off an impulsive reply: You would be an amazingly boring lover, Abu Dhabi Achchan. How can anyone put up with your holding forth like this? A man with no poetry in himself quoting couplets. Intolerable! Your clumsy chivalry would make anyone laugh. And then those predictable bits of advice. I've read better stuff in my civics textbooks in school.

After she had posted the letter she wished she hadn't. The poor man, waiting and longing to hear from her, all those seas away, wouldn't he be devastated by her cruelty? But immediately she had corrected herself. I know this man only too well. An ice-block that can't melt even in the heat of the Gulf. A simpleton who would not only offer his other cheek if his daughter slapped one, but would regret he hadn't a third to offer.

Sometimes I am very cruel. Yes, sometimes there are no limits to my cruelty. Just one remark and I can hurt so many people. Why am I like this? That's what Ashwin wants to know too. There is no apparent reason for your being like this, he says and then bursts out laughing. It's obvious you weren't thrashed often enough as a child.

Anyway that's not the point. I'm trying to understand what Ashwin meant this evening.

From where I sit I can see my face in the mirror. There is no cruelty in that face at all. Is it because the devil isn't in me right now? At the moment I am very very normal. After I left the college hostel I haven't broken any crockery. Haven't fought with the warden here. She has not had to call Abu Dhabi Achchan. Anyway she doesn't seem very enamoured of cheques from Abu Dhabi. A woman with the demeanour of a midwife. When she does her rounds at night, her hands clasped behind her back, surrounded by an aura of earnestness, I feel very tempted to say,

No, the pains have not started yet. When they do, I'll come and call you. Can you guarantee an easy delivery?

Once I must have muttered something like this and my roommate Alice Kalappurakkal hears me and, Delivery? Whose? she asks in a puzzled tone.

Then Urmila explains gravely to Alice Kalappurakkal. Twenty-nine pregnant women in this hostel. All at different stages of pregnancy. Women throwing up all over the place. Think of it, just one midwife for *twenty-nine* pregnant women. And then, suddenly, seven women go into labour at once. What a situation for the poor woman. She doesn't have fourteen hands after all.

Sweat breaks out on Alice Kalappurakkal's pretty face. She is terrified. Urmila, what are you saying? Are you all right? She comes up close to Urmila. Examines her eyes and face minutely. Brings her nose to Urmila's face and sniffs.

Liquor? Drugs?

She remembers Matilda Fernandes, expelled from the hostel long ago, and she is afraid. She lights a candle to St. Anthony. Poor girl, she believes the intimacy between friends should be as abundant and flowing as the rubber sap in the plantations of her native land.

No Alice, Urmila laughs. I haven't touched any of that. I'm not into that sort of thing. This is just good old inherited madness. That's what my chief, Pandurang Vinayak Sartre, probably thinks, too. But Ashwin. I don't understand it at all.

The letter that recently arrived from Kizhedath Cheriamma. No advice. No endearments. No bravado. Just small bits of news from the neighbourhood. About toddy-tapper Kunhappan being possessed by the village exorcist's ghost as he returned late at night from a film-show. About the collection that had been started for the renovation of the Bhagawati temple. For the first time, there's a headmistress at the local school. Very good-looking, by all accounts. People gather on the roadside to see her pass ... A letter written by a woman widowed at thirty-two, surely irrepressible sobs must arise from between its lines. But no, nothing of the sort. Perhaps she hid it well. After she was through with her news, she asked question after question about the wonders of the city. The city never ceased to amaze her. She wanted to know all the small details of urban life. Really? Is that so? Amazing! That you should have the good fortune to see all this, my child.

She firmly believed that Urmila wrote every word published in her big English paper, so much more important than the local Malayalam ones. Urmila had once sent her a copy. She would never understand that I am just a little cog in our establishment, a small-time reporter wandering about, jhola on my shoulder. She can have no conception of my chief, Pandurang Vinayak Sartre.

Oh no, that can't be true. You're just pulling my leg. Whatever you may say, they do publish all the English that you write. Isn't that enough to judge the capability of a person? I couldn't write two correct lines of English if I wanted. I've forgotten it all.

What radiance in that meek figure, covered in white, drew Abu Dhabi Achchan to her? Or was Achchan, too, in search of peace?

Stop that. You stupid person, roars Ashwin from behind my reflection.

Urmila winks at me from the mirror. You had better stop. If Ashwin gets angrier, he'll let fly "stupid" after "stupid." He thinks it's an obscenity worthy of the Bharani songs sung for the dark goddess of Kodungalloor.

But there must be something to it. Otherwise, Ashwin would never say that about anyone. A man so much more knowledgeable, more experienced than I am. Despite his first rank, his scholarship to go to the States, he chose to stay on and teach in a college. Swears never to register for a doctorate here. The universities, the professors, the evaluation system ... And then this barrage of "stupids."

She wrote to Kizhedath Cheriamma. How can we make our *Ashwin learn some serious swear words?*

When she asked Alice Kalappurakkal, she clapped her hands over her ears, knelt and crossed herself. And Urmila did not have the courage to ask Pandurang Vinayak Sartre.

Whenever I think of Kizhedath Cheriamma, it's a yogini's face that I see. I long to throw myself at those feet and seek sanctuary. Press my face into them, wash them with my tears ... If I carry on like this, I fear I may take up sanyasam. Oh yes, a great fear, that I, who have no interest at all in leaving everything and going off into another world; I, who have never been to an ashram, never attended a bhajan session; yet, deep inside me, it's always a white robe. Sometimes it is ochre.

Stupid. This time Ashwin says it laughingly. You don't have the pureness of mind for all that. You won't find it so easy to shake off the habits of a lifetime, the habits of an ordinary, careless young girl, the spoilt only daughter of a Gulfwalla.

But with whom can I share this? Something swells up within me. Whatever happens on the outside, something inside me is swelling up. I know very well I don't have the guts to leave everything and go off. What am I trying to run away and hide from? Am I transforming sanyasam into another romantic fantasy? I am thoroughly confused, Ashwin. I have never seen an idiot like me anywhere in the world. This kind of confusion about every little thing. I stuff all sorts of ideas into myself and when they rise to the surface, it's in strange and distorted forms, to trouble me, steal my sleep. It's been so long since I slept well.

No one tries to understand me, not even you, Ashwin.

At this, there's a slight change in Ashwin's face. He has been lost in thought, stroking his chin. Suddenly, unexpectedly, he reaches out and presses her hand gently. Although they have known each other long, this is the first time he has touched her.

Calm down, child, calm down, he murmurs. Everything will be all right.

After a thoughtful silence, he starts speaking in a low voice: There is no point in analysing your crazy thoughts. In any case, the human mind doesn't fit easily within the definiteness of theories, although so-called psychiatrists would like to convince us that it does. We're ordinary people. We just happen to be born, not because we will it or because someone wants us. On our long journey we connect with many people. We love them. Hate them. We're angry. We fight. And then we regret it. And so it goes. There is no point in thinking so much about relationships and working oneself up. Just let them be.

Such facile words. These aren't Ashwin's words. They are the kind of words Abu Dhabi Achchan might scribble on his blue paper to comfort me.

That night for no reason at all she cried in bed. She couldn't understand why. It was as if deep inside her, tears wandered aimlessly, looking for release. And when they welled up, Urmila couldn't hold them back.

Perhaps it's the sound of suppressed sobs that wakes Alice Kalappurakkal. Without putting on the light she gropes her way in the darkness to Urmila's bed. Puzzled, she strokes Urmila's back, asking anxiously, What is it, Urmila?

No reply.

It helps to pray for a while when you feel such pain.

To whom?

To your gods, of course.

And if I have no such gods?

Shh ... Alice Kalappurakkal shuts her ears. Don't say such blasphemous things, dear.

I just don't understand anything. That is the truth.

Abu Dhabi Achchan, Meḷedath Amma, Kizhedath Cheriamma, Ashwin, they all say different things. They buzz around my head like little wasps, and then they fly away after giving me sharp little stings. Honestly, I don't understand anything.

Stumbling in the darkness, she goes to stand by the window. Watching the star-sprinkled sky, she is reminded of Meledath Amma. In memories of childhood, it's always only her. It was she who used to point out the stars shining in the darkness of night. Every star is a soul, she would say. Love those stars. When we need them, they will appear to protect us.

That was how she started as a child to know the stars by name. In the cool of night, after Meledath Amma had fallen asleep, she would press her face to the bars of the window and call out to each familiar star by name. Hundreds of names. Hundreds of faces. To the lonely, they offer solace. Light years away, they twinkle at one another in silent communication.

How can you bring yourself to forget me, my daughter? There is sadness in Meledath Amma's letter. It was with me that you shared the warm intimacy of the womb. The midwife's cutting of the umbilical cord which bound us was only a temporary separation. Isn't it a knot that ties you to me for a lifetime? However far you wander, won't that moist length of nerves and veins join you to me?

Sometimes she feels Meledath Amma is right. And yet, why is she so cruel to Kizhedath Cheriamma?

Everything all of them say is right. Ashwin who says I should not glamourise unconventional relationships also tells me to let relationships take their own course. After all, one cannot foresee the havens one might arrive at in one's search for peace.

Meledath Amma said once: I pray with all my heart that your father never comes on leave. There was a hardness in her face. I noticed an uncharacteristic flush on her pale skin.

Never again? But when his job in Abu Dhabi is over?

I pray it never ends. Amma's eyes fill. She lowers her face. I can't bear to think of it, child.

When they met the next day, Ashwin was very serious. And Urmila too was still a little angry.

I fought with him again today, she says.

With whom?

With my chief, Pandurang Vinayak Sartre, of course. Who else? God, what a name. No patches on his body. Nor Vinayaka's paunch or appetite. As for the original Sartre, he's never even heard of him. What a totally inappropriate name.

Ashwin acknowledges her prattle with a brief, indifferent hmm.

He wants to cut out all my good stuff and push in his rotten Angreji. Do you know how beautifully he speaks English? In impeccable Marathi. I only have one ambition now. Just once I want to be Pandurang Vinayak Sartre's chief and turn his Angreji lines into a sea of red ...

Urmila stops short. Ashwin is not listening. Lying on his elbows on the grass, he's smoking one cigarette after another. Then suddenly he asks, Did you think about what I said yesterday?

Urmila nods silently.

And?

I didn't sleep a wink. All night I was at the window, counting the familiar stars. Whatever you say Ashwin, my mind is full of the presence of Kizhedath Cheriamma. Sometimes I think I should have taken shape in her womb.

Ashwin's face is still very serious. He says as if to no one in particular, If it were possible to choose one's mother at every turn in life, things would be so simple. To select a womb in which one can grow ...

That's right. A flash of mischief in Urmila's eyes. In that case, maybe Alice Kalappurakkal would have taken shape in Mother Teresa's womb. And you, Ashwin, in Jiddu Krishnamurti's. But what about poor old Pandurang Vinayak Sartre?

Nonsense, growls Ashwin. He is silent for a while. Then he sits up, cross-legged. His eyes are half closed. He strokes his beard.

Thoughtfully, he begins to speak: I don't see anything wrong in women being possessive. The desire to keep one's mate to oneself is primeval. It's something that cannot be explained in organic terms, but it is very real. Maybe when you reach a stage like that in your own life you will understand.

Urmila stares at him fixedly, as if not understanding at all.

To tell you the truth, I am one hundred percent with your mother. It's not because of the rules of good behaviour or because I accept the limits set by society. But something is definitely wrong. Actually it is you who should be saying all this. It is the woman's mind which feels separation most painfully. Somehow, in my eyes, your Kizhedath Cheriamma grows smaller and smaller as the days go by. I don't see her as a person of any great significance.

Urmila does not want to accept this. Nor does she know how to convince him. But I do know this. I see her very differently from the way all of you see her.

Ashwin says nothing.

Urmila sits, her legs stretched out, munching peanuts. Slowly, she begins to tap out a rhythm on her thigh. Inside her a unique melody unfolds itself. A melody she has never heard before. A melody which rouses her from deep inside.

She is lost to everything in its enchantment.

As for Ashwin, he doesn't like this at all. Stop it, he says loudly. You just don't understand what I am saying.

He sounds helpless.

I am a foolish little girl you just cannot straighten out, no Ashwin? Someone who should never have made it to a PG class. How on earth did that college take me in?

Stupid, grumbles Ashwin.

And, at exactly that moment, there is only one thing in my mind's eye. Spotless, pure white clothes. Head covered, the whole body covered, all that is visible is a thin face. And it is filled with peace. Eyes half closed. Lips trembling slightly. Perhaps they move with the telling of a shanti mantram. I see all the whiteness of day in that dress. A whiteness undimmed by all the dirt of a lifetime. The dazzling purity of a thousand thumba flowers, a thousand doves. The radiance of the sun.

White is the colour of widowhood, of separation, someone inside her murmurs. But it doesn't matter. Let's say I was born a widow; that I grew up as one. That I lost my mate at birth. A widow by birth ... In my childhood dreams there were always a lot of white feathers floating around. There they would be, in the little square of sky I could see through my window. I long to tuck these uncontrollable, random little memories into white sheets. As darkness falls, I find myself burrowing deeper and deeper into the security of my white hermitage.

Ashwin is thunderstruck. His lips are dry, his face has turned grey. He is unable to say anything, as if his voice has dried in his throat.

Slowly, he gets up.

Urmila notices the tremble in his fingers as they escape into his pockets. He is standing tall, with an air of having much to say. To Urmila, to her alone. Something very special. Perhaps something which only an Ashwin can articulate. But he does not say anything. Suddenly, her face looks unfamiliar to him. He moistens his dry lips with his tongue. As is his habit when uncomfortable, he smokes continuously.

After taking a couple of steps, he shakes his head in response to some thought, as if to someone else. He murmurs, Come, let's go. It's getting dark.

Silently, Urmila gets up. She starts walking. Her legs move faster. And then even faster. When some passers-by come between them, Ashwin who is now well behind, cannot see her at all.

Urmila is aware of her feet swallowing space. Something rises to her head and fills it. Deep within her, someone hums that glorious melody. Enchanted, she speeds on.

Around her, night begins to bloom in the city. And, in the distance, growing clearer, are the lights of her white hermitage.

KANJI PATEL

THE BEEHIVE

TRANSLATED BY SARALA JAG MOHAN
NOMINATED BY SHIRISH PANCHAL

First published in Gujarati as "Madhapudo" in *Gadyaparva*,
May-July 1992, Bombay.

In his new shirt and dhoti, a brand new cap on his head, he stood in the front room of the house, surrounded by the people of his village. His name was Bhagwan. From beyond the threshold his mother stepped out. She placed her hand on his head in blessing. Bhagwan's wife, who stood with her left shoulder squeezed against the door jamb, shuffled a little, for a better look.

The son rested his head on his mother's feet, not unaware that bringing a new wife to live under the same roof as his first wife was inviting trouble.

His mother helped him to his feet. Gently she stroked his head though he had his cap on and murmured, "May you live in happiness and have a large family."

Someone now brought a plate containing kumkum and grains of rice and placed a tika of wet kumkum on Bhagwan's forehead before going around, to do the same for the others gathered there. As the kumkum dried, Bhagwan felt the skin of his forehead stretch. His eyebrows twitched. His forehead rippled for an instant. A few grains of rice fell on the dhoti that draped his crossed legs. His eyelids dropped and through almost shut eyes he saw the grains of rice on his lap. They were tinged orange with the kumkum. At that moment, Parbhabhai came with a plate of gud, making his way through the people seated there, to place a small piece of gud on the tip of Bhagwan's tongue. A little sweetness slid down Bhagwan's throat with his saliva.

Akham, the watchman, was bustling about on assigned duties. He had pushed a packet of potash into a long iron tube with a stiff wire and, with great precision, banged the tube on a flat stone. Five times he repeated the operation and five blasts were heard, flying over the village roofs, the fields, the ridges that lay between individual fields, sending everything reverberating. Guests trembled. They pushed their fingers into their ears and shut their eyes tight. The walls of the crowded room rocked. But Akham the watchman had a heart of steel. He was about to push the sixth packet in when Bhagwan said, "Akham, bhai, hold on. You can do it on the way to the bride's house."

That same night, before the break of dawn, Bhagwan's hurried wedding was over and he was back home with a widow as his second wife.

His first wife, Santok, had delivered four sons. But one of them had a skin disease. Another had asthma. The third came under the evil spell of the witch, Fuli. And the fourth ... well, one way or another, winged Death had entered the portals of the house and purloined each one of them away.

Bhagwan was already forty. How far was that from middle age? Of course the mother wanted a second wife for her son. She pleaded with Santok. Then she did everything to humour her son so she could persuade him to tie the knot. Twice she convinced Govindbhai that he must take the responsibility of talking to her son.

Many months came and went before a decision was finally made, and one day, during the bright fortnight in the month of Margashirsha, the mother said to Santok, "Daughter-in-law of mine, one woman can't bear too many children. How long can we wait? May God grant male progenies to both my daughters-in-law."

Jamna, the new daughter-in-law was younger than Santok by about ten years. Poor woman, she had had the misfortune of being widowed. She had, of course, touched Santok's feet as she entered the house, but that didn't stop Santok from observing each act of Jamna's with eagle eyes. She longed to be in Jamna's body, draped in the fragrance of the clothes which had just been taken out of the big trunk.

Twelve long hours had passed since the new daughter-in-law's arrival. Twelve hours of the night still remained.

The new wife's charpai was laid in Bhagwan's room and

Santok brought hers to that portion of the house where her mother-in-law slept, close to where the grain jars were stored. Women from the village who had dropped in to talk to the new daughter-in-law about her father's family had, one by one, left for their homes, barely in time for their evening chores.

Santok snuffed out the lamp.

Whatever distance there was between her and the bridal bed vanished. Santok's eyes and ears, her total and undivided attention, were fixed on the cowdung plaster under the charpai in the room where the new daughter-in-law slept. Santok's bosom heaved under Jamna's charpai. With her eyes wide open, she stared at the patterns on the plastered floor. Could Jamna hear Santok's frenzied heart?

In her fury, Santok sees and hears every single move, magnified a million times. There, Bhagwan is moving towards Jamna's charpai. Jamna's big toe digs gently into his side. Then the charpai creaks. The strings at its head stretch. The legs of the charpai shake. Those two are now one. The pox on them!

A thousand nights have come, but never has there been one such as this. Jamna was in the house, there was nothing she could do about that, but there still raged a fire in the rib-cage of Santok's chest. At last the night, which a whole lifetime would not be able to erase, was over.

Morning came at the end of such a night. Santok felt neither fatigued nor as if she had lost sleep. Yet, when the sun waded in through the darkness, she continued to lie full length on the plastered floor, her heart thumping painfully, her eyes and hands and calf muscles unimaginably tired, unable to concentrate on anything.

In the afternoon, while weeding the wheat field, the mother-in-law spoke to Santok.

"Dear daughter-in-law," she said, "why do you look so drained? Don't you know I depend on you and Jamna to build on this strong and beautiful foundation that I have laid with great care? Soon I will be gone, fading out of your lives like your

father-in-law. Don't you know I took on this burden for your sake? May the Omnipotent One who gives, give you both many children. You shouldn't feel distressed, child."

Bhagwan had come to that side on the pretext of bringing his oxen to water. Now he stood by the wild cactus near the narrow gap in the hedge. He understood everything.

"You gave birth to four sons," he said, "but not one of them was fated to live. Ah, these evil days of Kaliyug! God did give, but he gave with the wrong hand. His will prevails."

Santok's hand was stilled. She could neither pull out the stalk of the cheel that she had grasped, nor could she let go of it. She kept staring at it. At whose bidding would the weed come off the ground? "Alas, it is my bad luck," she said in a voice so low that not only her mother-in-law but she herself could barely hear the words.

"Child, don't make yourself miserable by thinking of your bad luck," said the mother-in-law, stroking Santok's back.

Santok reached out for another cheel.

Bhagwan came through the gap. He stepped down from the raised ridge that bounded their field, walked between two rows of wheat plants to squat beside Santok and start weeding. He asked, "Has anything gone wrong, Ma?"

"Nothing."

"Is this daughter-in-law of yours unhappy about something?"

"No, you keep out of it, my son. It's between us. Don't scare her. You two must settle it quietly between yourselves. Let what passes between you be a guarded secret," said the mother.

And so it remained.

The days wore on. It was the eighth day after the wedding. Jamna made rotis in the evening and bathed the buffaloes with hot water as her mother-in-law had asked her to. But, even eight days after the arrival of the new wife, Bhagwan was not available to Santok.

"What do I care?" muttered Santok as she loosened her

clothes and lay down on the bare floor. Even if water were to flow over her head to the height of twenty feet, Santok would not move. Come what may! Such was Santok.

According to custom, on the ninth day, Jamna's brother came in the evening to take Jamna back to her mother's house for a brief visit.

Not having slept a whole week, Bhagwan fell fast asleep the moment he stretched out on the charpai.

Santok went up to him. She shook him violently. He did not even stir. Jerking his body angrily, she hissed into his ear, "You're fast asleep, hn? So that you can keep awake whole nights with her when she returns?"

Bhagwan stirred.

Santok twisted his ear. "The new is new for barely nine days, but the old one is yours all your life – do you hear? There are many who bring in a second wife when the first is still alive, but no one can be as heartless as you!"

Bhagwan almost jumped to his feet.

He sat up, blinking, as though the smoke of burning dung-pats had got into his eyes. Santok was offended. She flounced off to her charpai and pulled her sheet tight over herself.

Bhagwan had to spend hours in endless pleading and entreaties before she allowed herself to be won over. The next four days saw the stifled breeze blow with new vigour. Bhagwan and Santok were as though newly wed, inseparable through day and night.

But on the fourth day, Bhagwan's mother sent Bhula Bhagat, her husband's younger brother, to fetch Jamna. Bhula Bhagat spent two full days, enjoying the hospitality that the parents of the bride lavished on him, before bringing Jamna back with him.

Bhagwan was now faced with the task of establishing a rapport with Jamna all over again. At the same time, he had to take care not to hurt Santok's feelings. He had to keep in mind the expectations and surging excitement of the new wife as well as the angry words, the sleepless nights of the old one and the hard work she continued to do for the family.

Bhagwan felt a fire raging within him. While ploughing the field, the reins would slip from his hands. The oxen would turn unruly and throw off the yoke. They refused to make the concentric circles they had always made for him. The furrows he made didn't lie neatly parallel to one another. Try as he might, though he pressed his plough, it did not make new furrows but just slid deeper and deeper into those already formed. The ridges remained untilled.

Soon the breeze brought along an exciting fragrance. The mango trees had blossomed again. Bhagwan woke up one morning at dawn, muttering to himself, "I can't hold out any more. That Manglo, that motherfucker, he says, I am more prosperous than Bhagwan. Don't boast too much, Manglo! You are not even equal to the dust off the sole of my foot. Do I have to hear such taunts from you, just because I don't have a son?"

Days went by and Bhagwan continued to speak to himself. The old woman became extremely worried. Santok took to blaming herself, and Jamna said, her eyes brimming with tears, "Santok my sister, has this ever happened before?"

Not knowing what else to do, Santok went to fetch Govindbhai. The moment she set eyes on Govindbhai, the old woman pleaded, "Govindbhai, do something about my Bhagwan. I can't make out what is troubling him."

Before Govindbhai could hear her out, before he could respond in any way, he saw Bhagwan running away – towards the outskirts of the village. Bhagwan ran, through the narrow lanes, running so fast that his feet struck against his buttocks. Fine dust came dancing up from the lane as his feet beat down on it. The earth fumed with the heat of summer. Bhagwan was still talking to himself, turning every once in a while to look towards his house, and at Govindbhai who was pounding the dust close behind him. Seeing Govindbhai only made Bhagwan run faster towards the hill.

Govindbhai thought that he would surely lose. He ran with determined energy till he caught up with Bhagwan. Bhagwan stopped abruptly. He stooped to pick up a hardened lump of clay and brandished it at him. Govindbhai had to step back. Meekly, he folded his hands and pleaded with Bhagwan. Bhagwan was one of those who would settle scores even if half a dozen ruffians turned against him. It was never easy to keep Bhagwan under control. It was with great difficulty that Govindbhai brought a stuttering and protesting Bhagwan back.

Those two summer months, Santok and Jamna were as close as blood-sisters. The old woman as well as the other women of the village were all praise for them. But as the monsoon and winter months followed, there were fiery exchanges between the two inside the house. Santok would order Jamna to do all the housework. When Jamna protested, Santok would threaten her, "If you want to give me cheeky answers, better go back to your father's house. Don't think I'm under your or your father's thumb."

Bhagwan would jump to Jamna's defence. "You're all on fire from the day she came to this house," he would tell a frowning Santok. "Be careful or you may have to go to your father's house instead."

The seasons moved as they are wont to and blossoms were soon to appear on the mango trees. Bhagwan's mother sent a message to the exorcist. "Bhai Arjan, by the time the mango tree blossoms, let Bhagwan get interested in one of the women. Cast a spell, any spell."

Arjan Bhuva sat cross-legged on the plastered floor. He blew air through puffed cheeks and cleaned the ground, just enough to place a leaf-plate. The mother picked up a basket containing a handful of corn, and standing before her son, she moved the plate in seven elliptical circles that stretched from Bhagwan's head to his feet. She emptied the corn on to the clean floor.

"Why, why is this happening?" Arjan Bhuva asked. "Is it a witch who has cast her spell? Is it an ancestor? A widowed female, maybe? Is she from the village or outside? Tell me, is it a relative or a guest? Ma Joginimata! Your word won't go in vain. You must bring the travails of this miserable boy to an end. I fall at your feet!" The bhuva arranged the grains of corn in pairs; then he broke the pairs and regrouped them. One grain was left single. Damn it! He plied the goddess with another question: "Has this poor man blundered in any way? Has any one of us erred in this house?"

Arjan Bhuva continued to arrange the grains, but could come up with no answers. "Oh Jogmaya, only you can harness the wind," he pleaded. "This poor creature depends on you."

Bhagwan sat there, chuckling to himself. Then, all of a sudden, he reached out for two bamboos lying there. They were of the same height and Bhagwan raised himself onto them, quickly, deftly, adjusting his feet so that he was balancing on them. The slits cracked and widened and each of his feet wedged snugly into them. Moving swiftly, he reached the other end of the courtyard, then stopped at the threshold of the house. He struck the bamboos repeatedly on the ground – thak, thak ... thai, thai. At that moment, he noticed Santok, Jamna and his mother peering at him from behind the doorpost. Just then, he lost his balance and came crashing to the ground, right under the eaves. Shaking off the dust and the gravel that stuck to his elbows, knees and forehead, he meekly went back into the house, even allowing Arjan Bhuva to tie a knotted consecrated string around his neck.

Things went back to normal again. Santok was back in the kitchen, looking after it, giving and accepting, attending to social obligations, doing this and that, washing earthen jugs and scouring milk pots. Jamna worked in the field, swept and dusted the house, and fetched water. There was not a single murmur from either of them.

Bhagwan and Jamna would leave the house early in the morning to harvest the paddy. After feeding the cattle and making rotis, Santok would join them in the afternoon, carrying their lunch in a bundle. But then there came a day when she found Bhagwan and Jamna seated close, nudging each other, their work forgotten, their sickles lying on the ground.

Santok's heart trembled.

From that day on, Santok saw to it that it was she who went with Bhagwan to the field.

Once during that time, Jamna who came carrying the food-bundle, did not find Santok or Bhagwan near the paddy field. She waited impatiently, resting the bundle on the ridge of the field. At last she noticed them emerging, one after the other, from behind a bush. And as they walked home that evening on the narrow ridge that ran around the field, Jamna seized the opportunity to tell Bhagwan, "You must put equal pressure on both legs when you walk on such high ridges."

Bhagwan tried to express his entire self through his eyes. But Jamna's pert remark had penetrated through Santok's ears right into her heart. "Don't keep all that knowledge to yourself, Jamna," she said, wryly. "I too want to learn some nice things."

Desire was beginning to wane. The blossoms withered on every mango tree. Tender mangoes appeared. Gradually they grew bigger; they hardened. In less than eight to ten days, bunches of ripening mangoes could be seen from a distance.

Bhagwan sat clinging to his hukkah – not unlike a suckling child that tugs at his mother's breasts – from daybreak, when he chewed the neem twig to clean his teeth, to midnight when Santok and Jamna, in their respective charpais, got tired of waiting for him.

And then a moonless night came when Santok went to sleep by Bhagwan's side and Jamna lighted the lamp in the niche in the wall. The dense shadows of the mango tree were torn asunder. The night lost its meaning. And Bhagwan saw all the fruits darken and drop to the ground in quick succession.

The next morning when Bhagwan woke up he had already worked himself into a frenzy. "You!" Bhagwan shouted. "You've taken away all the golden cattle of the forests and you have pushed the Earth far away. Wait, just you wait!"

He rushed out. He was not walking but running. He was not running but flying. He was not flying but was being carried like a mote of dust by the mighty wind.

"I hear," he called out, "I hear the call of the gleaming mountains. I hear the call of the well."

The vav was at the end of a grove of mango trees with luscious golden fruit. A straight and narrow path ran alongside. But staggering and faltering, Bhagwan ran between two tall and thorny hedges, through a gutter that lay between them, raising a whirl of dust.

Soon, the dust reached the end of the grove where the steps leading down to the vav were. Clinging to a wooden beam above was a beehive – a thick, rugged lump like a protruding tongue, oozing gleaming honey.

From this there was a sudden rain of bees. In a startling second, the vav was covered with bees, their backs yellow as the kuvech plant. Ebony heads. Fluttering wings ...

Dust and bees swirled together. Then settled.

A drop of glittering honey loomed low and dripped. It mingled with the water that lapped the stone steps.

Vav: Step-well.

ꝺ

MEENA KAKODKAR

ONE'S OWN, YET ALIEN

TRANSLATED BY SACHEEN PAI RAIKAR
NOMINATED BY CHANDRAKANT KENI

First published in Konkani as "Aaplem ... Parki" in *Chitrangi*, Annual Number, 1993, Volvoi-Ponda, Goa.

The stars shine so brightly that every leaf on the trees can be seen clearly. Aatibai sits on the porch after her evening meal. As she always does. On such beautiful evenings, memories brush past her like the cool breeze, and later at night, the insects will play her memories in their nocturnal orchestra.

But today is different. She has Banu for company. Banu, who chatters endlessly. Banu, who has loads of questions that leave Aatibai breathless trying to answer them. Banu, who is her daughter Sunanda's only child.

"Aaje, tell me about your childhood," Banu asks suddenly.

Childhood? Aatibai's thoughts traipse off to her parents' home with its mogra in full bloom ... the endless games of langdi and her jumping from square to drawn square on the pathway that led to their front door ... the long string of abolem flowers tucked into her plaits that would sway as she jumped ... darkness descending and she running to the security of her mother's saree, to follow her from room to room and finally into the puja room.

"Aaje, tell me!" pesters Banu.

For a moment longer she hesitates, then, "I ... I couldn't say *re* when I was small," she says, lamely. "I remember I used to say the Sanskrit shloka, *Shubhankaroti kalyanam.* You know it, don't you? I would say *Shubankayoti kayyanam, aayogyam dhanasampada* ... "

Aatibai's next words are drowned in Banu's laughter.

"My mother promised to give me anything I wanted if I would only say *aarogyam* properly. And one day, I did!"

"So? What did you ask for?"

What did she ask for? Aatibai cannot remember. But Banu is waiting. "I asked for those red, yellow and orange coloured, sweet-and-sour lemon peppermints," she says. "Do you know what they look like?"

As Aatibai picks up Banu's pudgy palm to draw on it the shape of an orange slice, her memory flies back to a time when she was a child, no older than Banu here, happily sucking on a peppermint. What possible connection could there be between this old Aatibai and that little girl? How different the two people are. Such different forms, such different ways of thinking.

"Then, Aaje? What happened then?"

She brushes away her memories ... becomes Banu's Aaji again.

"Banu!" calls Shubha, walking up to them from inside the house. "You naughty girl, why aren't you asleep? Do good children stay up so late?"

Shubha is her son Prakash's wife. Even though her questions are playful and directed at Banu, Aatibai knows they are meant for her and, in an instant, she is overcome with guilt.

But Banu has come with a firm resolve to break all rules.

"Shubha Mami," she says, bouncing up to her aunt, "did you know that when Aaji was small, she couldn't say *Shubhankaroti Kalyanam, Aarogyam Dhanasampada*? So ... "

And Banu repeats the story all over again. But somehow, somewhere in the telling, the simple story is robbed of its sweetness and sounds trivial, foolish. The little girl that Banu and Aatibai had created, and left happily sucking on her peppermints, grimaces and flounces off to sulk in a corner.

But Shubha is still there, listening, a smile on her face and the right mmms and oohs, till Aatibai gets up abruptly.

"Let's sleep," she orders Banu, pulling the child to her feet.

Before long they have spread the mattress on the floor and are lying down on it together.

"Aaje, when you were my age, did you go to school?"

"No," says Aatibai, turning to face her little grandchild. "In those days girls were not sent to school."

"Why not?"

Banu's unending questions goad her into remembering long-forgotten details about the past. Sunanda used to be exactly like this daughter of hers, Aatibai thinks, smiling fondly. And then a thought rises unbidden to her mind: I was never like this.

I never asked questions. Why do boys learn to read and write and girls to cook? Why do boys always belong to the family while girls do not? Why are boys special? And girls? Well, girls are girls! Aatibai can't remember how young she was when such ideas had been drummed into her. This was how it was meant to be, how it would always be. Who could think otherwise? She had never questioned any of it till this moment, lying next to Banu.

No one, reasons Aatibai, no one ever questioned why heirlooms were for daughters-in-law, estates for sons. I worried about higher education for Prakash, but for Sunanda, what I prayed for was a suitable match. Sunanda had somehow managed to graduate before I married her off, refusing to listen to her pleadings.

"So," asks Banu's voice, breaking into her thoughts. "Why were girls not sent to school?"

Aatibai realises that she has not answered Banu.

"Back in those days, girls were married off at an early age."

"When they were as old as I am?"

"Yes. Now, if you do not sleep, I shall ask Sunanda to marry you off. *At once*!"

Banu rolls on the mattress, giggling and jumping around, then suddenly she has snuggled up against Aatibai and is fast asleep.

Morning finds Banu up on the guava tree.

"Banu, get down this instant!" says Aatibai. "You'll break a limb if you fall down. How can we give you away then, you naughty girl?"

"What do you mean by that?" Banu demanded.

"Nothing. Get down now!"

"No. First *you* tell me what you meant."

"You should have been born a boy."

"Why?"

"Get down right now," says Aatibai adding, "or I won't show you the toys from the glass cupboard."

Banu is down in an instant. An invitation to examine the contents of her Aaji's cupboard is something she cannot refuse.

Aatibai opens the glass cupboard. She carefully picks up the delicate porcelain dolls and the china cats and dogs that crowd the shelves and places them on the floor beside Banu.

"Aaje, will you give these dolls to me?"

"To you? You greedy child, these are for your Prakash Mama's children."

"But Prakash Mama doesn't have any children!"

"He shall. Soon."

Banu looks at the toys as if she would like to break them, each one of them. But she can never do anything that would hurt Aaji. Sullenly, she plays with the dolls wondering why her Aaji wishes to save them for Prakash Mama's unborn children. She notices a trunk under the bed.

"Aaje, what is in that?"

Aatibai smiles. "Do you want to see?"

"Yes!"

"But you will have to keep this a secret."

Banu nods vigorously. She loves doing secret things with her Aaji. She jumps and prances around Aatibai as she closes the door and bolts it. "Quick, quick, Aaje."

"Sit, child!" Aatibai scolds the child fondly. "How can I show you anything unless you sit still!"

Promptly, Banu squats on the floor, waiting impatiently for Aatibai to drag the trunk from under the bed, pull out the bunch of keys that hangs at her waist, select a key and open the trunk.

The scent of attar wafts from the thin linen cloth that Aatibai removes to reveal a magenta shaloo. Gently she places the cloth aside, her hands lingering over the soft silk.

"Is that yours, Aaje?"

But the tiny Aatibai, wrapped in the saree and standing in front of the antarpaat, cannot hear Banu's question.

Shaloo: A bridal zari sari. **Antarpaat:** A piece of cloth held between the groom and bride while the mantras are being chanted and before they exchange garlands.

"Aaje tell me!"

"Yes, Banu," murmurs Aatibai, as she turns her attention back to the box and the other sarees there. Under them is a sandalwood box. Aatibai removes it with great care.

The fragrance of sandal fills the room.

Banu rubs her nose on the box.

"What is in this?"

"Have some patience and I'll show you."

Aatibai opens the box with another key from her key-bunch. There's the glitter of gold ornaments lying on a bed of red velvet – gontt, pattalio, todde, kantto and the pakhe.

"Aaje, are these all yours?"

"Yes, child," Aatibai says, watching Banu try out one of the bracelets. It slides up almost to her shoulders. Aatibai laughs.

Banu grins as she picks up the pakhe.

"How do you wear this, Aaje?"

"You must get your ears pierced to wear those," explains Aatibai. She opens a secret drawer and takes out a necklace of gold sovereigns. There is a small delicately-crafted gold conch nestling between every sovereign and two small coral beads.

"Aaje, can I try this on?"

Aatibai places the necklace around Banu's neck explaining how she got it. "My mother-in-law received this from her mother-in-law and she gave it to me. I shall give this to your Shubha Mami and she will give it to her daughter-in-law."

"You won't give this to my mother?"

"Your mother?" Aatibai cannot suppress a smile. "How can I give this to your mother? Now that she's married, she is no longer part of this family. She's an outsider."

"Why? Is my father an outsider?"

"I didn't mean that, Banu. She's no longer part of *this* family She belongs to a different family now."

"How?"

Gontt, pattalio, todde: Different kinds of bangles; **Kantto:** A gold hair-pin, with a filigree flower at the apex. **Pakhe** : Studs, usually made of gold, that cover the whole ear.

"Banu," Aatibai says gently, "when a daughter gets married, she becomes an outsider."

But Banu's eyes are already brimming with tears. "Will my mother too think of me as an outsider after my marriage?"

"No, I did not mean that."

"Then what did you mean?"

Aatibai cannot find the words to make Banu understand. But of course Banu is right, says a voice inside her. A daughter is not an outsider. Yet, how can you give a piece of family jewellery to her? Shouldn't heirlooms stay within the family? But then, sons and daughters are conceived in the same womb, aren't they? If so, can such relationships be changed by merely marrying into another family?

Questions which had never occurred to Aatibai before, start nagging her. Was I unfair to Sunanda? Did I really love my two children equally, she wonders as she caresses this little daughter of her daughter. Banu did have a way of putting people into a quandary!

The holidays are over. Banu has gone back home, to her mother. Aatibai sits every night in her old ancestral home, all by herself, her mind slipping quickly, easily into nostalgia.

She has always found it difficult to get along with Shubha, her daughter-in-law. Sunanda, when she came to know how much Aatibai hated visiting her son's house, had suggested to Aatibai, coaxed and commanded her in turn, to stop staying alone in the huge rambling house. "Please come and stay with me, Aai," she said repeatedly. But how could Aatibai do that? Stay with a daughter? What would people say?

There are no such distinctions between sons and daughters, Aai, Sunanda had said, trying to convince Aatibai that times were changing. There's no difference at all between daughters and sons, she had insisted. But finally, even Sunanda gave up. Aatibai was impossible to convince! Aatibai is still sure that the family jewels must be handed down to Prakash. But, she finds herself asking, Am I really right? What if I am wrong?

And perhaps, it is this worry that makes her careless. One day she slips in the bathroom. It is a bad fall. Aatibai is bed-ridden with a fractured leg. As expected, Prakash rushes to her side with Shubha as soon as he is informed. And though Aatibai hates it, she is forced to accept Shubha's help, for she cannot do a single thing on her own. And then, as if by telepathy, Sunanda arrives. In her usual brisk way, not heeding Aatibai's weak protests, she packs Aatibai's bags and takes her home with her.

Of course Banu is thrilled to have her Aaje with her all the time. She now has someone who has nothing better to do than to listen to her endless chatter.

But this still leaves Aatibai enough time to think. And so a day comes when Banu returns from school and starts off on her usual stories about her class, her teachers, her friends.

Aatibai is not listening. Her mind is busy making plans. As soon as she goes back home, she will divide the contents of her trunk equally between Prakash and Sunanda. And the necklace must go to Banu, she decides. "For my daughter's daughter," she tells herself, aware that she is going against a time-honoured family tradition. Having reached the decision, she feels a great weight being lifted off her conscience. That day, she finds an answer to Banu's question.

"Banu, you were right," she murmurs.

"About what, Aaje?"

"This house is no longer alien to me."

Banu, who usually remembers everything, looks puzzled. "Alien? Of course it isn't!" she says, "Who said it was?"

Bending down, Aatibai hugs Banu tightly to her bosom. Words and laughter spill out of her. "There was once this mad woman who thought that ..."

N. S. MADHAVAN

THE CAPTAIN'S DAUGHTER

TRANSLATED BY NARENDRA NAIR
NOMINATED BY K. SATCHIDANANDAN

First published in Malayalam as "Kappithante Magal" in *India Today*, December 1993, Madras.

When, after a long interval, Malavika came to stay with us, Thelma and I felt a sense of relief. Since Thelma and I belonged to different faiths, hardly any of our relatives ever came to visit us. Life in our flat was unvarying, without any ups and downs, stretching ahead, "Like a dead man's ECG," as Thelma put it. Often we didn't know what day it was unless we switched to the serials on television. Even the soiled clothes in a corner of the bathroom, repeated themselves with monotonous regularity. Thelma's blue night dress with the white dots and my striped Shangu-Mark lungi appeared amongst them every other day. The thought of Malavika's blood red T-shirt and blue jeans invading and shaking up that heap filled me with a kind of joy.

Even though she lived with her father barely three kilometres from us, Malavika's visits were no more than occasional. She and Thelma were from the same village; for many years they had been to the same school. Each time I saw Malavika, I would recall something she had said to Thelma while at school. During one of the vacations, she had been to sea with her father, the ship's Captain. It was while sailing the Pacific that she first came to know of the still waters that covered most of the Earth, and of the vast and brooding silence that lay over them. Afterwards, whenever she looked at a map of the world, Malavika had said, all her thoughts would be of this bleak and enormous expanse of water and its giant shoreline, that huge and empty tract of silence that someone had obviously forgotten to invest with colour and life.

The day Malavika arrived happened to be a holiday, so she and Thelma spent most of the day together, chatting. Since the topics of their conversation were entirely alien to me, I withdrew to the bedroom and stayed there. After dinner, when Thelma got down to cleaning the kitchen, I went off to the balcony as was my custom, to relax in my armchair and gaze into the night. The sound of cars had ceased; soon the huge trucks would begin to rumble past. Far away, the furnaces of the power stations sent up their orange and red glow into the night sky. Though this was a scene I witnessed every night, it still fascinated me.

"Give me a cigarette," said Malavika suddenly, from behind me. "Where have you been all this while?" I asked, holding out the pack. "In Delhi?"

"No, I've been travelling all over the country with Anna Maria. By train. Showing her India."

"Anna Maria?"

"Yes. She's English. I got to know her while I was in France. She's living with me at the moment."

"You're smoking too much," I said.

"I smoke so that I can stop smoking."

"Meaning?"

"When I give up smoking," she explained, "I get the same pleasure as I do from smoking itself. I just love what happens to me when my addiction is being broken. All those withdrawal pangs – the dry lips, the cramps in the gut and that searing blaze along the veins ... Eesh!" Malavika said with a dramatic shudder, eyes closed in an orgiastic trance.

I could not help laughing.

Suddenly, pointing to the sky stained orange from the furnaces, she exclaimed, "Look, a Rembrandt sky!"

"Rembrandt indeed! Oh yes, you studied painting in Paris, didn't you?"

"Yes, for some five, six years. But then, I realised that I was not talented, was mediocre, and wouldn't amount to anything."

There was such an uncompromising finality about that statement – like a determined suicide – it made me uncomfortable.

Nonchalant, Malavika sat in the balcony, looking out at the neighbouring buildings, observing the various lives unwinding in preparation for sleep. Leaning against the terrace wall, she said, "See that flat over there? The husband and wife are quarrelling. Notice how the wife makes repeated visits to the toilet."

"So? Couldn't it just be that she has diarrhoea?"

"Not at all. Her walk to the toilet is slow. It's not the walk of one who has diarrhoea. No, when wives begin to hide in toilets, the marriage is on the rocks. That's for sure."

I laughed soundlessly. Encouraged, she continued her stories about the lives of our neighbours.

"Look at that trimurti over there," she said, pointing, "husband, wife and that purest of all souls, the mother-in-law. It's pretty obvious that hubby is a twerp who dances to mamma's tune. Even when he occasionally glances at his wife he does it as if he's committing a crime. There, the wife has moved towards the bedroom; he stands, doubtful, at the entrance to it and asks, Amma, may I go in too? Mother says kindly, Why not, son? Darling son asks, Amma, may I close the door? Mother says, Certainly. Gaining a little more courage, he asks, all in one breath, Amma, may I do it? Oh no, says Mother, anything but that, my son. Haven't you done it four times already this month? If you carry on like this, your delicate little stem will rot and wither away."

She said all this with appropriate gestures, acting out both the mother's and the son's parts. It was hilarious and I went back to the kitchen to retail it to Thelma. As expected, she burst out laughing. I returned to the balcony to find that the lights in many of the flats had been switched off, in an apparently abrupt termination of Malavika's story session. Whole buildings were receding into darkness, till eventually there was just one lighted window to be seen – in the central flat of the ten-storeyed building opposite us – spreading its 60-watt illumination all around.

Malavika said, "That is Rilke's house."

"You mean Rilke the poet? But he died ages ago."

"No, not the poet. The poet was Rainer Maria. This is his younger brother, Wilhelm Rilke. While Wilhelm was studying in Berlin, he enlisted in the Young Nazis and rose rapidly to become Hilter's right-hand man."

"From where did you pick up all this?" I asked, half expecting yet another funny story.

"Oh I know everything. I even know why Wilhelm has come out to this place."

"And why, may I ask?"

"To hunt me down," she said. So grim did she become all of a sudden that I shivered involuntarily.

"When the War ended," she continued, "Wilhelm, like other Nazi war criminals, sought asylum in Argentina. He's turned ninety now and is out to kill me."

"But why should he want to kill you?"

"He knows all about my relationship with Jesus Christ. He knows I can talk to Jesus without any go-between. This is something the Nazis do not like. Wilhelm came to know in advance that I was coming to stay here and so he took the flat opposite. From there he directs uranium rays at me."

She went inside, put a few ice cubes into a glass, poured whisky over them and came back to the balcony with it. We sat silently together, watching the twilight glow of the whisky over the ice, reflecting the moonlight.

Malavika said, "Wilhelm killed the poet. Imagine killing your own sib! Do you know how Rainer died?"

"Yes," I said, once more attempting to make a joke of it. "He was pricked by a thorn from a rose bush."

"Are you crazy?" Malavika downed her liquor in one gulp. Wiping her lips, she asked, "Does any one die of a prick from a rose bush? Actually what Wilhelm did was to smear uranium ointment over its thorns. He tried the same stunt with me too. He mixed uranium in my paints. But Jesus protected me. He also helped me by giving me information about this fellow's whereabouts from time to time. Now, Wilhelm has begun this business of directing uranium rays at me."

Her voice had sunk to a whisper. "If it weren't for Jesus, I wouldn't be here today," she mumbled. "You are lucky you are married to a Christian."

I got up and walked to the bedroom looking for Thelma. She was already fast asleep. I switched off the light in the bedroom and suddenly – I don't know why – I felt all alone.

When I came back to the balcony, I found Malavika huddled in her chair, looking tense and scared. Gently, I helped her to her feet and walked her to bed. She lay down but her thin arms held me tight. The grip loosened only after she was fast asleep.

When morning came, Malavika appeared to have calmed down, like the sea at ebb tide.

As we sat drinking coffee, Thelma said, "Raghavan told me all about last night. When did all this start?"

"All what?" Malavika asked, staring fixedly at me.

"These ... these phobias," said Thelma, uncomfortably.

Malavika did not reply immediately.

Then she said, "The first time I fell sick was in Paris. I was on therapy for six months. At the end of that everything returned to normal. Of late, I've once again come under the spell of these rays. I've also begun to intercept messages."

Thelma was concerned. "Are you seeing a doctor?"

"Yes. Malini. My analyst. When I am in Delhi, I see her every Wednesday evening. Two hundred an hour. I tell her all that is on my mind and Malini, her narrow Bengali eyes shut behind black framed spectacles, listens quietly to everything I have to say."

"Are you on any medication?" I asked, making my first contribution to the conversation of the morning.

"Yes, I do take some tablets. But the main therapy is the talking."

During breakfast Malavika told us more about her conversations with Dr. Malini, about her childhood, and her relationship with her father.

"To me Achchan was no more than a number of postage stamps, stamps of all kinds: Lincoln's ash-grey, mournful face on a ten cent U.S. stamp; Queen Elizabeth's grouchy face on a British one; the stamps of the newly rich countries with their loud and startling colors; the Saudi stamp carrying Degas's face; the Yemeni stamp of Hogarth's *Crab Seller* ..."

Malavika's story continued. Her father had been a Captain in the Merchant Navy. When she was seven, her mother died. Leaving her with her grandparents, her father went away to sea and made the ship his home.

"Achchan would write to me from every port," she said. "He always wrote the same things. Study well. Don't hassle grandma and grandpa. What gift would you like me to send? There are so many things a sea Captain can talk about, but no, his letters to me were all of the same mould. Finally I wrote back – I am delighted to receive your letters; there are so many new stamps on them. In my class no other child has as large a collection as I have."

With that, her father stopped writing altogether. Instead, he sent her empty envelopes with different stamps each time.

"I used to take those envelopes and go and sit beneath our jackfruit tree. I would fantasize that they smelt of the harbour at Sydney; sometimes of Hongkong noodles. At other times, I imagined I smelt Achchan's aftershave; at such moments, I would burst into tears."

By evening, we noticed that Malavika had become very restless. She began pacing agitatedly from room to room. Round and round she went like a caged animal, breaking off each cycle to peek surreptitiously at the ten-storeyed building opposite us. At eight o'clock she announced to Thelma, "I'm leaving. Achchan is alone at home. Besides, Anna Maria arrives from Jaipur tomorrow."

Thelma did not protest and frankly it didn't surprise me.

Four, five months went by before we saw Malavika again. During this time, we never spoke of her. On one occasion, however, Thelma told me that she thought there was a connection between madness and Jesus Christ. An uncle of hers, during a manic phase, would wrap his bedsheet around him like a robe and parade grandly up and down inside a locked room, declaring that he had been on earth two thousand years ago.

We met Malavika at an art gallery where her paintings were being exhibited. It was Thelma, who had come across the announcement in the Engagements Column of the morning paper.

As soon as she saw Thelma, Malavika asked, "Is there a loneliness greater than sitting all by yourself amidst your own paintings in an art gallery?"

Thelma consoled her. "Never mind. Once reports appear in the newspapers, people will come. Don't worry."

"Oh, it has already appeared in the papers. One or two measly lines, buried in the inside pages."

A white woman walked in. She had copper-coloured hair and deep brown eyes, and looked young and immature, like a tender bamboo shoot. This was Anna Maria.

Anna asked in English, "Sold anything today?"

"No," said Malavika. "We've stopped sales." She pointed to the board listing the prices. She had scored a thick black line across it and to its left, she had hung a notice that said in bold letters – PICTURES GIVEN FREE HERE.

"Oh Mala!" Anna Maria ran up and tore the notice to shreds. "Mala! What are you doing?" She held Malavika and began to kiss her forehead repeatedly. Malavika just clung to her and wept. They stood thus, in a corner of the gallery, forlorn amidst the huge canvases of birds and flowers and snake temples.

On the day the exhibition ended, Malavika visited us again. She appeared strangely subdued, as if the ability to speak had deserted her. But soon after dinner, she suddenly became loquacious.

"It was Achchan who got me into painting," she said.

"How?" asked Thelma

"Actually it was something trivial," she replied, "but it grew inside me like a worm. One day – I must have been nine or so at the time – Achchan's ship came in to dock at Cochin. I went, all spruced up, to see his cabin, my hair plaited tightly with a ribbon. The Mattancheri wharf at Cochin was quite a place. I can still remember the glittering yellow mounds of sulphur and the tall cranes ambling along, sniffing the sky. My father took me to see the synagogue and the Dutch Palace. At the Dutch Palace, he told me of a famous woman who had lived and painted nearby. Amrita Shergil. Can you believe it? There in *our* Mattancheri town! That was when for the first time I felt the desire to become a painter."

"What were you doing in Paris ?" I asked.

"While I was studying at Shantiniketan, I won a scholarship from the French Government to study Art. At first when I wasted time going round with my friends, drinking wine and mocking at art exhibitions, I was pretty sure what my future would be. Much later, when several of my companions became people of substance from being merely people of promise, I began to worry. I changed my friends. I began to associate with people who were perpetually 'growing.' But that didn't help, either. I was lucky if I managed to sell four or five pictures in a year. And even those were to the Gujaratis who came down from England. All they wanted were my paintings of Shiva and Ganapati. When I realised that they were destined for their puja rooms, I returned to Delhi. But even here, my exhibitions have stayed empty."

Thelma and Malavika continued talking long into the night. I decided to turn in early, having stayed up late the previous night. Around 3 a.m. Thelma shook me awake.

"Malavika ... " She was breathing hard.

"Malavika?"

"She has locked herself in the bathroom. It's been a long time. I can't hear anything, and I'm scared."

I ran to the bathroom. Not a sound from within.

Suddenly there was a startling crash of breaking glass and over it came a strange litany from Malavika. "Tuk Tuk Tuk Tuduk Tuk Tuk."

"Malu, what are you doing?" asked Thelma.

Ignoring her, Malavika kept up the weird chant. "Tuk Tuk Tuk Tuduk Tuk."

Beating the door with the flat of my hand, I said, "Malu, come on out."

"Don't disturb me," she said breaking her silence. "I am sending Jesus a telegram ... in Morse ... Tuk Tuk Tuk."

The dots and dashes continued.

"Why did you break the window pane?" asked Thelma.

"Jesus' replies were not coming through clearly. Too much disturbance. After breaking the glass, I'm able to receive Him loud and clear."

"Please Raghavan," begged Thelma, "please get her out somehow. I'm frightened."

"What message are you sending?" I called out.

"About Wilhelm Rilke," said Malavika. The Tuk Tuduk Tuk continued.

I tapped on the door with my forefinger. Tuk Tuk Tuk.

"Who is that?"

Changing my voice to a falsetto, I said, "Haven't you recognised me? I am Jesus, son of Joseph. Open the door, Malu."

Malavika fell silent for a moment, then resumed her conversation in Morse. The tempo of my own tapping accelerated. Thelma stayed close, anxious and hopeful, waiting for the door to open.

"Malu," I ordered. "This is Jesus. Open the door at once."

Malavika laughed out loud. "You who turned water into wine – is a closed door such a big problem for you?"

I decided we would need help to break the door down and was about to leave the flat in search of our stout watchman, when we heard Malavika pull the flush. When the water ceased to run, she opened the door. As soon as she caught sight of Thelma, she hugged her and began to cry.

"That old man Wilhelm attacked me today. Kept relentlessly throwing those rays at me. I had no alternative but to seek His help. It was easy to lock into Jesus' wavelength from your bathroom."

Next morning, Anna Maria came and took Malavika away. We

did not see her for some time after that. On a couple of occasions though, I did come upon Thelma standing motionless before the telephone with the phone book in her hand, opened at page M.

One Sunday morning when I opened the door in answer to the bell, I found an elderly gentleman standing outside. From behind me, Thelma said "Oh, come right in Menon Uncle, do sit down." To me, she said, "Do you know who this is? This is Malavika's father."

Mr Menon was panting heavily. He stood well over six feet, straight and tall, but with each laboured breath the veins in his yet uncreased neck stretched and distended. He was trying manfully to not give in to his asthma, his face reddening with every effort.

"Malu's phobias are worsening day by day," he said. "I saw Dr. Malini yesterday. I told her that I was advancing in age and that my asthma made matters worse. If it hadn't been for Anna Maria, I couldn't have held on. So the doctor said if it was a problem to look after her, she could get her admitted to the new hospital at Mehrauli."

"Oh no!" Thelma cried. "Won't they give her electric shocks there?"

"I don't know. But they say it is a very humane place. Yet I wonder ... Once inside the hospital, will she ever come back home?"

The old man had been speaking between gasps. Now he stopped to catch his breath. He stood at the window gazing out unemotionally with his cataract eyes. What visions did he see, I wondered, from those ancient eyes full of images of flying fishes and sharks?

"Malavika is my only girl," he said. "She was born at sea in the ship's hospital. I had engaged one of my men to note down the exact latitude and longitude at the time of her birth, so that I could get a horoscope made. My child was born over turbulent seas and the heaving coordinates must have been impossible to fix. So now, the planets trouble her."

Mr. Menon stopped speaking and began to cry quietly.

Thelma lowered her eyes.

With great difficulty, Mr. Menon continued. "Every time a ship touches port, it is said the sailors rush out in search of whorehouses. And I? I used to go in search of post offices. To send letters to my Malu." Sighing, he turned, preparatory to leaving the house. "Maybe we should wait, don't you agree?"

"Yes," said Thelma. "Let us keep the hospital as the last resort, if everything else fails."

"After all," said Mr. Menon, "Insanity is not a fatal illness is it? That is the tragedy." This was the first time the word "insanity" had come up in the conversation and it made my mouth go numb as if I had suddenly bitten on an iron filing in my food.

A week later, Malavika's father telephoned to say that he would be obliged if we would go over to his house right away. When we arrived, Dr. Malini was there as well.

"I've given her a sedative," said the doctor.

Mr. Menon said, "Anna Maria has left. She must have got fed up. One morning, she left a note and just went away. After that, Malavika's condition has worsened."

Thelma asked, "Any particular reason why Anna Maria left?"

"No, no particular reason," said Mr. Menon. "This isn't an illness that can sustain a friendship for long."

Afterwards, Mr. Menon left to drop Dr. Malini home and we went into Malavika's room.

"Anna Maria betrayed me," she said, as soon as she saw us.

"Betrayed you?" asked Thelma.

"Yes. She ditched me because she wanted to move in with Janet. I know."

"Malu," said Thelma, "I think you had better try and sleep."

Malavika seemed not to have heard. "I don't sublimate my craving with drink or drugs. I do it with my body. I have slept with a number of men and women. When making love I keep up an incessant flow of crazy talk. Only Anna Maria would respond to whatever I said. My most satisfying relationship was with her."

We didn't say anything but stood by quietly, looking at one another. Malavika said, sleepily, to Thelma, "You know Thelma, for men even love-making has to be a conquest. If we women ever take the initiative, they tend to panic." Unable to hold out against an overpowering drowsiness, her eyes closed.

We went back to the living room to await Mr. Menon's return. As soon as he came in he said, "I have decided to put her in a hospital. Anna Maria had been a tremendous help. But now I won't be able to manage alone, all by myself."

"No uncle, don't," said Thelma. "As it is, Malavika feels everyone is deserting her. If you put her in hospital it will only aggravate her condition."

"Then what am I to do?"

"Let her stay with us for some days," I offered. Thelma looked gratefully at me.

Two days later, Malavika came with her easel and paints. Each day she would begin to paint as soon as it was light. Most of the time she painted pictures of Shiva ... An overjoyed Shiva doing the Tandava ... Shiva the destroyer, his matted hair flowing, battering the ground with his feet to release his little demons ... Shiva in the act of creating his son with Parvati in a scene from the *Kumarasambhavam* ... A little tonsured child painted against the backdrop of the Mattancheri wharf, resembling the *Brahmachari* by Amrita Shergil. The only clue to the child being Shiva was the small third eye in his forehead.

While she painted she would keep up an incessant chatter with Lord Shiva.

"Mahadev, I will shampoo your matted locks today and make them shine."

"You need a good stud for your left ear, but only for your left ear."

"I am going to draw a big madhdhalam around your neck and make you into a Manipuri dancer twisting and turning to the beat of the Cholam drum."

One week later Malavika declared, "I have lost my fear of Rilke." Her conversations in Morse had also ceased. For the first time in many days, Thelma brought three chairs out to the terrace that night. She made Malavika kneel in front of her and began to plait her hair. Malavika said, "You know what, Thelma, I think my mind is healed now. Because I feel enormously hungry. That is the sign. It's ages since I ate stuffed aloo parathas."

In plaits, she looked like a little schoolgirl. Thelma patted Malavika on the back, indicating that she could rise, and went to the kitchen to make the parathas for her.

"Why is it that you are always drawing Shiva's pictures?" I asked.

"That again is because of Achchan. When I came down from Shantiniketan once during my holidays, he and I motored down to Kottayam. When we reached Ettumannur, he stopped the car in front of the temple. He showed me an old mural of Shiva inside the gatehouse and I felt myself tingle all over just as I did years later when I beheld my first Picasso."

Malavika began crying softly.

Then, abruptly, she wiped away her tears. Head held high, she said, "I will tell you a secret no one has known till now. I am actually a reincarnation of Lord Shiva. Half man, half woman. With my male half I have slept with several women – Anna Maria, Julie, then Nagalakshmi ... and with my female half I have slept with innumerable men." The tone had become detached, impersonal. She suddenly seemed a stranger. I felt faintly alarmed.

She rose and pointed to the opposite building. "Here, come and take a look. There is no bloody Rilke or anything in that flat. It is only a poor old Parsee woman." Malavika shivered in the cold and seemingly without thinking, moved closer to me.

"In the cold of the night ..." she murmured.

"In the cold of the night?"

"In the cold of the night, in the cold of the night – come on *you*!" she said, addressing me disrespectfully for the first time. "Say something, dammit! Like Anna Maria used to. Something."

I hazarded, "In this dark and freezing night ..."

"Shabash! The roads ..."

"The roads that lie lifeless and still as if in shavasan ..." I completed.

Malavika moved in close against me. She seemed to have been transformed. Like women I had seen before, performing a ritualistic propitiation to the snake gods, her voice had become hoarse and sibilant. Rubbing against me, she intoned harshly like one possessed. "In the cold of this night, in the cold of this night, in this dark and freezing night, on the streets that lie lifeless and still, the Word rolls on, a single Word, the only Word ..." Like waves that gathered and rose at sea, her breasts expanded, heaved and hardened against my chest. She panted like one in heat. I pushed Malavika away from me and moved back into the house only to see Thelma in the dining room speaking into the telephone. "This is Thelma, Menon Uncle, Thelma. I am calling about Malu. I think it may be better if you put her into hospital. She needs therapy, Menon Uncle. All said and done, nothing else can be an adequate substitute for therapy, no?"

She put the phone down and without meeting my eyes, walked back into the kitchen.

ଶ

PRATIBHA RAY

THE CURSE

TRANSLATED AND NOMINATED
BY SACHIDANANDA MOHANTY

First published in Oriya as "Shapya" in *Jhankara*,
April 1993, Cuttack.

Pari would not have been an outcaste had she not been addicted to paan. Nor would she have had an identity without it. In fact, it was paan that stained her reputation and saved it as well.

When the fifteen-year-old Pari first came to the house as a bride, she was no addict to paan. She was just perpetually hungry. Whenever she missed a meal, her beautiful face would turn pale, just as the moon does with the rising of the morning-star.

But why talk only of missed meals? Does anything happen on time for a girl, especially if she's also a daughter-in-law, new in the house? Pari would wake up long before daybreak but could go to bed only around the middle of the night. She would bathe early in the morning but had to go without food till well into the day. She could bear delay in all things. But when she missed her meal, her face would shrivel up like a fresh green plantain leaf left near a hearth.

How can a woman, soft as butter, carry the burden of life? A girl ought to look like butter, no doubt, but she should be able to endure like a rock; only then can she conquer life. Indeed, if there is anything that a woman can fall back on, it is sorrow, for happiness is ever-deceitful. And hunger (there are so many hungers in life) is the root of all sorrow. It is said that we can learn to control all other hungers by first learning to control the hunger of the stomach. Yet, when old age comes, changing not only one's appearance but also the nature of hunger, the hunger of the stomach stays on like a perennial bird, pecking at man from birth to death. Hunger has no respect for age.

A daughter-in-law cannot be good unless she can curb the hunger of the stomach, said Pari's grandmother-in-law, who had experienced various hungers at various stages of her life till now it seemed as if a thousand hungers had settled beneath the folds of her wrinkled skin. For all that, she muttered, I can never get rid of this damned hunger in my stomach.

But like the mind and the body, our tongue and stomach seem to pair off quite well. The stomach feels hunger and the tongue savours taste. So, to appease the stomach's hunger, paan is offered to the tongue as a bribe. When there isn't enough rice in the pot, one takes paan to stave off the thought of food. But the problem with a bribe is that it turns into an addiction and unless it is there after a meal, the stomach remains half-filled. Yes, paan is the best friend of both scarcity and plenty, said Pari's grandmother-in-law. I'd rather push aside my plate of rice but never would I give up my paan.

For Pari, it all started when, as a new bride, her face would shrivel up with hunger beneath her veil, and her grandmother-in-law, Ketaki, would thrust a paan into her mouth, saying, "It will not only add colour to your lips but also excite the mind; not yours alone, but of anyone who sees your reddened lips. It will not only control your hunger but also my grandson, Jadua. If you don't cast your spell well in time, my child, you'll repent later."

Pari began to like paan. She realised it brought flavour not only to the mouth but also to the mind. Her red lips added lustre to her radiant face. To Jadunath, she looked like a true pari, an angel straight from heaven. Pari could not say if her hunger was ended by the paan but her red lips definitely killed Jadunath's hunger. As his eyes stayed rivetted on her face, his meals often got delayed. He was reluctant to leave Pari behind and go back to the town where he worked. Jadunath had taken thirty days' leave for his marriage, and like the short-lived winter sun, the thirty days were soon to be over.

But what else could Jadunath do without stepping out of the village? Could he plough the field? Grow crops? Could he, like his father, carry those loads of vegetables to the haat? Is that how he would flaunt his qualifications of a ninth class failed? Besides, Pari's father would not have let him off so easily. It was only out of respect for Jadua's town job that he had given his docile and delicate daughter in marriage to this landless and half-literate Jadua. No one had ever bothered to know anything more about his job. Hundreds of young men like Jadua went to work in distant towns, but when they came back to the village in their new clothes and new shoes, one could easily tell them apart from the country bumpkins. It was certain that if Jadunath gave up his job and took to farming, even Pari would not have the same regard for him. It is not money that makes the difference between a job in town and agriculture; it is a matter of appearance and demeanour. The fact that the husband works in a distant city or town and people address him as Babu, is enough to fill a wife's heart with pride. So what if he is always so far away, that she's left constantly pining for him; so what if his town-bought dhoti, umbrella, wrist-watch and cigarettes never make up for the woman's longing for her husband.

Too soon, it was time for Jadunath to leave his village. The husband and wife parted amidst oaths, promises, kisses, embraces and tears. One cannot bare one's heart and show one's true feelings to others. If that were possible, Pari would have shown the world how her heart harboured the picture of Jadunath, etched in blood. Jadunath too would have proved that Pari sat like a queen on the throne of his heart, surrounded by a thousand beautiful women who served at her feet. However, such revelations do not seem necessary at such times and seasons; both of them can clearly see each other's soul. With that assurance, Jadunath goes off to some distant place where women tend to charm all men and Pari stays back in the village amidst a dozen flirtatious brothers-in-law, younger and older.

Our Jadunath is truly effeminate. At the time of parting, while touching the feet of her husband, Pari shed copious tears. That was the sign of her devotion to her husband. Jadua shed tears too! "Pari, my dear," he said, "this life has absolutely no meaning! Is it not much better to stay back here and plough the field? Only a worthless man can leave a wife like you behind and go to the town for work. Tell me, how will I survive without you?"

To console her twenty-five-year-old husband, the fifteen-year-old Pari fought back her own tears and placing a scented paan in his mouth, she said, "Even if my body is left behind, my soul will always be with you." Perhaps Jadunath would have said something, too. But he restrained his thoughts and fell silent.

The family members were waiting to bid farewell to Jadunath. The men stood outside the courtyard near the doorway, while the women were at the entrance to the room. The longer the couple took to bid farewell to each other, the spicier was the gossip among the women. Does no one else get married and go out, or is Pari's the only beautiful face in the village? This was truly embarrassing! What would people say? The auspicious time for departure was nearing, and these two showed no signs of coming out! There was an impatient toot from the bus which stood under the big banyan tree. And the grandmother-in-law called out, "Come on Jadua, your wife will be my responsibility from now on. Don't start spoiling her, child. An excess of lime always tastes bitter, so also an excess of love."

Pari's sister-in-law, who lived next door, said, "Jadunath is delaying deliberately. If he misses the bus he can stay on for one more day with his moon-faced wife!"

There was plenty of sniggering.

Pari gently pushed Jadunath away. Wiping his nose and eyes with his handkerchief, Jadunath stepped out. His eyes were red like those of the kumbhatua bird. Looking sheepish, he headed straight towards the bus, forgetting in the process, even to touch his grandmother's feet. But isn't this the story every time lovers part?

Pari had no way of knowing how Jadunath would bear the pangs of separation. Thankfully, no one had heard any gossip about Jadunath as they had about the other young men who worked in the town. Jadunath's love for his wife must be the reason. Why were Pari's lips tinged bright red with paan? Why did her eyes shine with kohl? Oh, that's just proof of a devoted wife! So many other women in this village took paan and applied kohl, but how many could boast of such brightly coloured lips?

Every year Jadunath came home on a fifteen-day leave. He brought gifts – more for his wife than for his parents and grandmother. At times, there was nothing for anyone barring the love he brought for Pari. No one felt bad about this. After all the more the son is devoted to the daughter-in-law, the more will he keep away from other women. It is the man who lacks interest in his wife who is likely to lose his way. He wastes money on wayward women and destroys himself.

As for Pari, her devotion to her husband was absolute. No one had ever seen her with her head uncovered or behaving disrespectfully. Like a busy bird she was constantly at work. But five years had gone by since her marriage, and she had had no babies; only a miscarriage. Pari is delicate, her in-laws said. She is young, yet. Let two or four years pass. After all, only a healthy and active daughter-in-law can provide elders with grandsons and grand-daughters to play with, they reasoned. Pari is rare indeed! They must have done great penance to have a daughter-in-law like her. So Pari continued to be the centre of every one's attention, just as Jadunath was the darling of the family.

Pari lacked nothing. Even when he could not visit, Jadunath was never late in sending his father money. The mother-in-law would shove five or ten rupees out of this into the hand of the daughter-in-law, and "For you," she would say coyly. Pari would ask, "What do I need money for? After all, what is it that I lack?" And her mother-in-law would reply, "Let it be. Next time a hawker comes, you can buy a few things – face powder, comb, hair clips." But Pari spent most of the money on betel nuts and elaichi; the sindoor and alta that Jadunath brought from town lasted her a long time. No one had seen Pari lack anything and that, said everyone, was God's grace.

Nor was she wanting in matters of chastity. The very sight of men of her brother-in-law's age, made Pari turn her face and walk swiftly away. It was as if Pari's tinkling anklets posed a challenge to her many brazen brothers-in-law. No one ever dared to joke with Pari. With a husband who was a wage earner and devoted to his wife, why would Pari care for anyone else? She had no hunger – neither of the stomach, nor of the mind.

You may say, A husband who works in a faraway town can send money every month and can take care of his wife's many visible needs, but what of her other needs that lie hidden from all eyes? Who ever keeps track of such needs of a woman, of her restlessness? These can be a source of such embarrassment to a woman, since they can be neither seen nor shown.

At times, Pari's mind did turn sour. When, after the day's chores were done, Pari sat down on the verandah at the back of the house, she was overwhelmed by the intoxicating smell of the aata flowers. In the deserted courtyard, with the cool breeze on her face, it was as if she alone could smell those flowers. The champak tree remained stunted. What unknown sorrow weighed it down, Pari often wondered. And then, as if in a dream she saw the barren branches bear tiny, tender buds. Soon bunches of little flowers would reveal their smiling faces. Isn't the human mind like the champak flower? Chaste white like a sanyasini and within it a hidden, colourful core.

Such thoughts often intensified Pari's loneliness. Would her longing disappear? Should Jadunath choose to stay back at home? Who could say? There were so many married people in the village. Their quarrels began right from daybreak. Women usually came crying to Pari. "What happiness is there in our lives?" they asked. "We are no better than cats and dogs. We must be prepared to eat, breed and wait the whole day, all decked up, to satisfy the hunger of a husband. And all because he's feeding you! You're a lucky one, Pari! Your husband is a city man. A real man. He is no rustic villager or an idiot like the others! But happiness is a matter of destiny. There is simply no point in our getting upset!"

Pari was quite content and proud to hear such praise about her husband. But this hardly removed her inner disquiet. Pari wondered, Should I tell them of my frustration? Perhaps she would feel relieved by opening her heart to someone. There are so many sorrows that one takes to the funeral pyre, so much gloom that can never be exorcised. It is easy to cut one's blue veins and reveal dirty blood but no one can tear open one's chest and reveal the wilderness within.

Jadunath was not able to come home every year as before. He was entitled to fifteen days' leave every year. But this is of hardly any use. It took him four long days of travel to reach home and the fare was no small amount either. Every one agreed that by travelling once in three years, one could save the fare of two years and stay comfortably in the village for one and half months. Is it not rightly said that one slogs abroad for the sake of the stomach, even if this *is* an ordeal?

Pari's world comprised a little backyard, a patch of garden, a pond and trees. A lot of things happened within this world: seasons changed, flowers blossomed and fruits ripened, birds grew wings and flew away to some unknown sky, the mongoose pair enacted its playful game, the bumblebee alighted on flowers and the snake raised its hood and hissed before slithering back into its quiet pit. In this little hidden world, Pari did not count days; it was years that she counted. Three long years! If Jadunath had merely lifted his head he could have seen the flowers and the sky and the birds and the snake. Why didn't he? What kind of a man was he? Was he blind or was his heart stone?

Pari sat, a number of thoughts crowding her head. The southern wind blew her sari off her head, revealing her bare back and beyond the heavy fence, a shadow stirred. Pari was startled to see her elder brother-in-law. She quickly covered her face with the end of her sari.

Jadu and his brother were sworn enemies. Nor were the wives on talking terms, as if the quarrel dated back to their previous births. Even the small opening in the fence that divided the two houses had been blocked by Jadunath's father. Nonetheless, Kunja, as Pari's elder brother-in-law, deserved to be respected, even if the brothers did not speak to one another. Yet, Pari wondered: What did Kunja do every afternoon in the backyard?

Kunja owned a cycle repair shop in the village market, where he earned some easy money every day. He was perhaps the only person who lived well in that area. Older than Jadunath by seven or eight years, he lived in style and God be thanked for that, for who would otherwise have looked at his dark and bony face with the protruding teeth, his tall, ungainly figure? Yet it must be said that Kunja's mass of curly hair was well groomed, and fell in many layers; not a single strand was ever out of place. He wore a neat set of shirt and pants, chappals and smoked a cigarette. Above all, he chewed paan unabashedly like a goat. To Pari, Kunja looked funny, perhaps somewhat like a joker in a folk theatre group. How often Pari had giggled while comparing Jadunath's looks with those of Kunja! People tended to take this cycle repairer for a city man. But did he stand any comparison to a real city dweller? No wonder, Kunja could never stand Jadunath! Wasn't that what Jadunath had told her? Kunja's hatred for Jadunath had a history that stretched back into their childhood.

Pari usually sat long hours in the backyard, her back turned to the breeze and the fence which was interspersed with knots of thorny bushes. She found that the places where the hedge was thicker were being haunted more and more regularly by Kunja's shadow. A gap, even a little bit wider than what existed, would have turned the shadow into a real human being. But this would have only led to bloodshed.

Kunja's wife, Tulasi, was younger than Kunja by fifteen years and was a dullard. She had three little sons and daughters. Tulasi was tied to her household chores day and night. Surely her mind must be active. But no one had ever heard her talk. A temporary visitor would have thought she was dumb.

In the whole family, Kunja was the only one who could afford a mosquito net. His had such fine holes that it was difficult to know in what position Kunja slept. People respected Kunja because he used a mosquito net while sleeping. This indicated the life style of babus. For instance, he preferred to eat chapatti and not rice at night, a common practice in the household of babus. Like the babus, Kunja drank tea not in a glass but in a cup and saucer.

Though illiterate, Kunja always had a fountain pen in his pocket, like the children of the babus. A corner of his shirt pocket always revealed an ink-stain, as proof of Kunja's knowledge of its use. He wore a wrist-watch, but to know the time he had to consult the passage of the sun in the sky and the lengthening of the shadow on the ground. But then, the babus sport watches, yet they seldom finish any work on time and everything about them is irregular. Hence they too wore wrist-watches not for keeping time but out of habit. All in all, though illiterate and plain-looking, Kunja had great taste. By his demeanour and manners he managed to cover up his ugly appearance. As a matter of fact, over the past few days, Kunja had not looked half as clumsy as he usually did.

Kunja's cultivated looks did not affect Tulasi, even when he began to pick on her without any reason. Kunja appreciated his wife's naive simplicity. Yet he would be the first to admit that Pari had an edge over Tulasi.

Kunja had never seen Pari's face directly. As she stepped out of the bathing ghat of the pond, her wet sari clinging to her body, she often saw Kunja breaking a twig from the tree near the fence to improvise a tooth brush. To Kunja, looking through the little gap in the fence, Pari's figure looked slimmer and more tempting than Tulasi's. Gathering the ends of her sari up to her calf muscles, Pari would squeeze out the water. Kunja would noisily clean his tongue and Pari, like a young sun-yellow butterfly, would be startled and hide behind the hollow of the flowering tagara tree.

In this game of hide-and-seek, Kunja's complexion always appeared dark. Dark males, we are told have a reputation for manliness. Jadunath was not dark, Pari thought. He is shorter and slimmer than Kunja. His appearance belied the fact that he was a city dweller. The cloak of city culture that Jadunath put on could seldom conceal the smell of his real rustic background. He stood straight as a cow. How could a man ever hope to get on with his profession and household affairs, if he was not manly? The evidence was right there for every one to see. Jadunath had a job but he claimed that his pay was not enough. Therefore he could come home only once every three years. Kunja, on the other hand, had a small shop and every two to three months he could make a trip to Cuttack in order to buy provisions. Perhaps it would have been better for Jadunath to open a shop rather than take up a job. This was Pari's assessment of the situation.

All this was hardly flattering to Jadunath.

As Pari remembered her husband in the faraway town, brother-in-law Kunja's shadow somehow merged with Jadunath's, making him in the process, shorter than he was. The loneliness of the dead afternoons enveloped the lonely body and mind of Pari even as she spent them increasingly in the backyard.

Once or twice, Pari had asked Jhatua, the ten-year-old son of Kunja to buy her a paan from the market. Older people might quarrel but children, after all, are loved by all. When Jhatua and Jhampi quarrelled at home while Tulasi was nursing her baby, she bundled both of them to the backyard of Pari's house, saying, "Go and listen to the stories that your new khudi will tell you." Predictably, the busy mother had little time for the children. On holidays, the children hovered around Pari.

Those days Pari got addicted to the paan sold in the bazaar. Without it she felt dizzy and uneasy. Somehow, a homemade paan did not taste as good. The bazaar paan had a special flavour, a unique aroma, even if at times, the excess of lime burned the tongue. It was the best remedy for the loneliness of dead afternoons.

On his way back from school, little Jhatua would fetch paan for Pari like the milkman with the monthly contract used to. But unlike the milkman, he would not accept money, for his father, standing in the paan shop thought it fit to pay for the paan that his sister-in-law ordered. He may have quarrelled with his brother, but was not Pari the daughter-in-law of the house?

Pari's heart would beat faster. Either out of fear of her mother-in-law or because of the excitement inherent in the forbidden. Initially Pari had firmly told Jhatua not to get paan from his father. Jhatua however never heeded her request. It was clear that his primary duty was to his father. With uneasy pleasure, Pari fell into the habit of taking the paan offered by her brother-in-law.

The first time Pari took the paan offered by Kunja, it seemed as if her whole body was on fire. She felt a great throbbing in her chest and was strangely delirious. Had she chewed a rotten betel nut by mistake, she wondered. No, this headache, heartache and unease must be of a different kind. Had any one sensed her pain? Whom should she turn to now? Man dies and is turned to ashes. There are many things that get extinguished with the body. No one is able to see the red hot flame within him ... If Jadunath did not come home this Raja Sankranti, he must be a real miser! Pari thought, annoyed.

One day, Kunja's mosquito net was fixed in the backyard. "It's too hot inside," said Kunja to his wife, "From now on, I shall sleep on the verandah. You can bolt the door from inside." Tulasi raised no serious objection. As everyone knew, Kunja had had a tough time finding a bride. He was well past his prime when he got married. Tulasi, on her part, was dark and came from a poor family. As soon as the marriage proposal was made, Tulasi's father felt as if someone had freed him from a grave burden. Now, Tulasi found no compelling reason to pester her husband regarding his sleeping habits. Nor did she ask why he did not want to sleep in the front verandah, where the soothing south wind blew and instead preferred the cramped quarters at the back. That was clearly not Tulasi's problem. She was quiet like the greenery of the house. The heat was unbearable inside the house. The backyard was full of trees and was cool, thanks to the pond. Perhaps that was why Kunja slept on the back verandah.

But why did Pari prefer to sleep in the kitchen in the height of summer? Pari was timid. She could never enter a dark room by herself, let alone sleep there. At times, her grandmother-in-law slept with her. Whenever Jadunath came home the old woman slept in the kitchen. But one day, while enjoying a paan from the market, Pari had said to her grandmother-in-law, "You get up at least ten times at night. My sleep gets disturbed and I have a terrible headache in the morning. Henceforth let me sleep in the kitchen. It's a small room but our ancestors are there. I shall never be scared!" The grandmother was happy that Pari was more confident now. She had been worried. She knew that her grandson was always away in the city and she herself was like an old palm leaf, ready to fall. If she were to die, how would Pari sleep alone? She could not possibly sleep with the mother-in-law. There was every chance that her sari might slip or her limbs may inadvertently touch her mother-in-law. The kitchen was a much better place. The souls of the ancestors resided there and she was bound to feel more confident.

Thus the old lady allowed Pari to sleep alone. The older one grows, the braver one should get, she thought. The kitchen was a warm place and there was usually a fire in the chulha till morning, enough to light it with the next day. If not, where would Pari go to fetch a little fire? In Kunja's house, Tulasi lit the fire by striking a match that Kunja bought from the market. But in the house of Jadunath, the city dweller, a matchbox was a far-fetched dream. Jadunath was truly selfish. Why did he not understand that a chulha that had died down can never retain a red-hot fire?

At night, when it was still warm in the kitchen, Pari cooled herself on the verandah. At such times, she noticed her brother-in-law's mosquito net blowing in the wind. Was Kunja inside the net? From afar, came the sound of someone's feet thrashing in the pond. Kunja must be in the pond. The pond was no source of contention for the men. Anyway, can one think of a fence in the middle of the pond? So only the bathing ghats were separate. The path from one ghat to the other might be slippery but it was definitely not long.

It is said that even darkness has eyes and solitude has ears and when it comes to gossip, even the inarticulate becomes audible. It did not take much time for suppressed gossip to leap from one thatch to the other. And such messages have a way of reaching swiftly from the village to the town.

It may not be possible to come home on leave when one's father dies. But, it takes no time to rush home to verify a wife's infidelity.

The day Jadunath arrived unannounced and got down from the bus, a stunned silence spread through the village. There was plenty of speculation. Would Jadunath's family be ruined, his world destroyed, Pari's life wrecked? What else could be her fate? At home there was only Pari's widowed mother. She had no father or brother. Who would come to her rescue now?

Needless to say, sensual and envious men are bound to feel a sadistic joy at this turn of events. Mocking at Jadunath's job and his urban finery, they remarked, "Let the blighter continue to work in the town! We peasants may be poor but at least we have family honour!" Similarly, some women of the village venomously exclaimed, "See, beauty is the cause of all misery. Pari may be beautiful but she is a piece of charcoal inside! How every one fawned over her beautiful face! Mark our words, it's the beautiful face that gets smeared the most. Better for you to end your life, you shameless woman!"

A sense of expectancy stifled the atmosphere. Not a leaf stirred. It was the lull before the storm.

Jadunath could not look at anybody. The proof of the gossip was all there in Pari's beauty. Could such a thing have happened if Pari was ugly and undesirable? And even if it had happened, would anyone have suspected a thing? The matter would not have spread like the smell of rotting fish, from the village to the town.

For once, Jadunath did not bow down before his parents and grandmother. Dropping his bag in the courtyard, he headed straight into his room. He even forgot to remove his chappals. Gently he shut the door from inside. Pari was standing in one corner of the room.

Jadunath said, "What is this I hear? Is it true? Whatever you say, I'll take as the truth. Am I a moron to ask the villagers about my household matters? I am asking you. If the answer is Yes, then I'll teach you a lesson, and if it is No, I'll teach the villagers one!"

Pari fell at the feet of her husband like a log of wood, wailing. People heard heavy thuds like the dropping of fruits from the palm tree. Like a demon gone berserk, Jadunath landed many blows on Pari's bare back. There was no sign of pity or compassion. It was as if he was possessed by the devil. Pari could hardly breathe because of the pain.

Outside, everyone was stilled and speechless. They seemed to be waiting for the final destruction, the last phase of the pralay, the Deluge. Surely, not only Pari's, even Jadunath's corpse would be lifted from this house today. For after beating Pari to pulp, Jadunath cannot remain alive. He will surely end his life. But who can stop Jadunath now? And how? What can the stupid Pari now produce in support of her innocence?

Writhing in pain Pari said, "Please don't beat me any more! Have pity on me. Believe me, it's no fault of mine!"

"If it's not your crime, is it your father's?" yelled Jadunath.

"I confess, but it is all the paan's doing. God alone knows what intoxicants were put in the paan that was brought by Jhatua. The trouble started from that day onwards." Sobbing bitterly, Pari fell silent.

Jadunath's raised hand, poised to strike, froze in midair and fell limply down. His whole body became lifeless. It was as if he had become a living corpse.

Jadua's grandmother suddenly opened the door. Standing firmly before her grandson, she said: "Yes, that cursed paan is the cause of all this misery. That scoundrel had sent paan so many times for his sister-in-law! God knows what that rogue had laced it with. So many times Pari had told me of the effect of the paan, but even an old experienced hag like me couldn't smell anything fishy. After all, Pari is a child. How could she fathom the complexities of the world?"

Jadunath, laden with dust, grime and tears, collapsed beside the pathetic figure of Pari. Pari continued to sob inconsolably, covering her face with both hands.

The old lady said, "Touch the feet of your husband, promise him that you are never going to take paan from that blighter again. Is there any dearth of paan and betel nut at home? Oh, what a lot of suffering for nothing!"

Once again, Pari fell at the feet of her husband and cried. They were tears of regret and repentance. There was a total lack of pretence in that crying. Why did I have to lose my balance, Pari moaned, albeit silently. And slowly, gradually, the injured and mauled husband within Jadunath recovered. After all, it was not as if his wife had deliberately turned towards the other man. She had been a victim of sorcery.

A small breeze stirred in the open courtyard. It was cool, wet and sympathetic. A mild whisper circulated amongst the gathering. After all, whoever had not heard of enslavement through paan.

Lucky Pari! She was saved in the nick of time.

The next afternoon, standing near the fence, Pari was heard showering the choicest of abuses on Kunja. There was no reply from the other side. It was clear that a stunned and dejected man was fading away like a shadow. Very soon, even the shadow disappeared.

Many such days followed. Pari's abuses were followed by silence from the other side. Thus, it was amply proved before all that the fault lay not in the character of Pari but inside the paan.

Gradually, Pari's wounds healed. There were no scars. And although the villagers had talked about it in whispers behind closed doors, they too began to forget the episode.

There was no further problem in the world of Jadunath and Pari. Their life of struggle, scarcity, joy and sorrow did not witness even one other conflict involving Pari's past. And as Jadunath looked at Pari, now a mature mother of five children, he admired her prowess.

Initially, despite his resolution, Jadunath was bent on tracing out the evil magician who had helped his brother-in-law to hypnotise his loving wife. But as we all know, it is always hard to find out such a culprit. Usually one lays hands on impostors. Jadunath, soon realising that he had neither the time nor energy to find out who that rascal was, took to soundly cursing the scoundrel to some nether world. Thus it came about that Jadunath's youth, manhood and anger gradually succumbed to time and the identity of the damned sorcerer remained an unsolved mystery forever.

[illegible]

[illegible]

[illegible]

[illegible]

[illegible]

[illegible]

[illegible]

ꝺ

BIBHAS SEN

ZERO-SUM GAME

NOMINATED BY RUKMINI BHAYA NAIR

No one would have imagined that the signing of the new GATT Treaty by India would trigger off a world-wide upheaval.

The epicentre of this cataclysm was an obscure town called Kisangunj (pop:17,000), tucked away in a dusty corner of U.P. Or, to be more precise, the dingy office of *Kisangunj Samachar* (circulation: 127 copies), a weekly tabloid owned and published by one Shewprasad Tiwari, BA, LLB. Mr. Tiwari's extended family had been wheat farmers for five generations and he was painfully aware of what TRIPS (Trade Related Intellectual Property Rights), with the possible increase in the cost of high-yielding varieties of wheat seeds, would do to his dwindling family income. And he gave vent to his feelings in an editorial which was essentially a tirade against the brazenness of the Americans.

This might have gone unnoticed but for the fact that the local stringer of a national newspaper, finding the piece outrageously funny, promptly sent it to his headquarters.

When Mr. Tiwari's fiery bit of journalistic salvo landed in the editorial department of *Hind Times* in Delhi, it was found both amusing and topical and so, instead of being tucked away in one of the inner pages, it appeared, unexpurgated, translated into English, as a box item on the front page of the next day's issue of *Hind Times*.

And since there was a paucity of hard news at the time, most of the national newspapers followed suit.

And instantly, all hell broke loose.

To understand the reason for the pandemonium, here is the full text of Mr. Tiwari's editorial:

THE UGLY FACE OF AMERICAN TRADE POLICY

We, in India, have been growing wheat for more than 5,000 years – long before Columbus misnavigated his ship to an unknown continent and created all the confusion about Red Indians, West Indians and Indian Indians. In short, long before America (let alone Americans) was 'invented' by carelessly compiled history.

And now we understand that soon we will have to pay more for HYV seeds because the Americans have done genetic engineering on them to increase the grain yield – the seed therefore, is now the "intellectual property" of America. We find this argument as convincing as that of a cosmetic surgeon doing a nose job on somebody and claiming the patient as his intellectual property.

We cannot help feeling that the American obsession with property (and a marked lack of intellect) have led to the coining of the term, Intellectual Property. Perhaps they would have been on safer ground if they had stuck to old-fashioned words like Invention, Patent and Royalty.

Let us give our American friends an example of what Intellectual Property is – or should be.

The greatest contribution to mathematics and by extension, to all branches of science, was the concept of Zero – given to the world by Aryabhatta, an Indian intellectual. The concept was first borrowed by the Arabs and from them, through the Phoenicians, it reached the western world. Therefore, the intellectual property right to Zero legally, morally and historically belongs to India and Indians. So far we have never even thought of charging royalty for this right. But in the changed circumstances, suppose we decide to charge a nominal fee for the use of the Zero, say at the rate of one cent per thousand zeros used per month by the people of America, we suspect that even the enormous wealth of America may not be enough to pay a single month's bill.

Mr. Tiwari was letting off steam; the stringer was doing his job and the editors of the various newspapers published this piece as a bit of comic relief from the daily humdrum of news vending.

None of them had contended with the hysteria that erupts so often in the Indian Parliament. Members of the Lok Sabha rushed to the Well of the House during Zero Hour, brandishing Tiwari's editorial before the stunned Speaker and demanding that the Government accept Tiwari's suggestion and teach a lesson to the arrogant firangis. A substantial segment of the Treasury Bench, already agitated

---

Zero Hour is at 12 noon, just after the Question Hour is over and before regular business of the House starts. By convention, this is the time when members raise matters that need urgent attention but are not included in the business for the day.

about the arm-twisting attitude of America, also joined in. Words like "economic imperialism" and "superpower hegemony" were being freely bandied about.

Business started again only after the Speaker agreed to have a half-hour debate on the subject.

The Leader of the right wing "nationalist" Opposition launched into a lengthy diatribe: "At a time," he thundered, "when the western worlds were populated by savages, only the genius of the Hindu tradition could have produced ..."

"Zero," an unidentified heckler completed the sentence.

A member from the minority community rose to point out that Aryabhatta's Zero would have remained an intellectual abstraction but for Arab mathematicians.

The Left Front Leader described the situation as another example of shameful exploitation by capitalist-imperialist forces of not only the material resources of India but even its intellectual treasures. And it was only fitting that a member of the proletariat (meaning Mr. Tiwari) should focus the attention of the nation on this gross injustice.

At first the Government tried to dismiss the whole thing with witty one-liners and inappropriate Urdu couplets. But this only added to the clamour. The few words that could be heard above the din were not just unparliamentary but scatological, leaving the Speaker no option but to adjourn the House more than once. This, however, had very little effect because every time the House reconvened, the members took recourse to walkouts. It was the last of these, which left only the Speaker and the Prime Minister sitting forlornly in the vast empty hall, that forced the issue.

The Government agreed to constitute a Joint Parliamentary Committee immediately to examine the entire issue and submit its report within six months. The members accepted the suggestion with the proviso that the JPC be constituted within twelve hours, the terms of reference be drawn up simultaneously and the final report submitted to the House within the next seventy-two hours. The fact that such speed of action was unheard of in the history of the Indian Parliament went unnoticed.

By now, the media, initially sceptical, had also become infected by the virus of patriotism. The Aryabhatta Zero became front-page banner headlines right across the country. International news agencies were quick to pick up the news and Shewprasad Tiwari's personal fulmination became thundering global news. In the diplomatic pouches of all the foreign embassies and consulates, encrypted reports and analyses sped towards their respective capitals.

The longest of these, understandably, went out from the American Embassy.

The President of the United States of America was prevented from finishing the last lap of his morning jog by a special messenger who informed him that his entire Cabinet had requested an immediate meeting on a matter of national emergency. In fact, they were already waiting for him at the Oval Office.

The Attorney General came to the point straightaway. She was looking haggard after spending hours in consultation with legal experts, including the Chief Justice of the Supreme Court and five of his eight colleagues. She had also spoken to the Chief of the World Court at The Hague. They were near unanimous in their opinion. Under the new clauses relating to TRIPS, it would be extremely difficult to dismiss the Indian claim on the Aryabhatta Zero. Unless of course, it could be proved that the said Aryabhatta was not the originator of zero.

The President said, "Then let me put it differently. Can the Indians prove their claim?"

The Attorney General squirmed. "Well Mr. President, the fact was documented primarily by Western mathematicians and historians, and no one has made any contrary claim since then. The Indians are simply trying to make commercial capital out of it."

The President turned to the Secretary of Commerce. "Dan, where do we stand if this infernal blackmail is allowed to go through?"

"There is no reliable census of the number of computers and calculators in use in America at this point of time," the Secretary of Commerce promptly replied. "Even assuming there are only a few million, the number of times the zero is used, every time someone punches the keyboard, will defy calculation."

The Treasury Secretary cut in. "No matter at what rate the Indians want to sell their zero, we simply don't have the kind of money to pay them."

In exasperation the President turned to the Secretary of State, "Mike, you've been very quiet. How do we get out of this mess?"

The Secretary of State took his time to answer. "You may not like this, Mr. President, but I think we'll have to settle for a little compromise. The easiest course for us, of course, is to ignore the whole zero business. After all, the zero is not a commodity which the Indians can pack and ship to us and slap a fat bill for. In other words, there's no way they can enforce this 'blackmail' as you called it."

The President not only relaxed but actually grinned. "Then what's all the hassle about, Mike? Forget the whole thing and let the bastards go to hell."

The Secretary of State looked uncomfortable. "We have to think of our image, Mr. President. Among the signatories to the GATT Treaty are many poor Third World countries whose sympathies are likely to be with India. I wouldn't like them to think of America as a cheat and a bully. We have many dependants but few friends, Sir. Why should we invite hostility if we can avoid it?"

"You may have a point there, Mike," conceded the President. "So, what do you suggest?"

"I suggest we make a show of magnanimity, Mr. President. Let's be a tad generous about items likes seeds, fertilisers, pesticides and such. May be we can throw in a few obsolete pharmaceutical products as well. I'm sure we can make up the shortfall by vigorously pushing Coca Cola, Pepsi, Burger King and Kentucky Fried Chicken ... not to mention our automobiles which no one seems to like ... and a few non-critical industrial plants and technology for good measure. I could add to the list but I'm sure you get the drift, Sir."

"Well if there are no serious objections to Mike's suggestions, gentlemen, I think we have a workable solution which will be acceptable to the Indians. Mike, will you please organise it – but keep it low-key, okay?"

The JPC Report was submitted to Parliament – incredibly, within the stipulated 72 hours – amidst wild jubilation. Various legal authorities, both at home and abroad, had confirmed that India's claim to the intellectual property right on the Aryabhatta Zero was legally tenable. But the first flush of victory was somewhat dampened by the realisation that the property right clause was not going to be easy to enforce even with legal sanction.

Once it was agreed that keeping track of the zeros used by American computers would be totally impossible, a solution was devised by a high-powered task force of financial experts, which most members of the JPC felt was worth a try.

Simply stated, the proposal was this: America will place at the disposal of India a sum of two billion dollars every year to be used by India exclusively to defray the additional import cost burden caused by TRIPS on sundry items like seeds, pesticides, pharmaceuticals etc. etc. (listed in the annexure). Items excluded will comprise soft drinks, chewing gum, cigarettes, denim etc. etc. etc. (listed in the annexure).

The Indian proposal was duly made through proper diplomatic and legal channels and was predictably rejected by America as arbitrary, frivolous and violative of the spirit of the new global trade treaty. After an unending spate of arguments and counter-arguments, injunctions, stays and appeals which only swelled the bank accounts of lawyers in both countries but achieved little else, the Indian policy makers felt the urgent need for a face-saving formula to end the impasse.

The formula, of course, was kept a secret from the public and a "working visit" was arranged for the Finance and Commerce Ministers of India to meet their American counterparts.

The two teams met on neutral ground at Barbados, where neither the local population nor the media paid them the slightest attention, since their arrival coincided with the last and deciding cricket match between the West Indies and South Africa in a three Test series. This helped a great deal in keeping the meeting low-key, as fervently desired by both sides.

India demanded a one-time payment of five billion dollars in exchange for revoking all future claims by way of property rights on the Aryabhatta Zero. This was grudgingly accepted by the Americans. Further, the demand of the Indian side for price status quo on specific items (as listed in the annexure) was also accepted by the Americans. The only condition that the Americans insisted on was that, in keeping with the earlier-issued guidelines of the World Bank and the IMF, Indian farmers should be asked to pay the full cost for electricity and water. "America is concerned about the set-back to the forces of liberalisation that could take place if India continues with such subsidies which distort free market mechanisms," said the leader of the American delegation, firmly.

It was 3 a.m. before the Indian delegation came to a conclusion. The Commerce Minister summed up the deliberations. "Let's face facts," he said. "Our economy is dependent on assistance from the World Bank and the IMF. As long as these two institutions are largely financed by U.S.A., it would be in the national interest to accept these conditionalities. I don't see why we can't give in on this electricity and water thing. It'll anyway help reduce the budgetary deficit. The Government should not lose the American offer and thereby miss the chance to achieve a greater degree of economic parity with the West."

The next morning, both sides felt greatly relieved at the mutually accepted and honourable retreat from a sticky situation and after the usual bonhomie and fixing up of their next meeting (at Monaco, to discuss the detailed modalities), they left for their respective homes.

In India, the positive solution of the Aryabhatta imbroglio was hailed as a tremendous moral victory. Most major newspapers and periodicals carried features on Shewprasad Tiwari and the national channel of Doordarshan telecast a fifteen-minute interview with him. He was described as the champion of the farming community (which he understood) and the embodiment of the spirit of Indian nationalism (which he did not). Various political parties were coaxing him to accept their nomination to contest for the State Assembly. There was even a rumour that he might get a Padmashree.

The adulation, however, had not changed the thrifty habits of Shewprasad. All in all, he was happy. Especially since his calculations had shown that he had saved at least Rs. 3780.00 on the cost of seeds. Quite an achievement.

In the meanwhile, the Finance Minister had acted double-quick on the American requirement. This was done mainly to expedite the one-time payment of five billion dollars. And, for the first time, Indian farmers were asked to pay the full cost of electricity and water.

In his euphoric state, Shewprasad had not paid much attention to these developments – in any case, the charges were bound to be nominal.

About a week later, Shewprasad received his first bills for electricity and water at the revised rates. For a moment the figures failed to make sense. A second look made him realise that he had to make an extra payment of Rs. 2,835.00 for electricity and an extra payment of Rs. 945.00 for water. The charges seemed to be rather high, certainly much more than he had expected, but they were still within his means.

Something niggled at the back of his mind.

Shewprasad took out his account book and jotted down his saving on the cost of seeds on a sheet of paper. Next, he totalled the extra amounts he had to pay for electricity and water and wrote this figure under the first. He repeated the exercise thrice. Each time the final result was the same. He was looking at:

Saving on seeds	3780.00
Extra charges on electricity & water	3780.00
	0000.00

CONTRIBUTORS' NOTES

ASSAMESE

Pankaj Thakur writes in Assamese and is known mainly for his satires. His collection of short stories, *Apuni Kiba Kaboneki* has been translated into Hindi. He has translated Ibsen, Strindberg, Sartre and Wole Soyinka into Assamese from English translations of their works. A former Associate Editor of *Ajir Asom*, a popular monthly, he is an honorary editor of *Paryatak*, a magazine on culture and tourism. He has edited works on developmental studies as well. Currently, he lives in Tinsukhia, where he looks after the TISCO office, and is editing a book on the Assamese short story for the Sahitya Akademi.

- The short story became a recognisable form in Assamese around 1892 with "Seuti," written by the doyen of modern Assamese literature, L.N. Bezborua. There was a fresh burst of creativity in the '70s, with the Natun Prithivi movement. Today, amongst the most promising writers of the new generation are those who were born after Independence. They include Kamala Borgohain, Bhupendra Narayan Bhattacharya, Jyotish Sikdar, Debabrata Das, Phanindra Kumar Debchoudhury, Sailendra Kumar Bhattacharya, Arupa Patangia Kalita, Manoj Goswami and Nabaneeta Gogoi.

  Manoj Kumar Goswami is aware of the reality that is Assam and the role of the true revolutionary. He has put them together here to come up with **"Samiran Barua Aahi Aase,"** which looks dispassionately at the north-eastern part of our country. Assam is in dire need of social change; but we find that most people are unable to accept that such change is a long and painful process. A difficult and sensitive subject of contemporary relevance has been dealt with courageously and skilfully in this story.

Manoj Kumar Goswami is a postgraduate in physics from Guwahati University. He taught physics for three years before he took up journalism as a profession in 1986. His first short story was published in 1979, followed by several collections of short stories:

This section is organised language-wise. It contains the biographical details of the Nominating Editor, the state of the short story in that language and the Editor's reasons for nominating the chosen story. This is followed by biographical details of the Author and her/his notes on the writing of the story; then the notes on and by the Translator. In languages where there is more than one story, the reasons for nomination of all the stories come with the Nominating Editor's note, while the Author's and Translator's Notes for each story have been placed together for ease of reference, and are alphabetical, according to the Author's first name.

Iswarhinata, Samiran Barua Aahi Aase, Moi Rajen Borak Samarthan Karon.

- The present unrest in Assam and the resultant deterioration of values in politics, academia and in all other aspects of society disturbs me. The rise of extremism purportly to wipe out social evils or to bring change in society, has no relevance for the middle class.

Jayeeta Sharma teaches at Lady Shri Ram College and is presently doing research in Modern Indian History at Delhi University.

- ... Some of the pithiness of the original comes from the very effective use of English slang words – I haven't been able to find a suitable mimetic device for this.

BANGLA

Sarat Kumar Mukhopadhyay is a major poet, fiction writer and critic, with twenty titles to his credit. His latest work is a travelogue on Europe. He is currently a counsellor in the Creative Writing Programme at the Calcutta Study Centre of the Indira Gandhi University.

- In Bangla, well-known writers are busy writing novels since collections of short stories do not sell. Young writers do experiment with the genre but most of them fail because they do not have the required command over the language.

  This story, **"Bimalasundarir Upakhyan,"** is an exception. The young writer has an eye for the obscure and, so far, he has not made compromises to earn mass readership. The author's brilliant craftsmanship weaves into the story an undertone of deep irony. The colloquial narrative embellishes the suburban atmosphere.

Swapnamoy Chakraborti, winner of the Manik Bandopadhyay award for *Bhumisutra* in 1982, and the Tarashankar award for *Vedio Bhagaban Nakuldara* in 1992, has so far, four collections of short stories to his credit. At present he is a Programme Executive with All India Radio, Calcutta.

- My curiosity was aroused by a middle-aged woman who was always followed by stray dogs and cats. Despite her poverty, she looked after her pets well and even bought fish for them. One day, I noticed her in conversation with an elderly man at the railway station. Some time later, she was weeping helplessly, seated alone on the platform bench. Although I tried to find out the reason for her sorrow, she gave me no answer and continued to weep. This is the source of my story.

Gopa Majumdar, a graduate in English from Delhi University, began translating short stories for *Namaste* magazine in 1987. Her other translated works include *The Emperor's Ring*, and *Twenty Stories* (Satyajit Ray's works, published by Penguin India) and *In the Same Boat* (UBS Publishers). She is currently translating more of Ray's stories for Penguin; a novel by Ashapurna Devi for Macmillan India.

- In this story ... great emphasis has been laid on sounds and noises. In the original text, they sound perfectly natural but any attempts at retaining those words in the translated version would seem contrived. Simply substituting one word for another, and making sure that every syllable from the original writing goes into the translation only serves to make the latter sound stiff and stilted. So certain portions had to be left out.

Editor's note: Certain portions that had been left out in the original translation have been incorporated in the published version.

ENGLISH

Rukmini Bhaya Nair was educated in Calcutta and Cambridge, where she obtained her Ph.D. in Linguistics in 1982. She has taught at Jawaharlal Nehru University, the National University of Singapore and the University of Washington and has been a visiting professor at the Indian Institute of Advanced Studies, Shimla. Currently she is Associate Professor in the Department of Humanities and Social Sciences, IIT, Delhi. A number of journals in India and abroad have included both her creative and her academic writings. She has one published volume of poems to her credit, *The Hyoid Bone*, (Viking, Penguin, 1993) after she won the All India British Council/Poetry Society prize. A second volume of poems, "Gargi's Silence," is to appear in 1995.

- Both the unpublished English short stories nominated for the Katha awards this year, I thought, truly lived up to their names. I chose Bibhas Sen's **"Zero-Sum Game"** not only because of the effervescent wit and extreme topicality, but because it was so pleasingly structured with its end seeming to meet its beginning in that effortless, circular movement characteristic of the figure zero. Indian writing in English has long been plagued by a lack of humour; stories like Sen's go some way towards lifting this pall of gloom by displaying the kind of combination of high farce and laconic irony which I feel humorists as diverse as Rajasekhar Bosu and Mark Twain might well have applauded.

  Vandana Bist's **"The Weight"** I selected for an almost diametrically opposed set of qualities. The story was full of gravities, rich in local specifications and gendered description. To me, this story was intriguing because its moral "weight" appears to derive not in the least from the fact of death itself, but from the intense effects of dark and light produced by the play of tradition, language, sexual desire and apprehension within the interior landscape of a woman's mind. Finally, as a writer who has always been concerned with the predicament of writing in the English language, I have to say that I was deeply impressed by the unselfconcious confidence with which Sen and Bist manage to keep at bay the spectres of both linguistic and political correctness. This seems to me to be a hopeful indication of English having now become a wholly Indian tongue.

Bibhas Sen claims that he cannot think of any academic or literary achievement in his life which could be of the slightest interest to the readers. In defence of his decision to write, he says that as an advertising professional, he has been writing "creative fiction" all his working life and simply wanted to find out if his craftsmanship was marketable.

- The inspiration for this story came from newspaper reports on the controversy arising out of the implications of signing the GATT Treaty.

Vandana Bist has a degree in Fine Arts from the Delhi College of Art and has specialised in illustration. In 1988, she was awarded the encouragement prize in the Children's Picture Book Competition organised by the Noma Concours Foundation, Japan. Her works have been exhibited in Japan and Bratislava. Since 1986, her writings and drawings have been published in various children's magazines and books. Her first book is *A Ticket to Home and Other Stories*, a collection for children (HarperCollins, 1994).

- The characters and situations woven into this story are inspired by accounts of the lives of people who belonged to the households my mother was born and married into. It is especially about women. The story has its origin in my resentment of the fact, that behind all facades of social progress, a cause and effect relationship persists in all dimensions.

GUJARATI

Shirish Panchal has a doctorate from M.S.University, Baroda and is presently teaching Gujarati language and literature at the same university. So far, fifteen of his books have been published which include a novel, a collection of short stories, critical works, and collections of essays. He edits the literary quarterly, *Etad*.

- The contemporary Gujarati story writer does not normally go in for experimental writing. But many writers have gained by their exposure to the modern short story in other languages and conscious efforts are being made by the short story writer to choose a different path.

The theme of **"Madhapudo"** is not unusual. It uses a traditional motif. But the conflict is rendered with fresh images and expressions. For the first time, we have here a tribal writer, exploring the dark regions of the human mind.

Kanji Patel is from the tribal area of Panchmahal district and is a postgraduate in English and in Sanskrit. A well-known poet in Gujarati, his first collection of poems, *Janapada,* was published in 1992. He has also written two short novels, *Kotarni Dhare* and *Dahelu.* At present he is a lecturer in English at the Arts, Science and Commerce College in Lunavada, Gujarat.

- The story emerged from my desire to narrate a simple story of a man, his wives, his mother, set within the confines of a basically agrarian society. The tragi-comic tensions, chosen consciously and unconsciously, have held great fascination for me since childhood. After twenty-five years, it's only now that I've found the language and the motivation to recreate the whole milieu.

Sarala Jag Mohan translates from and into Gujarati, Hindi and English. Recipient of an award from the Bharatiya Anuvad Parishad for translation, she has translated books for National Book Trust and the Sahitya Akademi.

- ... Since a few colloquial expressions were unfamiliar, even though I am quite conversant with such regional expressions, the story did pose a challenge.

HINDI

Vijay Mohan Singh has taught in different universities for twenty years. He has had published three collections of short stories and six books on literary criticism. For eight years he was in charge of *Vagarth,* the literary wing of Bharat Bhavan, Bhopal. He has also served as secretary of the Hindi Academy, Delhi Government.

- The Hindi short story is undergoing many changes, though traditional trends still exist. Social themes dominate.

  The story **"Palang"** was chosen for its symbolic realism and its powerful descriptions.

Priyamvad is a postgraduate in Ancient Indian History and Culture with a novel, *Weh Wahan Quaid Hain* and a collection of short stories *Bosidni* amongst his published works. Presently he owns and runs his own industry.

- As long as Ma was alive – for nearly forty years – I slept on the same bed with her ... Sometimes I saw her in states of undress. Lying on that bed, before falling asleep, we often shared some of our joys and sorrows. That bed had begun to take on the characteristics of a real person. After Ma's death, I slept on that bed, alone. During one of those nights, I thought that if ever another woman were to sleep here with me ... in Ma's place ... would I be able to accept her? I felt not ... Ma will always remain here ... even in that woman. Suddenly I saw a psychological problem. It is this emotion and its psychological aspect that I have attempted to convey through the story.

Nivedita Menon, a lecturer in Political Science at Lady Shri Ram College, Delhi University, has completed her doctoral dissertation on the interaction between feminist and legal discourse in India and has published several articles in her field.

- This dark and disturbing story is deceptively simple. Translating it presented no particular difficulties as its power to leave us shaken derives really from the spaces its creates around what is written, rather than from the words themselves. I did find it difficult though, to retain the inexorable rhythm of the last two paragraphs. The best I could do has lost something of the original.

KANNADA

Ramachandra Sharma has a doctorate in psychology from the University of London. He has worked as a high school teacher and a psychologist in India, England and Africa. Sharma is considered one of the pioneers of the modern movement in Kannada literature. His publications include *Gestures*, a collection of poems in English. He has translated English poetry into Kannada and both prose and poetry from Kannada into English. A recipient of the Karnataka Sahitya Akademi Award, his own poems and short stories have been translated into several languages.

- "**Meenu Maruvavanu**" handles with sensitivity, the theme of the symbiotic relationship between Muslims and traditional Hindus in a small community. The comic mode of the narration is subtle and makes the events more convincing. The story proceeds in a low mimetic mode and recommends itself to the discerning reader.

  "**Ondu Osage Oyyuvudittu**" is an intensely moving story. The control the writer exercises in telling the story is outstanding. The narration is rich in details which are both significant and convincing. The writing is powerful with a certain quality of immediacy about it.

Bolwar Mahamad Kunhi is the first writer to depict the travails of Muslims, in Kannada literature. He has to his credit four short story collections, a novel and two documentaries. Among them are *Devarugala Rajyadalli* which won the Karnataka Sahitya Akademi Award (1983), *Anka*, a collection of short stories which won the Bharatiya Bhasha Samsthan Award (1986), and *Akashakke Neeli Parade* which won the Sahitya Akademi Award for the Best Creative Book (1992). He is a Senate Member of the Kannada University, Hampi. A gold-medallist from Mysore University, he is with the Syndicate Bank, Delhi, as Personnel Officer.

- My stories – including this one – are set in the small but vibrant village of Muthuppadi in coastal Karnataka and are in-depth studies of Hindu-Muslim relationships. I see the story as emerging from the convictions and professionalism of the two prime characters, developed through the impressions of people who are unable to understand the strength of the two main characters. The climax brought back for me the Malayalam saying, "A fish vendor shall buy a ship and when the ship sinks he sells fish."

H.Y. Sharada Prasad was Information Adviser to Prime Minister Rajiv Gandhi. He has translated two of K. Shivarama Karanth's novels and his autobiography into English and R.K. Narayan's *Swami and Friends* into Kannada.

- I did not encounter any special problem in translating Bolwar. He writes in a simple standard Kannada and does not take recourse to any regional dialect. Also, his economy in the use of words makes the translator's work easy.

Mithra Venkatraj had her first collection of short stories, *Rukmayi*, published in 1991. Several of her short stories have been published in major Kannada magazines. She lives in Bombay and is actively associated with the literary and cultural activities of the Kannada Sangha of Bombay.

- The basic idea came from a childhood memory of a liaison of the type described in the story. In the conversations, I have consciously used the dialect of Kannada spoken in the Kundapura area of South Kanara where I was born and brought up.

C.N. Ramachandran is Professor and Chairman of the Department of Postgraduate Studies and Research in English, University of Mangalore. Three of his critical works in English and four in Kannada, besides a novel and a few short stories in Kannada, have been published. Some of his published translations include poems of Kuvempu (*Selected Poems of Kuvempu*) and two short stories, for the Sahitya Akademi.

- The story is written in a regional dialect of Kannada, which gives it authenticity. But this regional flavour is lost in translation. Precise kinship terms and names of food items peculiar to Karnataka are difficult to translate and have been retained.

KONKANI

Chandrakant Keni has been the editor of a daily newspaper, *Rashtramat* since its inception in 1963. A proficient writer of short stories and essays in Konkani, Marathi and Hindi, his short stories have been translated into English and other languages. A recipient of the Sahitya Akademi Award for his collection of short stories, *Vhoukal Pavnni* in 1989, he has also received the Dr. T.M.A. Pai Foundation Award for his collection of personal essays, *Bimbam Padbimbam.* He is a member of the General Council of Sahitya Akademi, and Chairman of the Editors' Guild and of the Gomantak Rashtrabhasha Vidyapeeth.

- Generally the output of Konkani short stories is limited, perhaps, because of lack of effective communication links between Konkani writers and readers living in different parts of the country. Distance is not the only barrier that separates a community that was fragmented some five centuries ago. Konkani is presently written in Devanagiri, Kannada, Urdu, Malayalam and the Roman scripts and this has become a barrier, restricting the output of a good writer. By and large, very few writers endeavour to sidestep the beaten path.

  "**Aaplem ... Parki**" reflects a problem that has caused many an upheaval in Konkani society. The theme is tackled by the writer in such a way that the story unfolds through conversation between a grandmother and her grand-daughter. It is a simple story.

Meena Kakodkar has won several prestigious awards including the Sahitya Akademi Award, the Dr. T.M.A. Pai Foundation Award and the Konkani Bhasha Mandal Award. She has two collections of short stories, *Dongor Chanvalla* and *Sapan Fulam,* to her credit. She is currently a Sub-Treasury Officer at Margao.

- Though the general attitude of people towards daughters is slowly changing, there is still some resistance from parents to accept sons and daughters as equals, particularly while accepting assistance from daughters in their old age. I strongly feel that ... a person who is affectionate and loving is one's very own.

Sacheen Pai Raikar graduated in Architecture from Goa University in 1993. He is a member of the Council of Architecture and works with Patki and Dadarkar Technical Consultants, in Bombay.

- The concept of a daughter being considered an outsider after her marriage is difficult to express in some ways, and it was especially so in the title.

MALAYALAM

K. Satchidanandan has fifteen collections of poems, plays and critical essays and an equal number of translations from world and Indian poetry to his credit. While some of his poems are in English, many which are in Malayalam have been translated into several Indian and foreign languages. He is the recipient of many awards including the Kerala Sahitya Akademi Award for Essays (1984), and for Poetry (1989) and the Sreekant Verma Fellowship for Poetry Translation (1989). He did his research in Post Structuralist Literary Theory for his doctoral thesis and was a professor of English at Christ College, Kerala, for twenty-five years. He has edited several magazines and anthologies in Malayalam and English and is at present editor of *Indian Literature,* Sahitya Akademi, New Delhi.

- I liked "**Kappithante Magal**" for its deft, artistic and controlled handling of an extremely complex situation ... The atmosphere of the story, with its texture derived from an interweaving of poetry, art, religion and sexuality, is more haunting than the resolution itself. Texts from various disciplines seem to flow here into one another dissolving their genealogical indentities to form an open and readable narrative which has cruelty at its core.

  I chose "**Velutha Koodarangal**" for its psychological subtlety and suggestive narration. Urmila's oscillation between ennui and renunciation, her substitution of her real mother with Cheriamma, and her feeling of being abandoned appear to be typical of a whole new generation in Kerala, compelled by frustration to look beyond the world of material comforts, to reach out to some fantastic world where love is inseparable from spirituality and where the polluted is magically transformed into the pure.

N.S.Madhavan started his career as a short story writer with *Sishu* which won the first prize in a competition held in 1970 by the literary journal, *Mathrubhumi.* In the next ten years he pubished ten stories which were later brought out as *Choolaimetile Savangal* in 1981. After more than a decade, he published *Higuita* which was chosen in a literary survey conducted by *Malayala Manorama* as one of the ten best short stories written in Malayalam in the last century. This story also fetched him the Katha Award in 1992 and the Padmarajan Puraskaram for the best short story in 1993.

Narendra Nair has an M.D. in medicine from Bombay University. A nuclear medicine physician, he is Chief of the Clinical Section at the Radiation Medicine Centre at the Tata Memorial Centre, Department of Atomic Energy. With no formal schooling in Malayalam, he says his love for the language is entirely due to his mother, late Smt. Janaki Amma's efforts. Dr. Nair writes occasional humorous pieces, poems and movie reviews for papers and magazines.

- I hope I have been able to transfer the sexual overtones in the girl's behaviour and speech into English without major losses.

Sethu (alias A. Sethumadhavan) has been writing short stories in Malayalam for the past 27 years with published works including eleven novels and thirteen short story collections. He has won the Kerala Sahitya Akademi Award twice; once for the highly acclaimed novel *Pandavapuram;* and again for *Petiswapnangal*, a collection of short stories. Another novel *Niyogam* received the Viswadeepam Award. His *Pandavapuram* is being filmed with NFDC assistance and is also to be published in English translation by Macmillan India.

- The story just happened. Probably some of these characters have been in my subconscious. This is the case with many of my other stories, too.

Nivedita Menon has also translated the Hindi story (see the Hindi section for biographical note).

- I found it difficult to translate the title. "Koodarangal" would be commonly understood to mean camps, encampment or tents. All these words have a martial ring. However, the story suggests the use of the word "koodarangal" in a less common sense, that is, as "tabernacles," the temples of the Jews in the desert. The heroine associates white with purity, spirituality and sanctuary – so tabernacle better approximates the sense in which she longs for, and fantasizes about, her "white koodarangal." But "tabernacle" is an uncommon word, Hence, "White Hermitage."

MARATHI

Ganesh N. Devy is Professor of English at the Maharaja Sayajirao University, Baroda. His publications include, *Critical Thought*, and *In Another Tongue: Essays on Indian English Literature*. His book, *After Amnesia: Tradition and Change in Literary Criticism*, received the Sahitya Akademi Award in 1993. He has held many distinguished fellowships including the Commonwealth Academic Staff Fellowship, the Fulbright Fellowship, the T.H.B. Symons Fellowship and the Jawaharlal Nehru Fellowship.

- During the eighties, the Marathi short story appeared to have become qualitatively less demanding. This picture is beginning to change. New voices are being heard today. Some of them – Sharankumar Limbale, Prakash Naryan Sant, Sumedh Vadawala Risbud and others – have started paying attention to short fiction. There is a freshness in the themes attempted, which transcend the by now conventional divisions of rural-urban, low- high, man-woman. The two stories nominated for *KPS 4* are by no means "representative"; they were nominated because they stand on their own as good stories.

"Bhijat Bhijat Koli," Gauri Deshpande's story, is so basic and simple that it reads like a parable. I found it unique among feminist stories in Marathi. She avoids the cliche about women's suffering by giving the story the form of a mock-parable. The bare and terse narrative depicts the violence in the situation without entering any rhetorical plot-strategies.

"Sharada Sangeet" by Prakash Narayan Sant is a psychological study of a young boy and his initiation into the world of adults. The author achieves a rare artistic effect by using the medium of music to depict the spiritual growth of his hero. Due to the special point of view and controlled style, the story acquires a spiritual depth which makes reading it a memorable experience.

Gauri Deshpande has ten novels, three collections of poems and one collection of short stories to her credit, besides innumerable uncollected essays (mainly on women and translation) and stories which are to be published in two volumes. Her translations from English to Marathi include Richard Burton's *Arabian Nights* in 16 volumes. Many of her books have won state and other awards. She also writes in English and translates into it from Marathi. A Ph.D in English Literature from Poona University, she taught undergraduate and postgraduate courses for a few years before turning to editing and freelance journalism. After a 20 year break, she has rejoined academics and presently teaches English at Poona University.

- The story originated from a discussion with a dear friend about the idea of 'self' or of 'soul' in Buddhist Philosophy. There was also a dissatisfaction with the way we could not resolve the difficulty of reconciling the 'self' and the 'non-self'. I didnot find any significant problems in translating the story.

Prakash Narayan Sant alias Bhalchandra Gopal Dixit has a doctorate in Geology and is a Reader in Y.C. College, Karad.

- My parents were both deeply involved with literature and music, and my mother, Smt. Indira Sant, is a well known writer in Marathi. I lost my father just when we were forming a very special friendship. But his influence was very strong, and as a result, I took to learning music. My memories of the music class, my friends (both boys and girls), a devoted teacher, the whole world of early adolescence and its magic came back to me forty years later when I visited Belgaum and found the building still there, though serving a very different purpose.

ORIYA

Sachidananda Mohanty, received his doctorate in English from IIT, Kanpur. A recipient of the British Council Award(1990), the Fulbright Fellowship at Texas and Yale(1991), the UGC's career award(1993), he has also won the Katha Award(1992) as a co-translator. He has published two books on D.H. Lawrence as also articles in leading magazines and journals. Currently, he is writing a book for USEFI.

- Of all the major literary genres, the short story enjoys the greatest currency in Orissa. Largely confined to the middle-class reading public, the short story has been the mainstay of most of the literary and semi-literary journals in Orissa. Because of its popularity many writers are attracted to it. However most of the stories are in the realistic mode.

  Through skilful narration, the story writer, employing a primarily comical mode, depicts a complex trade-off between the need for sexual identity and social respectability.

Pratibha Ray has to her credit, 18 novels, 17 collections of short stories, one travelogue, nine books for children and 10 books for neo-literates. She has received numerous awards and honours including the Orissa Sahitya Akademi Award for her novel, *Shilapadma*, in 1985. She is the first woman to receive the Moorti Devi Award of the Bharatiya Jnanpith(1991) for her novel, *Yajnaseni*.

- I witnessed a similar incident in my village when I was about thirteen or fourteen. Often, I would remember the incident and it disturbed me: Why was that young and beautiful woman attracted to paan and what was her exact relationship with the ugly brother-in-law. This ultimately took shape as "Shapya."

Sachidananda Mohanty (See above section for biographical note).

- The main problem in translating this piece lay in transferring the idiom and nuances that belong primarily to rural Orissa. Also, the comical mode, frequently employed by the writer, involves a lot of repetition which strike a discordant note in English.

TAMIL

Gnani is the pen-name for K. Palanisamy. A retired Tamil teacher he is a respected critic who has written, besides numerous essays in

Tamil relating to Marxism, two collections of poems: *Kalligai* and *Tholaivilirunthu.*

- As we look back, we find that short stories in Tamil far outstrips the novel in quality. They can be easily classed with the best in the world. Short stories handle the multifarous problems inherent in Tamil society though we find that commercial magazines drag the reader back onto the beaten path. But Tamil is lucky to have a flourishing small magazine culture which serves to bring out the creative talents of budding writers.

  Fine language and an imagination of a very high order contribute greatly to the literary quality of this story, "**Patri Erintha Thennaimaram.**"

Thanjai Prakaash has been writing for the last forty years. A Tamil Vidwan and a Sanskrit Shiromani, his published works include two collections, one of short stories(1970) and of essays (1990).

- This story was written for a brochure that was to be published for the seventieth-year celebrations of the K.C. Muthupillai Leprosy Hospital. Since they could not include a story section there, I was asked to narrate it in the celebration function. After a repeat performance at the Tanjavur Storytellers Association, the story was chosen for publication by the editor of *Subhamangala.*

Lakshmi Kannan writes both in English and in Tamil. Using the pen-name Kaaveri for her writings in Tamil, she is best known for her novel, *Athukku Poganum.* Her publications include fiction in Tamil and three collections of poems in English. She studied American and English literature at the Universities of Delhi, Jadavpur and California at Irwine (USA) and wrote her Ph.D dissertation on the Nobel Laureate Saul Bellow. Orient Longman has recently published *India Gate and Other Stories*, a translation of her short stories.

TELUGU

Allam Rajaiah is a prolific writer with over 100 stories and six novels published. Some of these have been translated into other Indian languages. *Bhoomi* and *Srustikarthaloo* is his latest published work.

- The Telugu short story presently is one that has conflict as its focus. Many stories come from the backward areas of Telangana and Rayalaseema. The Communist, the Dalit and the women's movements have made a great impact on the Telugu short story. The written word has identified itself with the spoken word of the common man. The Telugu story has thus come nearer to the working class.

  "**Nalugukalla Mantapam,**" is representative of the cruel reality of the plight of the poor, not necessarily confined to Rayalseema alone. Hence the selection.

Madhuranthakam Narendra has a Ph.D in English and currently teaches English at Sri Venkateswara University, Tirupati.

- Nalugukalla Mantapam is the name of a junction in the town Tirupati. It is a market where labour is bought and sold. The story is an attempt to portray a scene, full of life and activity, which depicts deep human dilemmas and relationships.

Vijaya Ghose is a professional editor. For many years she was associated with *Target*, a children's magazine that is published by Living Media. For the past few years she has been the editor of *Limca Books*. Her other publications besides *Tirtha*, are *A Guide to Complete Home Care* and *Women in Society - India*.

- The story is a narration of what happens at the four-pillared mandapam. Inextricably, Rangamma's life is woven into this texture of routine happenings. I found it distracting to have so many elements in the story which did not have any future impact on the story.

Editor's note: I saw Rangamma as a survivor, one who would not give in easily. But the original story had lapsed into a rather cliched ending. Working from a suggestion given by Katha, the writer has rewrittten the ending which appears in the revised translation.

URDU

Anisur Rahman translates from and to English and Urdu. At present a Reader in the Department of English, Jamia Millia Islamia, New Delhi, he has worked and published in the areas of new literatures in English and literary translation.

- The Urdu short story scene is not very encouraging. Only a few remarkable stories appear within any given year. The ratio of pulp fiction as compared to serious fiction is frightening. Maybe this is a time of transition for the Urdu short story which is in search of real authors who will help it emerge with greater resilience.

  "**Aaghori**" has been selected for its immense readability, for its effortless narrative brilliance and its linguistic ease, and above all for its effective use of symbols to recreate a difficult time in India's history.

Surendra Prakash, the pen-name of Surendra Kumar Oberoi, won the Sahitya Akademi Award Winner for Urdu in 1989. Born in Lyallpur, Pakistan, he migrated to Delhi after the partition and made his living as hawker, rickshaw-puller, flower seller and travelling salesman. His works include *Doosre Aadmi Ka Drawing Room* (1968), *Baraf Par Makalma* (1980) and the award-winning anthology, *Baz Goyi* (1988). He now lives in Bombay and writes scripts for films and television plays.

- Partition brought about the death of a composite culture. This story, as I have said in "Aaghori," is "a story ... but remember there is a story within a story and that in turn leads to another story. Grasping the identity of the story, finding the essence of that which is a figment of the imagination, is your business. This story is such that it cannot be put into words."

C Revathi is registered with the Pondicherry University for a Ph.D degree which is to be submitted shortly. She is currently working as an assistant editor with Orient Longman.

- A word-to-word translation seems to rob the life of the story while a certain amount of liberty leaves one with the fear of misinterpretation of the original. Translating speech or customs peculiar to this region into a language like English proved difficult at times.

A SELECT LIST OF REGIONAL MAGAZINES

ASSAMESE

Ajir Asom, Omega Publishers, GS Rd, Ulubari, Guwhahati
Anwesha, Konwarpur, Sibsagar, Assam
Asam Bani, Assam Tribune Bldg, GN Bordoloi Rd, Guwahati
Budhbar, Shahid Sukleswar Konwar Path, Guwahati
Prakash, Publication Board of Assam, Bamunimaidan, Guwahati
Prantik, Navagiri Road, Chanmari, Guwahati
Pratidhwani, Bani Mandir, Panbazar, Guwahati
Sadin, Sadin Karyalaya, Maniram Dewan Path, Chandmari, Guwahati
Sreemoyee, 'Agradut', Agradut Bhawan, Dispur

BANGLA

Aajkaal, 96, Raja Rammohan Sarani, Calcutta 9
Ananda Bazar Patrika, 6 Prafulla Sarkar Rd, Calcutta
Amrita Lok, Binalay, Dak Bungalow Rd, PO Midnapore
Anustup, 2E, Nabin Kundu Lane, Calcutta
Bartaman, 76A Acharya Bose Road, Calcutta 15
Bartika, 18A, Bollygange Station Rd, Calcutta
Basumati, 166 Bepin Behari Ganguli St, Calcutta
Chaturanga, 54 Ganesh Chandra Ave, Calcutta 13
Desh, Ananda Bazar Patika Ltd, 6 Prafulla Sarkar Rd, Calcutta
Ekshan, 73 Mahatama Gandhi Rd, Calcutta 12
Hawa, 49, Brahmapur, Bansdroni, Calcutta 70
Kaurab, Jamshedpur, Bihar
Kuthar, Flat 87, Cluster 14, Purbachal Housing Estate, Calcutta 91
Ganashakthi, 31, Alimuddin Street, Calcutta 16
Manorama, 281 Muthiganj, Allahabad 3
Madhuparni, Sitbali Complex, Balurghat, South Binajpur, WB
Parichaya, 89, Mahatma Gandhi Road, Calcutta
Pratidin, 14 Radhanath Chouduri Road, Calcutta15
Pratikshana, 7, Jawaharlal Nehru Road, Calcutta
Proma, 5 West Range, Calcutta
Yogasutra, TG 2/29 Teghoria, Hatiara, Calcutta 59
Yuba Manas, 32/1, BBD Bag (South), Calcutta

GUJARATI

Abhiyan, Chunilal Gandhi Vidyabhavan, Athwa Lines, Surat
Buddhiprakash, Gujarat Vidya Sabha, Ashram Road, Ahmedabad
Dasmo Dayako, Sardar Patel University, Vallabh Vidyanagar
Etad, 233 Rajlaxmi Soc, Old Padra Road, Baroda
Gadyaparva, 12A Chetan Apts., Rajwadi Rd, Ghatkopar East, Bombay
Kankavati, 24 River Bank Society, Adajan Water Tank, Surat

Khevana, 9 Mukund, Manorama Complex, Himatlal Park, Ahmedabad.
Navchetan, Narayanagar, Sarkhej Rd, Ahmedabad.
Navneet Samarpan, Bharatiya Vidya Bhavan, Kulpati Munshi Rd, Bombay
Parab, Gujarat Sahitya Parishad, Govardhan Bhavan, Ashram Rd, Ahmedabad
Shabdasrishti,, Gujarat Sahitya Akademi, Sector - II, Gandhinagar
Vi, Dept. of English, S P Univeristy, Vallabh Vidya Nagar
Sanskriti, Sandesh Bldg, Gheekanta, Ahmedabad

HINDI

Dastavej, Viswanath Tiwari, Dethia Hatha, Gorakhpur
Hans, 2/36 Ansari Road, Daryaganj, New Delhi
India Today (Hindi), F14/15 Connaught Place, New Delhi
Indraprastha Bharati, Samudaya Bhavan, Padam Nagar, Delhi
Kathya Roop, 224 Tularam Bagh, Allahabad
Pahal, 763 Agarwal Colony, Jabalpur
Pal-Pratipal, 372 Sector 17, Panchkula, Haryana
Pratipaksh, 6/105 Kaushalya Park, Hauz Khas, New Delhi
Samkaleen Bharatiya Sahitya, Sahitya Akademi, Rabindra Bhavan, New Delhi
Vartaman Sahitya, 109, Ricchpalpuri, PB 13, Ghaziabad

KANNADA

Lankesh Patrike, 9, East St, PB 416, Basavanagudi, Bangalore
Mayura, 16 MG Road, PO 331, Bangalore
Prajavani, 66 MG Road, Bangalore
Rujuvathu, c/o Kavi Kavya Trust, Heggodu, Sagar, Shimoga Dist
Samvada, Samvada Prakashana, Malladihalli, Chitradurga Dist
Shubra, Shubra Srinivas, No 824, 7th Main, ISRO Layout, Bangalore
Sudha, 16 MG Road, Bangalore
Tushara, Press Corner, Manipal
Udayavani, Manipal Printers & Publishers, Manipal 19

KONKANI

Chitrangi, Apurbai Prakashan, Volvoi Ponda, Goa
Kullagar, PO Box 109, Margao, Goa 1
Jaag, Priol, Mardol, Goa
Rashtramat, Margao, Goa 1
Sunaparant, BPS Club, Margao, Goa 1

MALAYALAM

Bhashaposhini, Malayala Manorama Co Ltd, Kottayam
Desabhimani Weekly, PB 1130, Calicut 32
India Today (Malayalam), 98-A, Dr Radhakrishna Salai, Madras 4
Katha, Kaumudi Buildings, Pettah, Thiruvananthapuram 24

Kala Kaumudi, Pettah, Thiruvananthapuram
Kerala Kaumudi, PB 77, Thiruvananthapuram 24
Kumkumam, Lakshminanda, Kollam
Madhyam, Silver Hills, Calicut - 673 012
Malayala Manorama, PB 26, Kottayam
Manorajyam, Manorajyam Press, T B Junction, Kottayam
Mathrubhumi Weekly, KPK Menon Road, Calicut

MARATHI

Abhiruchi, 69 Pandurang Wadi, Goregaon East, Bombay
Anustubh, Anandashram, Near D'souza Maidan, Manmad
Anuradha, Vitthal Society, 138, Hanuman Road, Vile Parle (E), Bombay 57
Asmitadarsha, 37 Laxmi Co Chawani, Aurangabad
Dhanurdhari, Ramakrishna Printing Press, 31, Tirbhuvan Road, Bombay 4
Dipawali, 316, Prasad Chambers, Girgaon, Bombay 4
Grihalaxmi, 21, Dr DD Sathe Rd, Girgaon, Bombay 4
Jatra, 2117, Sadashiv Peth, Vijayanagar Cly, Pune 30
Kavitarati, Vijay Police Vashat, Wadibhikar Rasta, Dhule
Lokaprabha, Express Tower I Floor, Nariman Point, Bombay
Lokasatta, Indian Express, Nariman Point, Bombay 21
Lokarajya, New Admn Bldg, 17th Floor, Opp Secretariat, Bombay 2
Maher, 2117, Sadashiv Peth, Vijayanagar Clny, Pune 30
Maharashtra Times, The Times of India, Fort, Bombay 1
Mauj, Mauj Prakashan Graha, Khatavvadi, Girgaon, Bombay
Navbharat, Pradnya Press, Wai
Pratishthan, Marathwada Sahitya Parishad, Sanmitra Cly, Aurangabad
Saptahik Sakal, Shanivar Peth, Pune 2
Satyagrahi, Kranti Niketan, 1468, Sadashiv Peth, Opp SP College, Pune
Samuchit, A/3 Univ Professor's Qtrs, Amaravati Road, Nagpur
Ugvai, Nirved, Kupwad Rd, Vishrambag, Sangli
Vasant, 2/8, Govardhan Building, Parekh Street, Girgaon, Bombay 4
Yugwani, Vidarbha Sahitya Sangh, Rani Jhansi Square, Nagpur

TAMIL

Arumbu, 22-A, Tailors Road, Madras 10
India Today (Tamil), 98-A, Dr Radhakrishna Salai, Mylapore, Madras 4
Kal Kudhirai, 6/162, Indra Nagar, Kovilpatti 2
Kanaiazhi, 245, TTK Salai, Madras
Kanavu, MIG 189 Phase II, TNHB, Thiruppatur
Kappiar, Kaliyakkavilai, K K Dist, TN
Naveena Vritcham, No 7 Ragavan Cly, Madras
Pudia Paarvai, Tamil Arasi Maligai, 84 TTK Rd, Madras
Puthiya Nambikkai, 13 Vanniyar II St., Madras
Semmalar, 6/16, Bypass Rd, Madurai 18

Subhamangala, 10 Appadurai St., Seethamal Cly, Madras
Virutcham, 7, Raghavan Cly, West Mambalam, Madras

TELUGU

Aahwanam, Gandhi Nagar, Vijayawada
Andhra Jyoti, Lubbipet Sunday Section, Vijayawada 10
Andhra Patrika, 1-2-528, Lower Tank Bund Road, Domalguda, Hyderabad 29
Andhra Prabha, 'Express Centre,' Domalguda, Hyderabad
Arunathara, 6-5-13, Kavali, Nellore Dist 1
Chatura, Eenadu Publications, Somajiguda, Hyderabad
India Today (Telugu), 98-A, Dr Radhakrishna Salai., Mylapore, Madras 4
Jyothi, 1-8-519/11, Chikadapally, PB 1824, Hyderabad 20
Mayuri, 5-8-55/A, Nampally, Station Road, Hyderabad 1
Rachana, PB No 33, Visakhapatnam
Srijana, 203, Laxmi Apartments, Malakpet, Hyderabad 36
Swati, Prakashan Road, Governorpet, Vijayawada
Vipula, Eenadu Compound, Somajiguda, Hyderabad

URDU

Aajkal, Publication Divion, Patiala House, New Delhi
Asri Adab, D7 Model Town, Delhi
Beeswin Sadi, D7 Model Town, Delhi
Gulban, 9 Shah Alam Society, 12 Chandola Lok, Davilipada, Ahmedabad
Kitab Numa, Maktaba Jamia, New Delhi
Naya Daur, PB 146, Lucknow
Shabkhoon, 313, Rani Mandi, Allahabad
Shair, Maktaba Qasruladab, PO Box 4526, Bombay
Soughat, 84 IIIrd Main, Defence Colony, Indiranagar, Bangalore
Zehn-e-Jadeed, 1D Ms Flats Type IV, Minto Road Complex, Delhi

N.B. This is by no means an exhaustive list of all the contemporary journals, periodicals, newspapers (the magazine sections), little magazines and anthologies which give space to the short story. But, for the most part, these names represent the range of publications consulted by the nominating editors in their respective languages. However, since the compilation of a more detailed list of publications is one of Katha Vilasam's objectives, the editors would welcome any additional information on the subject, particularly with respect to languages not covered in this list.

ABOUT KATHA

KATHA is a registered nonprofit organisation devoted to creative communication for development. Katha's basic objective is to spread the love of books and the joy of reading amongst children and adults. Our activities span from literacy to literature.

KALPAVRIKSHAM, Katha's Centre for Sustainable Learning, develops and publishes quality material for neo-literate children and adults, and works with teachers to help them make their presentation and teaching more fun, creative. Amongst our publications for neo-literates (in Hindi) are a health and environment magazine for first-generation schoolgoers called *Tamasha!*, and teaching/learning packages, specially designed for use in nonformal education – *Hulgul Ka Pitara* is a basic Hindi language package which is already published; "Anmol Khazana," a kit on sustainable living and "Chaand!", an integrated kit for the teaching of science, maths and language are in the making. The *Katha Vachak* books and monthly tabloid are for the reading pleasure of neo-literates, particularly women.

A part of Kalpavriksham is the KHAZANA EXPERIMENT, a project in Delhi's largest slum cluster at Govindpuri, started in 1990. This "deschool" and income generation programme caters to almost 1200 working children and about 100 women.

Any extra income that comes from the sale of our various publications (including this one) go to support these projects.

KATHA VILASAM is the Story Research And Resource Centre of Katha. One of our main efforts is to foster and applaud quality short fiction being written in the various Indian languages. The Katha Awards were instituted in 1990. The Katha Awards for Creative Fiction are given to writers. Stories are nominated by eminent critics and scholars. The main criteria are that they are world-class and have not been translated into English before. The Katha Awards for Translation go to nominated translators. The Katha Journal Awards go each year to magazines that had initially published the stories selected for the Katha Awards. Magazines that would like their stories to be considered for the Awards are requested to put the Editor, *Katha Prize Stories* on their subscribers' list. We are also making an attempt to get more information about translators and about magazines that publish quality short fiction in the various regional languages. Any information that you can provide would be welcome.

Please address all correspondence to:

Katha, Post Box 326, GPO, New Delhi 110 001.